THE ANGER
OF THE BELLS

Virginia Rath

THE ANGER
OF THE BELLS

VIRGINIA RATH

COACHWHIP PUBLICATIONS
Greenville, Ohio

The Anger of the Bells, by Virginia Rath
© 2019 Coachwhip Publications

Published 1937
No claims made on public domain material.
Cover image: Bell © inf1n1ty

CoachwhipBooks.com

ISBN 1-61646-473-9
ISBN-13 978-1-61646-473-8

THE ANGER OF THE BELLS

CHAPTER I
KITTY FEATHERSTONE-QUINN

All the other envelopes were long, white, neatly typewritten and promised to be officially uninteresting. But the green one smelled faintly of violets, and no matter how often he examined it, the red design on its back still persisted in looking like a feather lying on top of a small boulder.

Rocky Allan pushed the other letters aside and opened the green envelope. Words staggered inkily downhill on the verdant sheet of paper inside:

To the Sheriff:

Dear Sheriff,
As I will be in Brookdale Wednesday—
not that I'd be coming there otherwise,
and nobody knows that I am, so I hope
you'll not say anything about it for a
while at least—I'll come in to see you
at two o'clock, and I hope that won't be

inconvenient for you because I really would like to talk to you about a matter of importance. At least, it's important to me, though I really don't think it's anything especially serious and no doubt you'll know just what to do, and that will be the end of it. Anyway, I'll be in your office at two and will hope to see you then—if the car doesn't break down so that I'm late, or anything else happens to keep me from coming at all, but I don't think it will, and I hope not.

Yours sincerely,

Kitty Featherstone-Quinn.

Rocky looked at the signature, then at the crest on the envelope again and chuckled. "Featherstone! I'm a son of a gun," he murmured. Then, aloud: "Cy, would a dame named Featherstone-Quinn be the one that bought the hotel in Slacktown?"

Cy Rand, who had been dozing stoutly in his chair—his by right of twenty years' persistent occupation—sat erect with a jerk.

"I just closed my eyes because the sun glares so. Slacktown? Well, if you mean Gold Gulch . . ."

"Ever'body calls it Slacktown."

"Not the old timers don't. It was Gold Gulch first, and just because there was enough Slacks one time to change the name doesn't change it to me. Yes, that Featherstone woman would be the one that bought the hotel. *And* married June Quinn. You know: Junius Brutus Quinn, the county poet?"

"Do you mean," Rocky said in accents of simple horror, "that a man an' a Gold Gulch Quinn writes that lousy, God-awful poetry that comes out in the paper sometimes?"

"It does seem kind of hard to account for. But June went to school and never did a lick of work and always was a lad for the women. He used to write a lot more po'try than he does now. Just signs it 'Junius.' He's got a brother, Cash Quinn—Cassius—"

"I've met him. I remember thinkin' about him that while all desert rats are liars he could give cards and spades to most of 'em."

"That's Cash. Spent all his life prospectin', struck pay dirt two-three times and spent it all up. He ain't been well enough to go out lately, but there's still people would grubstake him. I might myself," Cy admitted sheepishly. "You never can tell. But he's up at the old place now. Why'd you ask about that Featherstone dame?"

"She's comin' here in about two minutes—if she's on time."

"Women never are. Was that green letter with the funny thing on the envelope that come in

yesterday, while you was away, from her? What is
that doodad, anyhow?"

"Her fam'ly crest—a feather on a stone," Rocky
said, grinning. "I think I'll get me a big rock
printed on my stationery. Ever seen her?"

"Not to know. She'd trade in Merton, and I
don't get down there—" Cy stood up hastily and
made a slight, creaking movement somewhat resembling a bow. "You wanted to see the sheriff,
ma'am? Right over there."

Rocky looked at his visitor with the peculiar feeling that he was seeing something out of
a toyshop come to life. A girl cousin of his had
had a favorite doll whose name was Guinevere but
should, he now thought, have been called Kitty
Featherstone. The doll had smoothly enameled
pink cheeks, large, round blue eyes and dusty,
brownish hair pinned up into a fuzzy pompadour.
So had Kitty Featherstone-Quinn. Guinevere had
a small, pinched-in waist, a round, swelling bust
and comfortably wide hips. Again, so had Mrs.
Featherstone-Quinn. She sat down in the chair before his desk, arranged flowered-georgette flounc-
es, loosened the molting feather boa about her
neck and said in a reedy, doll's voice:

"It is such a relief to find you in after making
the trip in this warm weather, and I am so glad
that you're alone so we can talk privately."

Cy's expression was a mingling of indignation and wistfulness, but Rocky shook his head and motioned toward the door.

"I do hope I didn't hurt his feelings. I try never to hurt people's feelings," Mrs. Featherstone-Quinn said earnestly. "But then I always think there's no reason at all for doing that as long as you just use a little tact. And I was just as tactful as I— Are you the sheriff? I thought he was an old man—not that I pay much attention, but—"

"He is. I'm his chief deputy, but he hasn't been in the county for more 'n six months. So you'll have to tell me your troubles, ma'am."

"Oh, you know I didn't mean I doubted you were the sheriff. I just wondered, and I wanted to go to the very top because it's my experience that's the only thing to do. Don't you think so? I'll just tell you what I came to tell—

"I can see you're thinking: 'Maybe she will, but she'll take a long time to do it.' Oh yes, you are," Mrs. Featherstone-Quinn said amiably. "And I don't blame you. I know I'm a talker. Mr. Barnhart says so. He says my style is discursive and diffusive, but he only says that to tease, and I tell him if he'd been an aunt as long as I was maybe he'd be discursive himself."

"What kind of an aunt?" Rocky asked.

"Oh, didn't I tell you? A newspaper aunt. Aunt Kitty's advice to the lovelorn, you know—when it wasn't to housewives—but mostly it was to the lovelorn, and they ask such silly questions, but you have to fill up space and manage to get in a lot of things like 'respect yourself, and the man will respect you' or 'do as your mother wishes, Sweet Sixteen.' I did that for fifteen years—after Mr. Featherstone died when I was just thirty—and finally I'd saved enough so I thought I'd find some nice little boardinghouse or hotel that wouldn't take too much of my time and help pay expenses, and I could do some serious writing in my spare time—though I must say I never seem to have any spare time."

"So you bought the Slacktown hotel?"

Mrs. Featherstone-Quinn shivered. "That awful name! Gold Gulch isn't so bad, but, as Ivy says, the very sound of the name Slack is enough to send chills down your spine—because she's sensitive to sounds, and so am I. I'm wandering again, aren't I?"

"A little," Rocky said politely.

"Oh, more than a little, I'm afraid. Well, this place was for sale cheap, and, although the man who built it nearly went bankrupt in the five years he had it, the place was in good condition and really a bargain—the only building in town but the store that isn't falling down. But I suppose you know the town?"

"I haven't been there for a couple of years."

"Well, it's undoubtedly just like it was then, except that a few more buildings are a little nearer tumbling down. Of course, it isn't actually a ghost town because there are some people living there, but it's almost one—and that sounds romantic, don't you think? I always mention that in my advertisements. Well, all I want to do is to make expenses, and there's no reason why I shouldn't, even if it is very quiet. There's good fishing, and some people like a quiet place, and one that's reasonable.

"I knew quite a few people in San Francisco who write, and some of them are tired of Carmel—and places like that—and would like it up here. That's one reason I call it El Dorado Inn. El Dorado: the search for spirit gold. Don't you think that's a nice thought?"

Rocky swallowed hastily, said it certainly was a very nice thought and did she have any guests yet?

"Three. Of course, I didn't mean I ever knew anyone really important or successful—except Mr. Barnhart, and he says he isn't really successful, and he never has much money."

"Is that Arthur Barnhart? The one that writes about the Civil War? I've read some of his books.

My grandfather talked to me so much about the war when I was real young that I've always been interested in that partic'lar time in history."

"I can just about guess which side of the Civil War you'd be most interested in from the way you talk," Mrs. Featherstone-Quinn said archly. "I do love those golden-honey Southern voices. Oh, don't be embarrassed; I really do. Yes, it's that Mr. Barnhart. He's thinking about writing a book about mining and ghost towns and things like that, and maybe he'll stay a month. Then there's Ivy Horne. She writes poetry, though she doesn't get much published—but then everyone says editors are so prejudiced against newcomers. I don't know about that; I'm no judge of poetry. Ivy's doesn't ever rhyme, and I can't see any sense to it—but that surely wouldn't be anything against it, do you think? Junius—that's my husband—says it shows a lot of promise, and he ought to know, because he's a poet himself. I suppose you've read some of his poetry?"

"I—uh—I've seen it in the county papers sometimes."

"What do you think of it?"

"Well, I'm no judge of po'try, either, Mrs. Featherstone-Quinn."

"That's exactly what I think of it myself." For just an instant a mischievous twinkle stirred the china-blue calm of Mrs. Featherstone-Quinn's eyes. "I think it's pretty bad, but don't you ever tell anyone I said so. Maybe you and I don't know, and, anyway, Junius is a lamb, and if it amuses him to write poetry I wouldn't stop him for anything in the world. It's just like I say about politics: if they amuse men let them have them. At least Junius' poetry rhymes. I guess I didn't tell you I went to live in the hotel in February and married Junius in March? I know everybody says *I* married him, but a woman usually can marry almost any man if she puts her mind to it, and Junius need-ed someone to look after him—and if he doesn't mind, why should anyone else?"

"Does anyone else?"

"I guess what you really mean is: am I ever go-ing to tell you why I came here. But maybe this has something to do with it. Junius's brother, Cassius, doesn't like me very well. I don't know why—I've been just as nice to him as I can be. Then there's Amelia Slack—"

"I don't believe I know who she is."

"Oh, she was born a Quinn and married a Slack. She's a cousin to the boys. I don't suppose she cared whether Junius and I got married or not, but she *does* look on me as an outsider, and so does Cassius and Tom Slack. He's the only real Slack left up there. Goodness knows what they want—I guess just to let the town fall to pieces without anybody trying to make a popular summer resort of it. That's the only reason I can think of why they might want to run me out of town . . ."

"So that's it? What makes you think someone's tryin' to do that?"

"A lot of things. Ivy Horne and Mr. Barnhart came up ten days ago, and my third guest, Leon Glidden, has been there a week. Well, for this last week someone's been trying to give the impression the place is haunted."

Surprisingly, Mrs. Featherstone-Quinn became almost terse. "Someone makes wailing noises in the graveyard around midnight or early in the morning. Unfortunately, it's on the slope just below the inn. Ivy says she saw a white figure flitting about from one gravestone to another one night. That sounds silly, doesn't it? But I can testify to the noise."

"Scare you?"

"Certainly *not*. They just went"—Mrs. Featherstone-Quinn's mouth became a pink O—"oo-oo-OOOhh! Just silly and very unconvincing if you ask me. That only happened twice. Then, someone's been ringing bells."

"Bells?"

"Well, one. They never took the bell out of the building that was a school and church. After the mining rush was over, but while there were still quite a few people living there they used to toll the bell when anyone died. One stroke for each year the person had lived. Of course, they still do that in some places. Anyway, the last three nights someone has rung that bell, and I don't mind telling you it sounds spooky—with the town so still at night, and all those old, deserted houses—up there all alone on the mountain top."

Rocky frowned. "How many times did the bell ring?"

"I thought about that; we all did. But so far there's never been any more than twenty, and all of us are older than that," Mrs. Featherstone-Quinn said cheerfully. "Mr. Barnhart says it rang twenty strokes Monday night. He was the only one awake to hear it begin, but he just laughed and didn't try to catch whoever was doing it. Sunday—the first time it rang—none of us thought of counting. It rang a few times before midnight, and we didn't do anything, but when it began again at three in the morning the men got up and went out to investigate. Of course, they didn't catch anyone."

"How do the folks up there take it?"

"They don't mind, except when it wakes them up. It makes Ivy rather nervous, but though she looks just like a poetess she has a lot of common sense. But I have some guests booked for next month—June—and I have to have this thing stopped before they come, because they'll be more particular. Besides, my cook doesn't like it, and I can't lose her, and she certainly doesn't want to leave me, but she's very superstitious. She's Chinese, mostly, and for pity's sake don't talk pidgin English to her. That insults her because she talks perfectly good English—though it may take a while for you to understand what she means. Monday evening someone started ringing a cowbell in the cellar. It's right under Mary Anne's kitchen—"

"Mary Anne?"

"Mary Anne," Mrs. Featherstone-Quinn said firmly. "And, of course, it scared her into conniptions, and she simply sank down on the floor and howled. So by the time I got into the cellar whoever it was had gotten away by the outside door, though they left the cowbell behind."

"What is it you expect me to do?"

"Scare the daylights out of whoever it is."

"Well, who do you think it is?"

"Tom Slack or Cassius. Only Cassius couldn't have rung the cowbell because we were at dinner then, and he was with us. But he could put Tom Slack up to doing it."

"I thought the Slacks and Quinns didn't used to be very friendly."

"Well, Tom's the only one left, and Amelia is his sister-in-law, and he and Cassius are friend-ly. He's a horrid old man. And Amelia is—queer. Her husband was killed in a mine he had, before they were married very long. She talks about him like he wasn't dead, and then other times she says Cash killed him to get the mine. Except for that, she's all right. Of course, I don't want any fuss. I wouldn't want you to arrest anyone—except may-be Tom Slack. Could you come up to dinner to-night, and I could tell them who you are but not say why you're there? And then you could look the town over and talk to me like you'd learned some-thing, and maybe that would be enough to scare whoever's doing it."

"I don't see why it might not work," Rocky said. "That's givin' them fair warnin'. If I have to arrest one of the old inhabitants on your say so—"

"People will resent it because I'm a newcomer. I want to avoid that, but I won't be scared away," Mrs. Featherstone-Quinn said placidly.

"Of course, if it keeps up I'll have to sneak up there an' watch till I catch someone at that bell. No one would try any tricks as long as he suspect-ed he was bein' watched. You suspect just those three people?"

"I knew it couldn't be anyone in the inn. They'd have no reason to do a thing like that—and, any-way, we've all been together several times while the bell was ringing. The Jameses are nice people, and young Mr. Murdoch, who runs the store, is just as interested as I am in making the town come to life. And those are the only other people who live there."

"What time do you have dinner? Six-thirty? Oh yes, I can get there easy enough by that time. Is this Leon Glidden you mentioned a painter? Lives in Reno and does pictures of the desert and sagebrush country? He sold quite a few of them in Merton."

"That's Leon. But he's been living in San Francisco for the last six months. He showed some pictures, but he didn't sell very many. People down there didn't care for them. I like them myself—but then I like those Nevada hills, and the sagebrush when the sun's just beginning to go down."

Rocky nodded. "I thought he did mighty well by those purple shadows you see out there that time of day. But maybe his pictures look too much like the thing he's painting to be popular."

"Well, he's a sweet boy. I met him before I left the city, and he and Ivy know each other. I thought it would be so nice if they— But then, I don't know what they'd live on, and they don't seem to like each other at all *that* way, and maybe one artistic temperament in the family is enough. Not that either of them ever acts very temperamental, but they probably are. And I must start back," Mrs. Featherstone-Quinn said, winding the feather boa around her neck so that its two dejected ends fell over her shoulders. "We're having fried chicken, and when you've eaten Mary Anne's fried chicken I guess you'll see why I don't want to lose her just because some silly, childish person goes around ringing bells in the middle of the night."

CHAPTER II
"A CLOCK THAT'S STOPPED . . ."

Rocky had spent the entire morning in Indian River, thirty miles from the county seat of Brookdale, and had had a very early and unsatisfactory lunch. It was past three o'clock now, and fried chicken at six-thirty seemed a long way off, especially with an hour's drive to Slacktown before him.

Brookdale's two lunch counters apparently brewed their coffee from some strange berry that had never seen Brazil, and all the food tasted of stale grease. Ham and eggs and coffee that was coffee, even if he had to fix them himself, were better than anything he could get at the lunch counters, and leaving the courthouse Rocky turned toward home.

Since the old sheriff, Jake Thompson, had gone to live with a son in San Diego eight months ago, Rocky and Eleanor had the use of the Thompsons' house. It was an old-fashioned, white dwelling with green, outside shutters and furniture that Eleanor declared "takes getting used to." Most of the chairs and tables dated back to the beginning of the century, and Mrs. Thompson had cherished as objets d'art several bearskin rugs, a number of very large vases resembling funeral urns, two, mounted, stags' heads and three stuffed owls.

When one of these became too much for Eleanor's nerves she carried it away to the attic. Rocky was thinking, as he walked toward the house, that if the Thompsons ever came back without giving advance notice they probably wouldn't recognize their living room.

Nor the yard, either—and they would have to take that as they found it. Mrs. Thompson's front yard had been a prim, orderly affair with flowers sternly confined in round, rock-edged beds. Eleanor planted seeds enthusiastically wherever there was a spare bit of earth for them, and when the flowers came up let them spread wherever they would. Just now there was a mass of color along the fence: petunias, sweet william, sweet peas growing tall, roses, verbena, marigolds.

Rocky stopped to look at a rose that had pushed its way through the picket fence; he lifted one of its satin petals against his finger because its color was so much like that of Eleanor's hair. Not so dark, but the same, shimmering orange-red. He

sighed unconsciously and then looked up, startled, as someone coughed dryly.

A lean, wiry man with weather-beaten skin was
sitting in a deck chair on the porch, half-hidden
by one of its pillars. He wore shapeless and very
expensive tweeds, a light-tan ten-gallon hat and
polished tan boots. His thin lips were curved in a
half-ironical smile; his eyelids drooped so that his
eyes showed as narrowed slits underneath short,
thick lashes. He said in a slightly nasal drawl:

"If you wasn't married, son, I'd think you was
in love—moonin' aroun' like that an' not seein'
folks watchin' you. How are you?"

Rocky snapped the rose's stem, dug a thorn into
his finger and said "Damn!" Then, with praise-
worthy nonchalance: "I'm fine, Dad. How are you?
Would it come under the head of an undue dis-
play of emotion if I asked just exactly where you
dropped down from?"

Robert Edward Lee Allan chuckled. "Sometimes
you don't talk like you used to. Learned a lot of
words since you was seventeen, I reckon. Well, I
decided to take a little trip, so I thought I might
as well drop in on you while I was at it."

"Quite a little drop—from Texas to No'thern
California," Rocky murmured.

"I was settin' in the livin' room one evenin',
and all the sudden I thought: Hell! Why don't I

get out and see some of the world again before I get too old to enjoy it? Nothin' to keep me home. So I packed up an' started," Allan said casually. "Spent a day in Los Angeles an' Frisco but they can't hold a candle to San Anton'. Where's Eleanor? Don't tell me she's up an' left you."

"If you'd only known it, you could 've seen her in San Francisco. Come on out to the kitchen, Dad. Had anything to eat lately?"

"Not since breakfast. I been settin' out there on the gall'ry ever since about eight this mornin'."

"Good Lord! Why didn't you come to the office?"

"The youngster that told me where the house was said you'd gone off early some place or other. So I just waited. Didn't want to bother you if you was busy, anyhow. I just set and watched what people went by an' took a little nap. Why's Eleanor in Frisco?"

Rocky grinned. "So long's she's there an' not in Reno— I think Eleanor's been readin' some of these articles about how married folks ought to take vacations from each other. An' she and Nancy Mitchell felt like they couldn't live any longer without some new clothes that wasn't bought in Reno. So they fin'lly decided to go to the city together for a few days.

"Jazz Mitchell hit it about right when he said we couldn't win. If we told 'em to stay home we were brutes, and if we said to go on and have a good time, then we wanted to get rid of 'em. I must say Nancy looked like she'd get off the train if you gave her an excuse. But then," Rocky said tolerantly, measuring out coffee, "Nancy an' Jazz have only been married about six months."

"Funny: that rose's just about the color of Eleanor's hair." The little sun-wrinkles about Allan's eyes deepened as Rocky turned red. "You two ought to be gettin' yourself some children," he went on indelicately. "You've been married more 'n a year. It didn't use to be considered hardly respectable unless you produced a baby in a year."

"You tell Eleanor you want a grandson."

"S'pose I'd ever say anything like that to a lady?—which Eleanor is. Well, what 're you laughin' at?"

"You," Rocky said frankly. "You ought to have a seat at some of the discussions Eleanor an' Nancy Mitchell get into. It 'd make your hair curl. Two eggs or three?"

"Make it three. You goin' to be next sheriff in this place?"

Rocky shrugged. "I reckon so. I wasn't opposed in the primary this month. The county attorney would 've liked to get someone to run against me, but he's pretty busy campaignin' for himself. He hasn't liked me any since that schoolteacher got killed up here last October. That's the case Jazz and Nancy was mixed up in. Eleanor wrote you about that? Things have been pretty quiet up here since then. Set up to the table, Dad, and pour the coffee while I get some bread. . . .

"You very tired?" he asked, when his father had tilted his chair back against the wall again and lighted a long, very thin cigar.

"Tired? Hell no. Why should I be? Think I'm gettin' old? If I cain't stand a little train trip at fifty-eight—"

"I was just askin' to be polite. I've got to go up to Slacktown pretty quick, an' you might just as well see some of the country while you're here. You ain't listenin' to me."

"Well—no, I wasn't," Allan admitted. "I was thinkin' you look more like your mother ever' day, an' she was the best-lookin' woman in Gillespie County. Also about the stubbornest."

"Good thing, wasn't it?" Rocky said bluntly. "Unless she was goin' to be a doormat."

"She wasn't. She come out visitin' from Virginia—she was a distant cousin of Mamma's—an' she was goin' to civ'lize me right away," Allan said unsentimentally. "But I reckon she never made a very good start on it. Yes, you look a lot like her."

He squinted impassively at the smoke curling from his cigar. Rocky thought: that's as near as he'll ever come to admitting he's been lonely sometimes. Well, it's sixteen years since Mother died, and I've been away eleven and only home once. . . . He said:

"You remember I wrote you when Jake Thompson first told me he intended me to run for sheriff this year?"

"An' I said, as I remember it, that I know county offices is good for four years, if not for life. Hell, you've made your place here; you'd be a fool to leave. I might 've felt diff'rent about it if you was still railroadin'. You may recall"—Allan's sardonic smile deepened—"I never had much use for railroaders."

"I have a pretty good remembrance of you tellin' that to Uncle Bill quite a few times."

"Well, him bein' one, he put it in your head to go. Though as I did some wanderin' aroun' when I was younger, I shouldn't blame Bill altogether for you gettin' the idea. Besides, you 'n me didn't get along any too well. You got an awful even disposition—so long's you ain't crossed."

"That's exaggerating," Rocky protested.

"Maybe a little. But I had experience enough with hosses that I should 've known there's times when a tight rein don't do no good. But about this notion of you an' Eleanor comin' down home 'to take care of Father'—if you ever had it—it wouldn't work. It 'd get on my nerves. I ain't in my dotage yet. An' while Eleanor's a mighty nice girl, she wants to pretty the place up an' keep the dogs out of the house. . . . What's the name of this place we're goin' to?"

"Slacktown." Rocky looked at his watch. "It's after four so we might as well start. I'd like to look aroun' up there while it's still light.

"The place used to be called Gold Gulch," he went on, when they were out of Brookdale. "It never was a real big mining town, but it was pretty busy once. That's more 'n fifty years ago. Old man Quinn owned a lot of mines aroun' there. Lode mining, it was, and, while there wasn't any big fortunes made, he must 've left a nice nest egg for Cash and Junius when he died. Which I suppose they spent up years ago. There was a brother of old Quinn's up there, too, and a whole mess of Slacks.

"I reckon in ten years' time most of the mines was worked out, and people began movin' away. Quinn stayed because he liked it, and I reckon the Slacks was too much like their name to move.

The only thing they ever did was to get the name of the town changed. But they fin'lly died off or moved away, and now there's just Tom Slack and an Amelia Slack who was born a Quinn. I think there's an old doctor named James and a young fellow that runs the store. There was a hotel built there about six years ago, and that's the one this woman bought."

"What woman?"

"She came to see me today. Kitty Featherstone-Quinn. Yeah, that's her name. She told me kind of a crazy story, but I've got no reason to doubt it. She said . . ."

He told his father Mrs. Featherstone-Quinn's story. "Kind of childish—spooks in the grave-yard," Allan commented. "Any reason to think she ain't tellin' the truth?"

"Oh no, I didn't mean to say she wasn't. Do you remember a doll Ella had that she called Guinevere?"

"Your cousin Ella? Yeah, I remember the fool thing. You 'n her got to playin' Indian one day, an' you scalped it. Ella's mamma come squallin' to me about it."

Rocky laughed. "I'd forgotten that. Well, Mrs. Featherstone-Quinn looks just like Guinevere, an' at first you'd think she didn't have much in her head but sawdust. I ended up by kind of likin' her, and she's pretty shrewd—in spite of the way she talks. She's O.K., but I thought I'd better go up and have a look. You can't ever tell."

"You wasn't thinkin' there might be some other reason for wantin' to run her out of town than just her bein' a stranger and tryin' to change things an' all?"

"I said you can't ever tell. She don't seem to be scared, and it does sound like just a practical joke. I suppose everyone up there knows it 'd frighten this Chinese cook. It's just as well to put a stop to it right now."

"This is kind of pretty country, at that," Allan said presently, breaking the silence between them. He took off his wide hat, showing black hair only slightly gray at the temples. "I can see how you might get kind of used to it and like it."

His eyes dwelt on the river, hurrying over hidden rocks, curling back in white foam from sleek boulders, then running quietly into still pools where late sunshine drowned slowly. From the river's farther bank hills rose steeply, dense with the dark and darker greens of tall pines.

"We turn off here," Rocky said and added unnecessarily: "The road's narrow an' steep, but it's not far to the town."

"Anybody live aroun' here?"

"'There's a few houses stuck back in the woods. If you don't turn off at Slacktown you wind up over at La Porte. But it's a hell of a road, and there's easier ways to get there."

"Damn fool!" Allan said grimly as a car came without warning around a curve in the road, swerved slightly and passed them without slackening speed.

"You get used to drivin' on mountain roads and forget to be careful. That guy probably knows ever' twist an' turn on this grade. I see someone's been prospectin' here."

Allan looked with interest at the small tunnel driven into the side of the hill. They passed more than one of these as the road climbed steeply upward through the silence of thick forests.

"No, most of 'em aren't worked, right now," Rocky said in answer to his father's question. "But you'll always find a few fellows takin' a chance. Cash Quinn's one of that kind, but he did most of his minin' over in Nevada or aroun' Downieville."

He pointed toward a small clearing where a few rough tables and cupboards had been built. "People camp down there sometimes, later in the year. The fellow that built the hotel must 've thought he could make a resort out of the place, but it's too quiet."

"Mighty high up. My ears is buzzin' like a bee-hive."

"It's right on top of the mountain. And this is it." Rocky swung the car around a sharp turn, turned again, and they were on Slacktown's one and only main street. He nodded toward a large, red, shingled building with stone foundation and said: "That's the hotel, El Dorado Inn." But he did not stop until he had reached the end of the street, a rickety white fence on the edge of a steep cliff.

Allan got out of the car, walked over to the fence, with the peculiar bowlegged gait of a man who has spent long hours on horseback, and looked down. "I sh'd think a concrete wall 'd be a better thing to have here." He turned and surveyed the town. "Is this all of it?"

"This is all. There was houses built on the hill, but they've fallen down. That was old Quinn's mill," Rocky said, pointing to what appeared to be two buildings, long and narrow, erected one below the other on two different levels of ground. "They had to build them that way. You can see it's hills above and hills below this one street. They piped the water down to run through the two buildings. They're connected, though they don't look like it at first glimpse."

"I wouldn't mind takin' a look aroun'."

"Better not—till I ask if it's safe. They're just about falling down. Let's see if we can find that old schoolhouse."

Their feet made no sound in the soft, reddish dirt. "It's funny," Rocky said, "but I always feel like whisperin' in a place like this. It's not because the houses are really in ruins. That 'd be all right. It's because they aren't, quite."

Those old white houses were like empty eggshells that had a break in them that you didn't see at first. Then when you took hold of the shell it would crumple up in your hand. At first you might think people were living in these houses. There were curtains at some of the windows, old rocking chairs on the porches, great reddish-purple lilacs blooming in dooryards and fence corners.

But if you stopped at a front gate it sagged under your hand. The curtains were mildewed and falling apart, window panes broken, doors swinging aimlessly on rusty hinges. Several two-story houses had signs: DANGEROUS! DO NOT GO UPSTAIRS! Another smaller house leaned tipsily against the huge timbers that propped it up on one side. When Allan spoke, his voice, too, was unconsciously hushed.

"I reckon nobody lives on this side of the street, exceptin' in the hotel. Maybe the hill bein' below these houses is dang'rous. There's a buildin' over there has a kind of cupola to it. Reckon that's your schoolhouse?"

They crossed the street to a faded red building somewhat like the caboose at the tail of a freight train. The door was open, and they stepped into a square vestibule. Just above their heads an old iron bell was hung, with a length of frayed rope dangling nearly to the floor.

"Like the one we used to call the hands to meals," Allan said. "You don't expect to find out anything just by lookin' at it, do you?"

"No, I just wanted to see where it's located. An' if the place's got more than one door."

"They mostly don't have—schoolhouses like this. Takes me back," Allan said, following Rocky into the schoolroom. "Just about like the one where I went to school."

He looked at the half-dozen old-fashioned double desks, ran his hand absently over the initials carved on one of them. At one end of the room was a small platform on which was a square, oak desk, its top thickly overlaid with dust.

"Nobody's touched that for a long time," Rocky said. He stared at the cracked, green blackboard behind the platform. There were still a few pieces of chalk and a dusty eraser in the trough below the board, and someone had written on it, written so heavily that the imprint of the words still re-mained, "Honesty is the best policy."

"That 'd be a writin' lesson," Allan said. "Teach-er's writin'—you can tell that anywhere. It don't seem hardly decent to leave it like this."

Rocky did not ask him to explain. He said: "No, it don't. If they'd tear things down an' make an end of them, that 'd be all right. But this way—it's like a clock that's stopped, an' nobody's bothered to wind it up. You feel like things would take up right where they left off, if someone did. The kids would be back in school, and someone would be settin' in the chairs on the porches—" He smiled deprecatingly. "Oh well. There's only the one door. Let's see who lives next to here."

A narrow space of hard earth that must once have been the school playground was bordered by a picket fence that separated it from the next house, a small white cottage.

"There's someone livin' there," Rocky said. "Smoke coming out of the chimney. I wonder whose place it is? Keep quiet a minute."

A woman carrying a green sprinkling can had just opened the front door of the cottage. Her hair was pure white, brushed straight up from neck and forehead and coiled on top of her head. She wore a white waist with a high, net collar fastened with a

painted, china brooch; a shiny, black, broadcloth
skirt trailed in the dust until she lifted it with one
hand to show a dust ruffle underneath its hem.

Even from that distance they could see that she
was painfully thin: her hands long and bony, her
collarbones sharply outlined under the net that
covered them. The thin face was strangely un-
lined, the blue eyes serenely devoid of expression.
She tilted the sprinkling can so that a fine spray
of water fell on a newly planted bed of pansies,
turned and went back into the house without having glanced in their direction.

"That almost has to be Amelia Slack," Rocky
said. "But she don't look like she was—"

"Touched in the head? Well, I suppose some
folks would call her that—from what this Mrs.
Quinn said about her. She ain't really been livin'
for a long time. Prob'ly not since that outfit of
hers was in style. That's why her face fools you.
She looks old to me. I reckon you think she looks
younger 'n she is?"

"Y-yes. Yes, I did think that at first. I see what
you mean, though. She keeps her place up pretty
well," Rocky said. "Let's see what's on the other
side of the school."

They skirted the back of the schoolhouse, passing a broken pump and decayed, wooden trough.
A chicken scratching in the dust raised its head,

squawked in alarm and scrambled through a gap in the fence to join half a dozen others in a pen roughly constructed of slats and wire netting.

"I deduce," Allan drawled, "that there's somebody livin' here, even if the place's fallin' down. Now let's see you deduce somethin'."

"That Tom Slack probably lives here. I know this isn't the old Quinn place—that's near the mill on the other side of the street." He studied the boarded-up windows on the house's second floor, the timbers holding up the front porch. "I'd be scared the place'd fall down on me, but from what I've heard about the Slacks, he wouldn't worry. He must just use this one back room. Well"—he looked at his watch—"it's six o'clock, so we'd better get over to the hotel. Might as well leave the car where it is."

"Here's another house someone lives in," Allan said as they went toward the inn. He read aloud the sign on the old gray building: "'OLIVER JAMES, M.D.' Funny a doctor 'd stick up here."

"I reckon he's a pretty old man—too old to want to make a new start. Must have a son: 'O. L. JAMES, D.D.S.' I don't see how a dentist could make a livin' up here, but he may have to look after the old man."

They crossed the street again. Rocky pointed to a small building with heavy, iron doors. "That was

where they kept the gold before they sent it away.
Kind of a Wells-Fargo office, I guess. That's the
store next to it. There was more stores and some
saloons where the vacant lots are. They all burned
down so long ago the grass has had time to grow
again."

A young woman came out of the store before
they reached it and crossed the street so quickly
that they had only a glimpse of her face. Studying
her back, Allan said approvingly:

"Now, there's a girl with what I call a good fig-
ger. Some meat on her—though maybe she's built
a little too much like a man. But pretty neat just
the same."

Looking at the girl's broad shoulders, slim waist
and flat hips, Rocky privately agreed with him.
But he said sweetly:

"You ought to be ashamed—at your age! You
come on along an' meet Kitty-Guinevere Featherstone-Quinn."

CHAPTER III
EL DORADO

Mrs. Featherstone-Quinn had put Rocky on her left, Robert Allan on her right and then placed Ivy Horne on his other side with the optimistic prediction: "I know you and Ivy will get along just splendidly."

Rocky watched his father with unfilial amusement. Allan, he thought, was handicapped by the fact that he'd been brought up to be polite to women just because they were women. But he must have been sorely tried by Miss Horne's dissertation on Van Gogh. And now Mrs. Featherstone-Quinn was asking if he had not been "a cowboy in your younger days? I'm just certain you were—there's something about you . . . So romantic—the wide open spaces and all the cattle and cowboys and everything like that . . ."

"When men were men, and women were scarce," Arthur Barnhart said blandly. "Would you like me to yodel, Kitty?"

Rocky was inclined to like Barnhart, mainly because of the only half-suppressed smile with which he had been listening to Ivy Horne a few minutes before. Barnhart was probably in his late forties: a big, round-shouldered man, just beginning to take on flesh. He had a square, pleasant face with a long, humorous upper lip, and although he had evidently shaved recently his jaws already showed the bluish-black shadow of a very heavy beard.

"But I'm afraid I interrupted you, Kitty," he added, "and didn't give Mr. Allan a chance to answer your question."

"I reckon you'd say I've been a cowboy," Allan said grudgingly. "My dad raised cattle and always found plenty for me to do, and I was over in Arizona once for a spell."

"They have some of the most priceless cowboy pictures in some of the secondhand stores in San Francisco," Ivy Horne said. "In a place on O'Farrell. They're positively comic. Do you remember them, Leon?"

"Yes, and the ones in that place on McAllister. Wasn't that where they were? We ran into it when we were wandering around the sacred book stores one night. They'd go well with my religious chromos. You'd like those, Barnhart. Especially the one that shows two impossible infants just ready to step off the brink of a cliff. All that restrains

them, apparently, is an equally impossible guard-
ian angel who is hovering above them. It's a very
inexpensive and interesting hobby," Leon Glidden
said. "I've started to make one of temperance pictures, too. I've several touching illustrations of
the 'Father, dear Father, come home with me now'
theme."

Glidden didn't look like an artist, Rocky decided, even while he admitted that his conception of
an artist as a man who wore a smock and always
needed a haircut was based on nothing more substantial than the memory of several novels read at
an early and impressionable age.

But Glidden was simply an ordinarily good-looking young man, sensibly dressed in slacks and
flannel shirt. It wasn't until you'd looked at him
several times that you realized his face was shaped
rather like a pear: narrower at temples than jaw.
With brown hair and eyes he had very fair skin,
burned just now to an unbecoming brick-red. He
remarked presently that he had been "trying for
fifteen years to acquire a decent coat of tan, but
all I do is turn red and peel and then burn all over
again next time I get a good dose of sun."

If Glidden did, disappointingly, look like any
young business man on a holiday, Ivy Horne perfectly fitted Rocky's preconceived idea of a poetess. He could imagine her intoning verses—some-

thing like 'Hail to thee, blithe spirit'—with one
long, white hand raised wearily to her slender
throat. Her skin was waxy-white; there were dark
shadows under her eyes, and curling, dark hair fell
nearly to her shoulders.

Although she was wearing a knitted, jade-green
suit you felt that she should be clothed in flow-
ing white. Her movements gave the impression
that she was gracefully managing invisible, floating draperies even while she ate a very substantial
dinner.

Mrs. Featherstone-Quinn had started a huge
platter of fried chicken on its way around the
table again. Cassius Quinn, sitting next to Rocky,
requested him to "hold the thing so's I can see
what's there." He forked over the contents of the
platter disparagingly. "Nothin' but bones left.
Seems to me I might 've got a piece of breast when
ever'one knows I can't eat bones. Oh well"—he
put a wing on his plate—"this 'll have to do."

Kitty Featherstone-Quinn looked at her broth-
er-in-law, then meaningly at Rocky. Her round-
eyed gaze said sadly: "You see? He doesn't like
me." Junius Quinn said:

"Never look a gift horse in the face, Cash. Kitty
invited you to dinner, and if you'd told her what
piece of chicken you wanted she'd have seen that
you had it."

"Think I don't know why your wife asked me to supper tonight? Wonder to me she didn't have Tom an' Amelia, too. Maybe that 'd looked kind of pointed, though."

"You don't need a special invitation, as a matter of fact. You probably would have come without one," Junius said impatiently. "That's way I said—"

"Now, boys! I know you don't mean a thing by it, and Cassius knows we're always glad to have him here. They always squabble like that, but it doesn't mean anything at all," Mrs. Featherstone-Quinn told Rocky. "It seems like, sometimes, men just never do grow up. Leon, I know you want some more chicken . . ."

"Thinks I don't know why she asked me specially for tonight," Cash Quinn said in Rocky's left ear. "I don't mind. She's got a good cook, an' I ain't afraid of you checkin' up on me. I got better things to do than stay up nights to ring a bell. Even if it is funny to see 'em all runnin' out, tryin' to catch whoever's doin' it and makin' believe they ain't scared. I've lived too long here to get scared. I'm at home with the ghosts." He laughed shrilly and tore the chicken wing to pieces with his fingers.

"And as far as me eatin' here is concerned, they'll tell you I'm living offen them most the time," he continued. "But that ain't so. I take a meal here now and then, but I don't have to do it. I managed to make a livin' all my life, and that's more 'n June, over there, ever did."

Junius Quinn's smooth, pink face took on a shade more color, but he appeared not to have heard his brother's last remark. Junius had soft, womanish hands, a rounded and unimpressive chin, a well-shaped, full-lipped mouth. His hair was thick, glossy and beautifully waved. Undoubtedly, he took very good care of it—and himself. Women would call him handsome, Rocky conceded, and though he must be past forty he looked a good fifteen years younger than Cassius.

You couldn't—if you'd ever known any prospectors—mistake Cash for anything but the desert rat he was. In one respect he and Robert Allan resembled each other: both had been burned and dried to the texture of leather by sun and wind and had squinted against these elements for so long that the protective drooping of eyelids had become habit. But Allan still moved lithely, and his back was straight as a boy's. Cash's thin shoulders were so bowed that his arms seemed unusually long.

He wore a large and ragged, mustache and that added to bushy eyebrows and the ragged, dirty, gray tuft of imperial on his chin, filled the eye so that most people had a very hazy idea of the features above and below the mustache. Cash wore a stickpin made of one large gold nugget thrust into his greasy tie. That nugget probably dated back to one of his early strikes.

"Well, if you don't mind bein' checked up on, where'bouts do you live? I've got the rest located," Rocky said, "if it's Tom Slack who lives in the big house to one side of the school."

"That's Tom's place. Someday it 'll fall down on him before he can wake up," Cash said hopefully. "I live t'other side of Amelia's place, if you spotted that. Two-story house with about the biggest laylac bushes in town."

"It didn't look to me like anybody was livin' in those three or four houses between Mrs. Slack's and the doctor's."

"You wouldn't call it exactly livin'. I just use the kitchen, like Tom does. The place we was born in, over next to the mill, got kind of dang'rous. I was scared it might slide downhill."

"Don't anybody aroun' here ever do anything when their places begin to fall down on 'em?" Robert Allan said unexpectedly.

"'Melia's kept hers up pretty well, and so've the Jameses. Tom Slack don't count. Slack by name an' slack by nature is a sayin' in this town. Our place 'd been all right if I'd been here to look after it."

"Do we have to discuss that again?" Junius said.

"Discuss what?" Cash said with a hairy and unpleasant grin. "It's the truth that June, over there, moved into this hotel the minute it was finished. The old place wasn't good enough for him."

"Cash doesn't mind rats—he's perfectly at home with them—I do," Junius said unpleasantly. "There are nine rooms to the place, and it would take a small fortune to keep it in repair. So Cash's looking after it wouldn't have done much good."

Cash gave up his futile gnawing at the chicken wing. "Damn these false teeth! June can talk about small fortunes. Talk's cheap. I'll admit he's always managed to live well enough—"

"Is everyone ready for dessert?" Mrs. Featherstone-Quinn rang the small bell beside her plate and said: "It's strawberry shortcake," in the tone of one announcing a special treat to children. "Yes, Mary Anne, you can clear away. And the chicken was delicious."

The dumpy little woman bobbed a curtsey, staring at Rocky with round black eyes. "Yes, that's the sheriff," Mrs. Featherstone-Quinn said indulgently. "And we aren't going to have any more of these horrid old bells ringing around here."

Rocky smiled reassuringly and tried to look as if he had the situation well in hand. He had

been curious about Mary Anne, but Mrs. Featherstone-Quinn explained that Mary Anne didn't like
to wait on table and only brought in the dessert
on special occasions.

Rocky watched her distribute oversized individ-
ual shortcakes and wondered what indiscretions
might have been committed by one or more of her
forebears. Mary Anne had a flat, yellow face, but
her eyes were round as licorice drops, and her hair
was a faded, light brown. She wore long, red earrings, a dress of checked gingham protected by a
voluminous apron and embroidered Chinese slip-
pers on tiny feet.

"Well, these practical jokes haven't spoiled your
cooking, Mary Anne," Barnhart said. He looked at
the island of crisp biscuit surrounded by crushed
red berries, sighed and then helped himself gener-
ously to cream. "Here comes another pound—but
who cares?"

Mary Anne bobbed again. "Thank you, Mr.
Barnhart. I hope it's like you say, only a practical
joke, but my ignition tells me it ain't. Those bells
are going to osculate again because it ain't no human hand that's ringing them. I tell you, if I hear
them again, it's absolutely going to prostitute me.
You can't tell what's going to sneak up on you in
the dark like a great, big, black pantheist."

Rocky glanced around the table, but everyone looked preternaturally sober. He said uncertainly: "Uh—pantheist, did you say?"

"One of them big, black beasts like a lion or tiger. You know? Miss Kitty, we ain't got enough coffee in the house for breakfast. I know it was very negligee of me not to remember it before . . ."

"I'll bring some over after dinner," said the young man sitting at the foot of the table. He had been introduced as "Lawrence Murdoch, who owns the store and has his meals here."

Rocky's private opinion was that Mr. Murdoch was cherishing a huge grouch about something. Until now, he had spoken only to say "thank you" or "please pass the salt." His reddish-brown eyes looked sulky, and he scowled unconsciously at his food. Now and then his nose twitched slightly. Rocky thought of a fellow whose nose did that when he was angry and decided that young Mr. Murdoch was still simmering for some cause or other. And what could be better cause than a good-looking girl who'd certainly been in the store just before supper? Rocky said innocently:

"Doctor James is pretty old, isn't he? Has he got any folks?"

"His granddaughter, Olivia. Such a nice girl and so unusual. It's too bad for a girl like that to be stuck up here," Mrs. Featherstone-Quinn said.

"Yes, that's all, Mary Anne. Olivia is really a won-derfully bright girl, but Doctor James needs her because his son—her father—is dead now, and so she feels she has to stay here, even if there are practically no opportunities for her here."

"I wouldn't worry about her. She believes in people making their own opportunities. Told me so again tonight—" Murdoch stopped, his square, red-brown face turning redder as he seemed to re-alize that his tone was somewhat violent. "Well, she's always telling me what a fool I am for stick-ing up here," he mumbled. "Maybe I am, but I've got the store, and I manage to live, and I might manage to get some trade for an auto camp some day. I call that planning ahead."

"Of course it is," Mrs. Featherstone-Quinn said consolingly. "We'll put this town on the map yet, you and I. Mr. Allan"—she lowered her voice—"it was nice of you not to laugh at Mary Anne. She was showing off for your benefit. She just loves words, but she never understands them, even when she reads them in the dictionary—which she quite often does."

Rocky laughed. "I b'lieve you. What's her igni-tion?"

"Intuition. I do wish," Mrs. Featherstone-Quinn sighed, "that I could break her of saying pros-tituted when she means prostrated. But I can't.

She's been with me since before Mr. Featherstone
died—though I don't know much about her. She
can't be pure Chinese, but she's never said, and I
wouldn't hurt her feelings for anything by asking
her. Well, are we all through? Then let's go out on
the porch. It seems awfully close tonight."

Mary Anne, reappearing suddenly, said: "It ain't
the heat; it's the humility. No, you don't need to
help me none tonight, Miss Kitty. I feel safe in
the kitchen as long as the sheriff's here."

"But I thought you said no human hand is
ringin' those bells," Rocky said. "I can't put handcuffs on a ghost."

"Well, I might be mistaken, and, anyway, maybe ghosts have some retrospect for law and order.
And you shouldn't talk about them irrelevantly,
either," Mary Anne said severely.

Rocky chuckled and followed Mrs. Featherstone-Quinn out of the dining room. Just ahead
of them Ivy Horne was saying to Robert Allan:

"It's too bad you were here tonight when Cassius was in one of his moods, Mr. Allan. That always makes things a little unpleasant. Of course,
he is a character . . ."

"One of them comic ones, like in the cowboy
pictures you was talkin' about?" Allan said suavely.

Mrs. Featherstone-Quinn murmured: "Oh dear,
I don't believe your father does like Ivy, after all.

She really is a sweet girl, but she does like to pose a little, and I should have known—"

"Dad can handle her, though he'd do better if he'd forget his manners. I'd like to talk to Amelia Slack. How about takin' me over there?"

"Well—" Mrs. Featherstone-Quinn stopped to light a large gasoline lamp in the living room, turned it low. "So inconvenient, not having electricity. At least, the water supply is good. Yes, I'll take you to Amelia's. She's always very polite to me. Maybe I only imagine she doesn't like me very well. I don't believe she really has any especial feeling for or about anyone most of the time," she added. "Except that she's very fond of Olivia James and doesn't ever seem to like Cassius."

They left the others sitting on the porch that ran across the front of the hotel and crossed the street. Mrs. Featherstone-Quinn picked her way daintily, shaking her little feet, in their high-heeled shoes, like a cat when she plunged deep into the thick dust.

"I do hope what Mary Anne calls the humility means it's going to rain. This dust is awful. Would you mind telling me why you want to see Amelia, Mr. Allan?"

"Well, she should be able to get a view of that schoolhouse from her side windows. Maybe she sets up late—"

"How did you know that?"

"I don't. It's a guess. She looks like time wouldn't mean much to her."

"It doesn't. She eats whenever she's hungry and sleeps when she's tired, which doesn't seem to be very often or very early. Look!" Mrs. Featherstone-Quinn pointed toward one of the front windows of Amelia Slack's house. A light had appeared in the window, shining faintly through the dusk. As they came closer to the house Rocky saw that a small, old-fashioned kerosene lamp had been placed on the window sill.

"It's pathetic, isn't it? She does that every night and keeps it burning until morning to light her husband home if he should come. I can't understand it," Mrs. Featherstone-Quinn, said. "She seems so sane about most things. Maybe that's just something that helped her when Andrew Slack died, and now it's gotten to be a superstition with her."

She lifted a rusted iron knocker and let it fall on the door. Amelia Slack opened it almost at once and said: "Good evening, Kitty. This is so nice of you. Won't you come in?"

Her voice had a faded sort of sweetness, an echo of some former vitality. She led them into a small living room, furnished in heavy mahogany and red

plush. Everything in the room was old, yet somehow the chairs and tables, carpets and bric-a-brac
glared with the newness of wedding gifts that had
not had time to become friends with the house.

Chairs and the one sofa were protected by large
tidies worked in black cross-stitch designs. Near
the stove was one shabby old rocking chair. Rocky
guessed that Amelia Slack sat in it, with a small,
worn rug under her feet, and saved the rest of
her furniture, dusting and polishing it carefully
and shielding the bright floral carpet from the sun
that would stream through the side windows in
the afternoons.

Those windows gave a clear view of the left side
of the schoolhouse and its front door. He walked
over to them and looked out while Mrs. Featherstone-Quinn was explaining that "Mr. Allan is investigating all this disturbance we've been having,
and he wanted to talk to you—if you don't mind."

"I don't mind. Though it hasn't disturbed me.
I've heard that bell ring before," Amelia Slack
said. "So many times: sixty strokes for my mother,
forty-eight for my father and twenty-five . . .
twenty-five . . ."

She seemed to forget that anyone was with her.
Rocky turned and said abruptly: "Mrs. Slack, have
you ever seen—from this window—anyone goin'

in or comin' out of the schoolhouse after the bell
had been ringin'?"

"I do sit by the window and look out—but
not after dark. I draw those shades then. And I
couldn't see anyone unless it was moonlight. The
moon hasn't been full for some time, and I've been
in bed before it rises. Besides, it's been cloudy at
night."

"Yes, it has. But haven't you been curious about
that bell ringin'? It's so close to you here."

"I'm never curious about anything," Amelia
Slack said gently. "The bell hasn't disturbed me,
and I've never tried to see who rings it. I didn't
realize you took it seriously, Kitty."

"Oh, I don't—not really. Only, of course, it is
annoying, and I have to think about its effect on
my guests. The ones who are coming later, at least,
and I'm afraid I'm a little stubborn and don't like
the idea of being forced to give up the hotel or not
make it pay just because somebody rings bells."

Amelia nodded. "I hadn't thought about that.
I'm not very practical. I wouldn't worry, Kitty.
If it's just somebody playing a joke on you, very
likely your calling Mr. Allan up here will stop the
joker."

"What do you mean—if it's only a joke?" Rocky
said quickly.

"I shouldn't have said 'if.' I should have said that as far as this practical joke is concerned, your coming up here should be the end of that."

"Do you mean there's something else I ought to investigate?"

"Nothing that you can, Mr. Allan. Not as long as the people up here won't change their natures. You look rather like my husband," Amelia said dreamily. "He's tall and blond, too."

Kitty Featherstone-Quinn got up abruptly and said: "Good night, Amelia. . . . There's no use," she explained to Rocky when they were outside, "trying to talk to her any more when she begins to talk about her husband. She always says he looks like every good-looking man she sees. Junius says Andrew wasn't any taller than he is and not particularly nice-looking. Mr. Allan, you don't think there's anything more behind all this nonsense than just someone trying to—well, to get my goat?"

"I don't think so. I'd like to know what Mrs. Slack meant about people not changing their natures, but I suppose you all have your little squabbles up here just like anywhere else."

"Oh yes. You know Cassius and Junius don't get along very well and Junius despises Tom Slack and— Well, things like that, you know."

"I admit this place has a funny effect on a person who isn't used to it. You begin wonderin' if there might be something more than a joke goin' on when you think of that bell ringin' up here at night."

"Are you psychic?" Mrs. Featherstone-Quinn said hopefully. She giggled at the look on his face. "Oh, now you do resemble your father. It's funny: you two don't look alike except for some kind of funny resemblance you can't fix definitely. You know, you can't put any faith in anything Amelia says, but if you think you should stay here tonight I'd certainly be glad to have you."

"There's no use in me stayin'. You've got a phone, haven't you?"

"When it works. A private line."

"Well, you can get me at Brookdale tomorrow till aroun' five-thirty. Then I'm going to a banquet at Merton, and I'll stay all night there, but I've had a phone put in our house there so you can reach me all right. I hope you won't have any more trouble. I've asked some questions an' tried to look official and that's about all I can do right now."

"I'm sure it will be enough. I don't think— Oh dear!" Mrs. Featherstone-Quinn stepped hastily back against Dr. James's picket fence. "Here comes Tom Slack, drunk again," she whispered. "Just keep still, and he won't see us, but if he does, sometimes he's quite abusive, and I— No, I don't want you to do anything to him. He's going home to sleep it off. Goodness knows where he gets the stuff—unless he makes it himself—because Lawrence Murdoch won't sell it to him, and he never leaves town."

"He cert'nly is carryin' a load tonight," Rocky murmured, watching Slack's wavering progress down the middle of the road. Presently he fell flat, got up, cursing fluently and brushing the dust out of his beard.

This beard was not an ornamental affair. In fact, as it would be excellent protection against cold and did away with any necessity of Slack's wearing tie or collar it could be considered a very utilitarian growth. A large nose jutted like a sharp, pointed stone from this underbrush of hair, and small, bloodshot eyes glared suspiciously at the universe.

"He's saved a lot of money on haircuts and razors the last twenty years," Rocky commented, looking at the bushy, salt-and-pepper hair that fell to Slack's shoulders. "An' I don't suppose he ever has to wash the back of his neck."

"I don't suppose he ever wants to. I don't see how Amelia stands him. I suppose his being Andrew's brother is enough for her, and she and Cassius are the only ones he'll have anything to do

with. We can go on now. We'd better," Mrs. Featherstone-Quinn said with her peculiarly childish
little giggle, "rescue your father from Ivy."

But Allan had already rescued himself, and he
and Barnhart were talking at one end of the porch.
"I'd like to talk to you again," Rocky heard Barnhart say. "Contemporary accounts like that diary
you say your father kept are invaluable. He fought
all during the war under General Forrest?"

"Yeah. He'd be a pretty old man if he was livin'
now, though he was just a youngster when he en-
listed. Nothin' would do but for us to name Rocky
after Forrest—Nathan Bedford. You see, my mother was from Virginia, and she was stubborn, so I
got named after Gen'ral Lee . . ."

Ivy Horne was looking, with effectively up-
raised eyes, at a new moon half veiled with misty
clouds. Junius was also conscientiously admiring
the moon and, Rocky suspected, Ivy's profile and
long, black lashes. Glidden, just behind him, took
his pipe from his mouth to say impatiently, evidently in answer to some suggestion of Ivy's:

"I never have any luck with effects like that.
For heaven's sake, don't try to tell me what to
paint, Ivy. I know what I can do. The moon over
the mountains is worse than your pet view of the
moon over Chinatown. You write a poem about it
whenever you simply can't restrain yourself."

Cash Quinn chuckled and shambled down the porch steps. "Good dinner, Kitty," he said ungraciously. "Thanks. You goin' home now, Sheriff?" he asked, when Mrs. Featherstone-Quinn had gone on up to the porch. "Not goin' to do anything more?"

"Not this trip. Do you think I need to?"

"Well, a word to the wise . . . I see old Tom just go by, roarin' drunk. But I'll be talkin' to him tomorrow," Cash said. "I see Kitty ain't so easy scared, and if it's me she's got her eye on— I ain't going to be up here much longer, maybe."

"Goin' off prospecting again?"

"I might. Wouldn't like to grubstake me, would you?"

"I know somebody who might."

Cash laughed. "Oh, I'll get along all right. You never can tell when or where you'll strike it rich. A greenhorn's as apt to do it as anyone else. I s'pose I'll always come back to this place. I'm used to it. So is June, though he's always talking about wanting to get out. He won't work, though; he'd rather marry a woman like Kitty than do that. She's all right. She kind of riles me, and she don't belong here, but I guess June probably got kind of the best of the bargain. She'll have to keep an eye on him when there's women around.

"Well"—he yawned—"I'm goin' off to bed. See you again sometime. Your pa got rid of that po'try-writin' female, but you'd better clear out if you don't want to have to admire the moon with her."

CHAPTER IV
"THEY'RE BOTH MISSING"

Old Doctor James had sneaked into the pantry that Thursday night to eat another very large piece of Olivia's lemon cream pie. The doctor had prescribed a diet for himself, when Olivia insisted that he do so, and had forbidden himself all the foods he liked best. But he was an old-fashioned doctor, and, though he knew his blood pressure was far too high, he really had very little faith in diets.

Olivia had made the pie because today was his seventy-fifth birthday and lemon cream pie was his favorite dessert. But she had cut him a very small piece at the dinner table, and he was afraid to ask her for more. That one piece had been just enough to give him a taste for another, and after Olivia was asleep he went into the pantry, cut a generous slice and ate it hastily, with one eye on the door.

He tried very hard, when he awoke at three o'clock in the morning, to convince himself that he didn't have a bad case of indigestion. But the gnawing in his stomach and the burning sensation around his heart persisted. His medicines were in the office at the front of the house, and he would have to pass Olivia's door to get there. And she left her door open and slept very lightly.

Olivia was a good child, and she meant to take care of him. But when you were old as he was and had seen so many people die you couldn't feel it was so important to prolong your own life. It wasn't just people. This whole town that his life had been bound up in was so near death that you had to listen before you were sure there was still a flickering heart beat in it. But he wished Olivia didn't feel she had to stay here, it was no place for her with all her ambition. . . .

He had to get up and mix himself some kind of dose, even if Olivia woke up and scolded him for eating that pie. And she did wake and did scold him, while she mixed white powder in water and handed him the glass.

"You shouldn't make pie like that if you don't want me to eat it, Livy," he said mildly.

"It was good, wasn't it? But I wouldn't have made it if you hadn't asked for it. I had to give you some kind of birthday present, and we're so damned poor," Olivia said rebelliously. She ran her hands through the tousled short hair that in daytime was brushed smooth and close to her head. "Everybody's poor in this town except Mrs. Hyphenated-Quinn, and she probably will be after she's been married to Junius and tried to make a go of the hotel a little longer. By the way, we haven't had any bells ringing tonight or last night."

"Very likely that's because the sheriff was here. It was a very foolish business, but I can't see why it should frighten anyone."

"It didn't frighten me, but it was a nuisance. I thought the sheriff would come to talk to you. Anyone could tell just by looking at you that you're a desperate character."

This was meant to be a joke so Doctor James smiled dutifully. "I saw him from the window. He seemed a very nice young man."

"Wonderful physique. Fine shoulders and not a bit of fat around his waist. If Larry doesn't take more exercise he's going to develop a bay window early. He's inclined to be chunky, anyway."

Doctor James winced inwardly. He hadn't become accustomed to Olivia's frank comments on the male physique. In his day girls as young as Olivia hadn't appeared even to know that men had legs. Of course, Olivia did know—naturally, she did, considering her education—but she might be a little more reticent about it.

"However, he looked to me like he might be pretty dumb," she went on. "Though I've heard he isn't. Do you feel better now? You'd better take some Allonal and go to bed. Go on, take it. You won't sleep if you don't."

She extinguished the lamp, and they went out into the narrow front hall. "It seems awfully close tonight. I think I'll see if it's any cloudier. It would be nice if it rained."

The doctor said: "What's that? Let me see!"

The shades in the office had been drawn to the window sill, but when the door was opened a ruddy light danced in the hall. They looked out and down the street, at flames just beginning to shoot high from a building near the old mill at the end of the town. . . .

There was a feud of thirty years' standing between the railroad town of Merton and the older, more sedate county seat at Brookdale. But at least once every year some wellmeaning citizen of one town or the other tried to promote good feeling, usually by arranging a banquet.

Tonight the Merton Kiwanis Club had entertained the Brookdale Lions. There had been a great deal of heavy, lukewarm food, several jugs of Dago red and a plethora of speeches. No one's feelings must be hurt, so everyone was asked to speak and did, with varying degrees of fluency.

It was midnight before Rocky and his father got back to the log house on Mariposa Street, and it seemed to Rocky that hardly ten minutes passed between the time he tumbled into bed and the moment when he rolled over and reached sleepily for the telephone on the table beside him.

He said "Hello!" several times before the operator's weary voice broke in: "Slacktown, here's your party. Here's your party, Slacktown."

The voice from Slacktown was very faint and faraway: a ghost voice from a ghost town. "Mr. Allan, can you hear me? It's Ivy Horne. Mrs. Featherstone-Quinn wants you to come at once."

"Why? What's happened?"

"I can't hear what you're saying. It's just a murmur. Oh, I do hope you hear me! Please come as soon as you can. The wires may not—" A crackling sound filled Rocky's ears for an instant, then Ivy Horne said again: "Please come as soon as you can," and the wires were silent. The Merton operator said:

"Rocky? Greenleaf says there's a fire at Slacktown, and she's been trying to get the forest ranger. She'll keep trying, but the wires may be down by now. Anyway, I can't get you a better connection . . . Oh, don't mention it."

Rocky groaned as he began to dress, then looked up to see his father standing in the doorway, buttoning his coat.

"Sure I woke up," Dad Allan said. "What 'd you expect? I wasn't sleepin' good, anyway. I thought my stummick could stand most anything, but that stuff they give us to eat along with that red ink give me bad dreams. I might sleep better after a ride. Where we goin' to?"

"Slacktown. Mrs. Featherstone-Quinn wants me to come right away. The phone girl says there's a fire up there. I wonder," Rocky grumbled, "if Mrs. F.-Q. thinks I'm a visitin' fireman."

"You don't b'lieve that, do you?"

"I wish I did. What I'm afraid of is that hell's broke loose up there in some form or other. Well, let's go. If you want a ride you'll get one."

They were perhaps two miles from Slacktown when Allan spoke for the first time during a breath-taking journey. "There's a fire, all right. I can smell it. I reckon it's because the trees are so thick we ain't seen it?"

"Yes. If we got far enough away we'd see the smoke. There may be a ranger there by now. It 'd be bad if the fire spread away from the town down

into the canyon. But there wasn't any use notif-
yin' the Merton fire department. They couldn't
get that old fire engine of ours up this grade."

Rocky set his foot on the accelerator again and
in a few minutes more took the hairpin turn into
Slacktown on two wheels. He thought he heard
his father mutter: "I reckon I was meant to die in
bed," and then they were out of the car, and Kitty
Featherstone-Quinn had thrown herself into his
arms and was sobbing hysterically on his chest.

"Oh, Mr. Allan! Oh, Mr. Allan!" She kept saying it over and over while Rocky looked helplessly
at his father over the woman's turbulent haystack
of hair. Dad Allan grinned in diabolical amusement, but he rose to the occasion and patted Mrs.
Featherstone-Quinn on the shoulder.

"Now, ma'am, you don't want to do that. You
tell us what's the matter. We can't do nothin' till
we know that, can we?"

"It's—it's— You see, the fire . . ."

Rocky blinked in the glare from dying flames
and the glowing ruin of the old mill and the three
houses nearest it. "We see it, all right. But they
seem to 've got it pretty well under control and—
Damn it! Will you stop cryin' and say what's the
matter?"

Mrs. Featherstone-Quinn drew herself up and
dabbed at her eyes with a blackened handkerchief.

"I know it's awful to go to pieces like this. It's Junius and Cassius. They're both missing. Their beds haven't been slept in, and we can't find them anywhere."

"Oh! When did you miss them?"

"Just as soon as we discovered the fire. Olivia and Doctor James gave the alarm. Junius wasn't in his room then, but I thought we'd just missed seeing him go out to warn Amelia and Cassius. But Cassius wasn't in his room, either, and we've had to fight the fire so we haven't been able to look for them very much, but they haven't turned up—and they would have by now, wouldn't they? With all this going on . . ."

She began to cry again. Rocky said: "Well, we'll look just as soon as it's safe to stop watchin' the fire. They don't need you any more. Where's some of the women?"

"I'll take her back to the inn," Ivy Horne said. She scrubbed at her face with the trailing sleeve of what had once been a white negligee. Her face was streaked with soot, her eyes red-rimmed and bloodshot. "We've worked like demons, and Mr. Murdoch says he thinks the fire is under control now. Come on, dear. They don't need us now, and we do need to wash our faces. . . ."

Rocky looked at the group strung out along the fire front. Mary Anne, in blue-cotton coolie coat and trousers, was pouring coffee from a large pot into the tin cup that Leon Glidden held out to her. Glidden wore a sweater, striped pajamas and his shoes, with the pajama legs rolled up to his knees. Olivia James had taken time to put on over- alls and stout shoes, and Barnhart and Lawrence Murdoch had a somewhat Russian aspect with pajama jackets hanging down over their trousers. All three of them had badly singed brows and lashes, and Murdoch shook a blistered hand while he still held a sodden sack in the other.

"Yes, Amelia came out," he said in answer to Rocky's question. "But her heart isn't so good, and Doctor James insisted on taking her back home awhile ago. He shouldn't exert himself, either. Tom Slack's so drunk we let him lay. Well, I've planned for years what I'd do if we had a fire, and it's a good thing I did."

"It's also a good thing there wasn't a breath of air, and that we've got a pretty good force of water." Olivia patted the hydrant by which she stood. "But I'll admit Larry got us organized. Gosh, I wish it would rain. I did feel a drop or two a few minutes ago."

"There wasn't any use trying to save these build- ings," Murdoch explained. "The four of them had to go, so we concentrated on the vacant lots here and the end of the street on the other side of the mill. Livy and I patrolled the back of the houses and kept sparks from getting down in the canyon. And we wet all the roofs of the nearest houses. Mary Anne, if you'll give me some coffee, I'll take a look down the canyon again."

"Here you are, Mr. Murdoch. I guess Mr. Glidden has had a sufficiency. My, it certainly was a colossus conflammation," Mary Anne sighed, staring at the molten mass that had an hour and a half before been weathered timbers. "If you gentlemen don't want any more coffee I guess I better go look after Miss Kitty. The poor dear's pretty near prostituted—and no wonder."

"Wait a minute before you go, Murdoch," Rocky said. "What do you think about the Quinn brothers bein' missing?"

Murdoch shrugged helplessly. "I don't know. It looks bad."

"Where could they be? Cash wouldn't clear out because he was afraid of the fire, and I can't even imagine Junius doing that," Olivia said. "What good would it do? Besides, his wife says his bed wasn't slept in."

"It wasn't," Barnhart said. "I ran in there myself, to wake him. He and Kitty have separate rooms. I think I was the first one to wake when Miss James started pounding on the door. I roused Kitty first and ran on to Junius' room before she was out of hers. So he didn't have time to slip away after the alarm was given."

"How far had the fire gotten when you discovered it, Miss James?" Rocky asked.

"It started in the old Quinn house, and by the time we got outside the building was a mass of flames. Of course, all these places are so old and dry that they burn like gunpowder. The first look I had at the Quinn house gave me the impression the fire had started at the back and was working toward the front, but I may have been mistaken about that."

Rocky turned to Lawrence Murdoch. "How do you think it started?"

"I think it was set. I don't— Glory be! it's going to rain. It *is* raining." For an instant they all stood with faces upturned to the first, slow, cool drops, then Murdoch went on: "No one ever went into that house. It wasn't safe. And we don't get tramps up here. There wasn't any wind, so a spark from one of our chimneys couldn't have started the fire—if we'd had any fires going at three-thirty. That was about the time Livy gave the alarm."

"Could Cash or Junius have decided to spend the night in the old-home place for any reason?" Glidden said. "And gone to sleep and set fire to the place with a cigarette?"

"Cash smoked a pipe, and Junius didn't smoke at all," Olivia said briefly.

"She's right. They might have used a lamp or candle in the place. But it doesn't seem reasonable to suppose they would both come here," Barnhart said. "One, perhaps, but not both of them. Well, what do we do about it?"

"There's nothin' to do till it's rained awhile longer," Rocky said. "When this has cooled off we can investigate."

"You mean you think there's someone in there?" Glidden looked slightly shaken. "But why—"

"I don't think, offhand, of any other good reason for anyone settin' a fire, when you consider two men are missin'."

"Will there be—anything left?" Barnhart said.

"There always is. If there's enough for two bodies, all right. If there isn't— Well, Cash and Junius were about of a size, so it 'll be hard to tell."

"I see," Barnhart said with a sickly smile. "I hadn't thought of that."

"Teeth are the best means of identification," Rocky added. "I reckon even Cash went to the dentist sometimes."

"I was the last dentist both of them had," Olivia said. "I have all the records."

"You—what?"

"I said, Mr. Allan, that I was the last dentist that Cash and Junius went to. Olivia Lucy James, D.D.S. That's me. Who did you think it was?"

"Your father . . ."

"He was a doctor, and he's been dead twenty years. There's no law against a woman being a dentist, is there?"

"No, ma'am," Rocky said meekly. But he looked at Lawrence Murdoch sympathetically. It must be tough to be in love with a woman dentist. Dentistry seemed like such an absolutely unfeminine occupation. "Well, if it turns out we need anything like that you'll have the information for us. Do you think you need us here, Murdoch? Then we'll look aroun' for a while. Come on, Dad. We'll be at Cash's place if you need us."

It was raining steadily now and very quietly. Mingling with the acrid smoke fumes was a wet fragrance from the old lilac bushes at the back door of the house where Cassius Quinn lived.

Rocky produced the flashlight that had come to be an inevitable part of his equipment and finally located a lamp on a rough, deal table, noting before he lighted it that there was very little kerosene left in it.

"He kept this place mighty neat," Dad Allan said.

"So do lots of old fellows like him who've bached for years."

Rocky looked around the room. Cash had not bothered with a bedstead: springs and a mattress on the floor had served him. The bed was neatly made up, though the blankets were dark with dirt and grease. One old-fashioned rocker, two rickety kitchen chairs, a small, rusted cookstove, two or three braided rugs and half a dozen, rather shaky shelves nailed to the walls completed the room's furnishings.

A scanty stock of canned goods was arranged on the shelf nearest the stove, with a stale loaf of bread, a bottle of souring milk and a rancid hunk of bacon. On a lower shelf, near the door, were arranged a tin wash basin and bar of soap, Cash's shaving kit, a nearly toothless comb and well-worn hairbrush.

Rocky stood looking into the washbasin for so long a time that his father finally said impatient-ly: "You gone into a trance?" and came over to him. "Why, the old fellow did some shavin' not so long ago."

"He shaved. What makes you think it wasn't long ago?"

"Any fool 'd know that. The hairs ain't all dried yet, an' the basin's damp in the bottom. You can see that as well as I can."

"Yes. I was just wonderin' . . . Cash shaved aroun' that mustache and imperial of his. Maybe he did it for supper tonight—last night—if he ate at the hotel."

"There's too much hair here for that kind of shavin'," Allan objected. "A lot of long ones on the floor. Maybe he decided to get rid of the chin whiskers."

"This pair of scissors has got hairs on it. But he'd wore those whiskers for years. Of course, there's no runnin' water in this place, but he could 've thrown the water outside and cleaned the basin if he wanted to leave things in order like he usually did." Rocky touched his thumb to the moist, soapy shaving brush. "He didn't even wash his brush or razor. See if there's any water in the teakettle, Dad."

"Full all the way up an' stone cold. There's a fire laid in the stove."

"A fire's got to be entirely out before you dare lay another one."

"I don't know where you get your brains from, Son," Allan drawled. "Either he shaved early, or he shaved with cold water. Is that it?"

"It'll do," Rocky said and examined Cash's wardrobe hanging from two hooks on the wall and consisting of one woolen shirt, an ancient pair of blue jeans and an old army overcoat.

He passed on to the bookshelf nailed up within easy reaching distance of the bed. Cash had read *True Stories, East Lynne, St. Elmo,* several of Pansy's masterpieces and odd copies of the Merton *Chronicle* and the San Francisco dailies. On top of the folded newspapers was an old account book filled with clippings, "mostly stories about gold strikes," Rocky said. "Here, Dad, you put this thing in your pocket. I'll read it through later on. And don't look so downhearted. I know you expected to find this place a wreck, like someone had had a fight in here. But it's just discouragin'ly neat. Well, look aroun' some more. You've got sharp eyes."

"Got to be somethin' to see, ain't there?"

"You might look for things that ought to be here and aren't." Rocky pointed to an oily ring on the floor near the stove. "Where's the coal-oil can?"

"Well, you don't need to smirk about it. Where's the cat?"

"Cat? All right, that makes us even," Rocky said amiably, bending over to look at the cushion in the rocking chair. "He had a cat, all right: a black one."

"Probably out seein' his lady friends. The cat, I mean. An' of course you're right about that coal-oil can," Allan said. "It 'd ought to be here, and it ain't, unless he left it over at the store. Not likely he did that with so little oil left in his lamp. Anyway, coal oil's good for startin' fires."

"That's what I was thinkin'. Damn it! There ought to be somethin'." Rocky sat down on the bed and looked discontentedly about him. "If someone was killed here it isn't reas'nable there aren't some traces of it."

"I'd make damn sure there wasn't, myself, if I was goin' to the trouble of burnin' up the evidence. In books there's usu'lly fingerprints."

"There may be some here. I was wondering if this place can be locked up. There's a key in that door—"

"Both doors. The one that leads to the rest of the house, too."

"Well, I'll lock up. I can't lug everything out of here to take a look at it. I've been studyin' fingerprinting, and we'll see how much I've learned. What're you looking at?"

"Under the stove. I s'pose I got to take my han'kerchief to this after talkin' about fingerprints. . . . It's just a poker," Allan said complacently. "You'd ought to look under stoves, Son. It's a good, substantial sort of poker." Holding it by its blackened point he brought it over to Rocky. "Take a look."

"I'm lookin'." Rocky regarded the heavy, knobbed handle grimly. "You could smash a man's head in with that. It looks like it 'd been polished off. No hairs or anything you could see on it without a microscope. You'd have to hold onto the poker part to use it."

"It's got soot on it, but it's kind of smudged."

"I had a hunch this business would get you, Dad."

Allan hastily put the poker down on the table beside the lamp. "I don't know what you're talkin' about," he snapped.

Rocky laughed. "And you with your nose up like a houn' dog scentin' a fox," he said disrespectfully. "Keep it up and—" He had put one hand flat on the bed to support himself; now he withdrew it quickly with a look of repulsion. He looked at the faint, pinkish stain on his palm, touched the blankets with the tip of one finger.

"The things are so dark an' dirty you'd never notice it unless you looked hard," he said as he got up and tried to inspect the back of his trousers.

"You didn't sit in it," his father said, more mildly than usual. "I didn't see it myself. The light ain't any too good in here. Quite a bit of it, ain't there?"

"Enough. Someone must've fell on the bed or been laid there. Bled quite a lot, an' it soaked in.

Well, let's get out of here," Rocky said abruptly. "I'll lock the door to the rest of the house an' this back one and keep the key. Look at the windows, will you?"

"I reckon the old man didn't care none for fresh air. They ain't been open for years. What are you— Well, we got a visitor."

The big black cat that had walked into the room as Rocky opened the back door arched its back and rubbed ingratiatingly against Allan's legs. Rocky grinned and picked the cat up as his father stepped quickly aside.

"I remember now that you don't like cats. I do." He rubbed the black head, and the small bell on the cat's leather collar tinkled thinly. "He's got a purr like a small steam engine."

"I wouldn't go so far's to kick a cat to keep it away from me—I've saw people who would—but I don't like 'em. What you goin' to do with him?"

"Take him to the hotel, I guess. He can't stay here and walk over things," Rocky said, locking the door. "The way this key turns I don't think Cash locked up very often. Be still, will you, cat? All right, scram." He watched the cat slink blackly away into the lilac bushes. "Let's go over next door. I want to see how drunk Tom Slack is."

To all appearances Tom Slack was very drunk. He lay on his back, snoring loudly, and did not open his eyes when Rocky directed the light from his torch across them. He grunted uneasily and burrowed his whiskered face into a filthy pillow.

"You could knock down a house with his breath," Rocky murmured. "He's drunk, all right—now an' for some time past. If someone— What's that?"

"It seems to be another pet. Maybe he used it for a alarm clock."

The elderly white rooster, perched on the back of a chair, eyed them with sleepy, ministerial dignity, descended to the floor with a flutter of wings and walked without haste across the room and out of the door that had been slightly ajar when they entered.

"This is a crazy place," Allan said. "Maybe you'll find out that woman, Mrs. Slack, keeps a cow in her kitchen."

"A pig would feel right at home in this hole," Rocky said, looking disgustedly about the incredibly dirty room. "It smells to me like he's let some beans go sour on the stove, but it may just be the booze. I don't see anything incriminatin' around here. Let's go over to the hotel and see if we can get some more coffee."

"This all you're goin' to do?"

"Till it's lighter, and the fire out there's dead enough to work in. You can't," Rocky reminded his father, "investigate a murder very well till you've got somethin' that at least kind of resembles a body."

CHAPTER V
"THOSE THINGS WERE PLANTED"

Rocky's tanned face had a curiously bleached look as he raised his head and threw a corner of the sheet back across the gruesome exhibit they had been studying.

"Well," he said to the group in Doctor James's office—four men and Olivia James—"you're agreed it's Cash Quinn?"

"So far as my evidence goes it might be Junius," the doctor said. "There's nothing here that can enable me to say positively which man this was. But Olivia—"

"They're Cash's upper and lower plates. I ought to know; I had them made for him and tried to fit them to his mouth. They were beautiful work, too; so were Junius'. But Cash expected them to fit like his own teeth the minute he put them in and to get used to them without wearing them." Olivia spoke so calmly that Lawrence Murdoch looked at her disgustedly, but when she struck a match to light a cigarette her fingers were shaking.

"That's his belt buckle, too," Murdoch said, indicating the blackened silver square with the initials C.Q. "He'd worn it for years. Funny it didn't melt."

"He must have been lying on his face, so the buckle was under him. You can't ever tell what will burn, and what won't, in a fire," said Mike Chapin, the fire ranger who had arrived at Slacktown not long after the Allans. "I remember a fire where all the silver but the teaspoons melted into a lump, but those kept their shape. Isn't that old Cash's nugget stickpin, too?"

"What's left of it. You can see there's been gold on it. Well, that would be under him, too. What about the—the skull, Doctor James?" Rocky said.

The doctor went on washing his hands at a small stand in one corner of the office. "It doesn't offer any evidence. After all, the house fell in on him; perhaps beams fell over the body. The back of the skull is badly crushed. I must say I'm rather surprised at the shattered condition of the lower jaw, but, as Mr. Chapin says, fires play odd tricks."

He sighed, drying his capable old hands. "Poor Cash. I was in charge in that house that's just burned down the night he was born. That was fifty years ago. I was twenty-five, and it was one of my first maternity cases, and I was very nervous about it. Olivia, my dear, suppose you bring out the whisky. I think we'd all be better for a drink. Yes, pour me one, too, a small one. I'll prescribe for myself this time."

"She'd do all the prescribing around here if you gave her a chance," Murdoch muttered. "Well, it was a dirty job, and I don't want any more like it. I'm going home and take a bath. But what about Junius?"

Rocky shrugged, still looking at the sheet on the operating table. "What can you think when one person's dead, and one's missing? Was there bad blood between those two?"

"They didn't get along very well, but I wouldn't have thought there was any danger of one killing the other," Murdoch said. "I can't imagine any of their squabbles—like you heard at dinner the other night—leading to murder. And where's June gone to? Where could he— Sa-ay! I was awake sometime last night, between ten and three-thirty. Ten's when I went to bed. I woke up for just a minute and thought I heard a car. Then I supposed it was thunder, so I went back to sleep without looking to see what time it was."

"I reckon you heard a car," Rocky said, "because Mrs. Featherstone-Quinn's is missin'. I looked in the garage before we started work out there in the ashes. But I can't tell you which way the car went because the rain's washed out everything. There's no use cryin' over that. That loose dirt probably wouldn't have held tire marks or footprints, anyway."

"Quinn must be pretty faraway by now," Chapin said suggestively.

"So far away that my startin' out right this minute ain't going to do any good. He'd be out of the county by now. If he was smart he went down through Greenleaf, Merton and over into Nevada. Besides— Well, I'll send out the alarm pretty quick."

"The phone's working all right, now?" Chapin said. "They couldn't get me for a while."

"The wires were bad while the fire was burning, and the service is never too good. I tried to get you," Murdoch said. "Then I was too busy to bother, but the operator kept trying. I guess the phone's all right now. Wouldn't you and your father like to come over to my place for breakfast, Allan? I get my own."

"I'll have breakfast for all of you in a few minutes if you'll wait," Olivia said.

"We won't bother you. You look like you could do with some rest. Mary Anne said for us to come back to the hotel. Thanks just the same," Rocky said. "I'll be back later. I want to talk to you."

Mary Anne had removed two leaves from the dining-room table to reduce it to a size more suitable for five persons. "I gave Kitty a sleeping powder," Ivy said, "without consulting her, after Leon came back and told me you were going to have to—what you were going to have to do. I was afraid she might insist on going outside again."

"Doesn't she connect the fire with the two men disappearin'?" Rocky asked.

"I don't know. I suppose she will when she thinks things over. It isn't like Kitty to be hysterical," Ivy said slowly. "She usually keeps her head in an emergency. Was it— Arthur says he thinks it was Cassius who was in the building where the fire started."

"I said we found a belt buckle and tiepin that were evidently his," Barnhart corrected. "'We' is not the right pronoun, however. Leon and I were very little help."

"You did what you could," Rocky said "After all, Chapin's used to that kind of thing and knows how to go about it."

"My spirit was willing, but my stomach was weak," Glidden said candidly. He examined a blistered thumb. "That James girl makes me feel like a weak sister. She did two men's work when we were fighting the fire and gave me the impression that I did everything wrong. For that matter, Ivy

pitched in and did yeoman labor herself. Didn't
think you had it in you, Sappho."

"I am really a very practical person. I shouldn't
have tried to fight fire in a negligee, but I hav-
en't any overalls. I don't look well in overalls, and
the James girl does. My appearance is all against
me," Ivy said. "I admit I pose. I was a child poetess, and I've never recovered. I can't help it if I
look like an ethereal being fed on dew. But why
am I talking about myself now? Habit, I suppose.
Someone has to tell Kitty what's happened. And
what *has* happened?"

"Apparently Junius has killed his brother and
cleared out," Glidden said. "Mary Anne says Kitty's car is missing. I didn't hear a car drive away
during the night, but the garage is on the other
side of the house from my room. Did any of you
hear it?"

"I sleep the sleep of the dead up here," Barnhart
said. Then, as Ivy winced, he apologized: "Sorry.
I meant to say that I sleep very soundly. I put my
light out about ten-thirty. Dozed off with a book
in my hand, so I was asleep at once."

"Did Cash have supper here last night?" Rocky
asked. "When's the last time you all saw him?"

"He was here and went away at his usual time,
about eight o'clock. He always went to bed early,"
Barnhart said. "Odd that his bed wasn't slept in.

We all went upstairs just a few minutes before ten, and since Junius hadn't been to bed, either, I suppose they must have arranged to meet each other."

"Did those two quarrel last night?"

"No more than usual. Cash made barbed remarks regarding Junius' dislike of work, and Junius retorted that Cash had been living on Kitty since she came up here. It didn't seem serious to me."

"It wasn't. And I simply cannot imagine Junius killing anyone," Ivy said.

"I can imagine him killing for money. He was a greedy little devil," Barnhart said. "On the other hand, he loved his own skin and probably wouldn't risk it by murder."

"Oh, I think you're unfair. He probably did marry Kitty for purely practical reasons, but you know she wanted to marry him, and he was always very nice to her. He was a misfit; he didn't belong here and never had. I was sorry for him."

"I imagine he meant you to be, Ivy. That was his line," Barnhart said satirically. "The misunderstood genius—and nothing personal meant by that remark. I'm a misunderstood, or at least an underpaid genius myself. But perhaps you have more questions to ask, Mr. Allan, and we're wasting time."

"I wouldn't say you were. What do you think it would have taken to make Cash turn killer?"

Barnhart did not answer immediately. "Gold," he said at last. "He was crazy about gold: not money, not even gold coins, but chunks of pure gold. He told me that nugget on his tiepin was the largest he'd ever found. Then he told me very interesting stories about all the fabulously large nuggets that have ever been found."

"I don't doubt that, after lookin' over his scrap book. Did either Cash or Junius carry life insurance?"

Mary Anne had just come in with fresh coffee, and she answered Rocky's question. "Mr. Quinn didn't have a bit of life assurance, Mr. Sheriff. People ought to have themselves assured, and I told Miss Kitty so, but she thought it would be kind of indelicate to elude to it. Goodness, she spent enough money on him that he might 've done that for her, and he looked to be a good risk. Not like Mr. Featherstone, who always had gastronomy real bad. He didn't have no assurance—which was funny, when he wasn't euphemistic about his chances of living long—but at least he had a saving disposition. You folks want any more hot cakes? Well, you call if you need me."

"The late Mr. Featherstone suffered from indigestion," Barnhart said. "However, I happen to have heard Cash say several times that insurance

and banks were both 'skin games.' But why bring
that up?"

"Motive," Rocky said impatiently. "No one's
given me any really good reason why Cash or Junius should 've killed each other. Besides, the setup
has all the earmarks of an insurance swindle."

"Wondered if you was goin' to miss that." Mr.
Allan speared three flapjacks from a big platter
and reached for the syrup jug. "Occurred to me
right away, soon as we got them teeth and the pin
and buckle all collected."

"Well," Barnhart said slowly, "I admit the same
thought occurred to me. It's been done so often in
just that way that one's suspicious of such means
of identification. But how can you be certain?"

"That those things were planted by Cash? I don't
know of any way to prove it," Rocky said, "but
you probably know Cash wasn't fond of wearin'
his false teeth. I noticed he had a lot of trouble
with them the night we was here, an' Miss James
said he didn't wear them enough to get used to
them."

"I've often seen him without them," Glidden
said. "In fact, he often wore them only at meals.
I've seen him slip them out and put them in his
pocket after dinner. So has Ivy."

"It certainly wasn't a sight I'd be apt to forget."

"Well, there you are. It isn't reasonable Cash would be wearin' those teeth late at night in his own place. If he was expectin' Junius he wouldn't bother to put the things in for his benefit. And someone shaved himself over there where Cash lived an' not very long before the fire. Gray hairs, like Cash would have. Was he shaved at supper last night?"

"He was not. And he very badly needed to be," Ivy said. "He had simply added another day's growth to the stubble he had the night before."

"Tom Slack certainly ain't shaved lately, and Doctor James is the only other one here that 'd have a gray beard—if there was any reason for him to shave anywhere but at home. Junius' beard wasn't gray—I guess. Did he dye his hair?"

"I don't think so. There was a thread or two of gray in it that wouldn't have been there if he had," Barnhart said. "And I know his beard was still black; I've seen him in the mornings before he'd shaved."

"It don't matter because there was too much hair aroun' to be accounted for except by Cash's mustache and imperial. A pair of scissors had been used to cut hair. I reckon you've wondered why I haven't sent out word to look for Junius?" Rocky said. "How can I, when it's prob'ly Cash we want?

And Cash without the marks it 'd be easy to identify him by."

"Clever," Barnhart muttered. "Get rid of his mustache and imperial, perhaps trim his eyebrows, and I swear I couldn't give a decent description of him under the circumstances."

"He had filmy blue eyes, high cheekbones with a small, half-moon scar on the right, a thin, straight nose and a pointed chin," Leon Glidden said. "Flat ears with large lobes, and the left one must have been chewed on by some animal. Anyone could describe his general build."

"Is that what you call a photographic eye?" Rocky asked.

"Not exactly. I'm no portrait painter, but I wanted to see what there was to his face besides eyebrows and whiskers. But look here," Glidden said, "if that's Junius, why aren't his own teeth in his mouth?"

"Miss James spoke about him havin' plates, too."

"O-oh! I don't believe it!"

"He did, though, Ivy. They were very good ones, and he always wore them," Barnhart said. "He was sensitive about having to have them, said rotten teeth seemed to run in their family. Well, that's not important. What are you going to do, Allan? I'll be damned if I could make up my mind."

"Oh, I'll send out a description of Cash and phone the cor'ner, though I doubt if he'll hurry about the inquest. He usually does get it over right away, but under the circumstances he might as well go slow. And I've got to phone to Brookdale for some stuff I want and talk to some more people and look aroun' a bit," Rocky said vaguely. "That ought to keep me busy for a while."

"It should," Barnhart agreed. "By the way, was there any proof that fire was set by someone?"

"We found a piece of what looked like it 'd been a coal-oil can, if you can call that proof. Chapin says it probably was blown out the back of the house. Another one of the fire's funny tricks. A can of coal oil was missin' from Cash's room; Murdoch says he got it filled up fresh yesterday afternoon. Of course," Rocky added, "there probably wasn't much coal oil left in the can before the fire was lighted. I reckon most of it was poured over the body to make sure it 'd burn."

He smiled apologetically, as Ivy shivered, and went out to the telephone in the hall. They could hear him talking to the coroner, who apparently resented the fact that nothing which could properly be called a body awaited his inquest.

"Well, take your own time about it," Rocky said finally. "Yes, there's enough people here for your jury. I can't help things bein' like they are. I'll be in Merton sometime this afternoon if you want to call and tell me what you've made up your mind to do."

He left Lorenzo Sloane to his perplexities, called Cy Rand and told him to send the fingerprinting outfit to Merton as soon as possible. "Pay somebody to take it up if Al Sully's too busy. Send my mail up, too. . . . What? . . . You ask the cor'ner for the details, Cy. I've got work to do."

Robert Allan, having finished his after-breakfast cigar, came out to the hall and found Rocky still sitting at the telephone, chin resting on his clasped hands, staring at the crude designs someone had scrawled on the wall.

"You cert'nly are a mighty busy man. Getting any inspiration from them curlicues?"

"I was just thinkin' . . . Well, let's go over to Cash's place again."

"It's stopped rainin', anyway," Allan said. "I feel dirty, grubbin' in them ashes. You expect to find anything more in this place? Who you goin' to talk to first?"

"I don't know," Rocky said, unlocking the door to the old house where Cash had lived. "Probably not to anybody for a while. There's no use."

"Why not? You ought to— Here's that damn cat again."

"I reckon he wants to be fed." Rocky found an already opened can of prepared food on the shelf over the stove, scraped some out onto a tin plate and put it on the floor. "He's a good-lookin' beast. Murdoch said Cash called him Sultan. If nobody else wants him I'll take him. Eleanor would like to have him. I wish she was here."

"Any special reason?"

"She gets acquainted with people." Rocky was taking the lids off the cans labeled TEA, SUGAR and COFFEE and looked into them as he spoke. "She'd be holdin' Mrs. Featherstone-Quinn's hand and being confided in. And it takes a woman to size up a woman. Still, she may be safer where she is." He took a dishpan from the top of the stove and emptied the contents of a sack of flour into it.

"So this is detectin'," Allan drawled. "Lookin' through a bunch of groc'ries. Want me to go through the woodbox?"

"If you don't mind." Rocky took the cushion from Cash's rocking chair, examined it carefully and then allowed Sultan to establish himself on it. "I suppose that's your special place, cat?" he said, stroking the round ball of black fur. The bell on the cat's collar tinkled as he uncoiled himself, stretched and curled up again. "Well, take your nap while you can because you aren't stayin' here long."

"There's nothin' in this box but wood," Allan reported, pulling a splinter out of his thumb.

"I didn't suppose there would be. Thanks." Rocky was pulling the blankets off the bed now. He turned the mattress over, looked at it disgustedly and threw it back on its springs, took the rag rugs from the floor, shook them and threw them in a heap in one corner.

His father said pensively: "This used to be a mighty neat-lookin' room." Rocky was going through Cash's library, fluttering the leaves of books and scrutinizing their covers. He unfolded all the newspapers, turned out the pockets of the garments hanging on the wall and finally stood still in the middle of the floor, looking about him.

"Well, there isn't any wallpaper an' the floor looks just like a floor," he said. "Everything was in order in here this mornin'. Wait a minute. I want to take a look at the rest of the house."

The look lasted not more than two or three minutes. "There hasn't been anyone in there for months," Rocky reported, locking the door again. "Dust all over everything, and it hasn't been walked in." He picked Sultan up and put him down on the doorstep. "Sorry, but you'll have to find you another home."

Sultan clawed affectionately at Allan's trousers and being told to "Scat!" sat down by a lilac bush and glowered at the world.

"You've hurt his feelings, Dad."

"That's all I did hurt. He can sharpen his claws on a tree. Well, the way you're starin' at this yard I expect you want me to take the dirt up and sift it?"

"No, but you might"—Rocky suggested, grinning—"crawl under the lilacs, an' see what you can see. Forget it. Let's go over and talk to Mrs. Slack."

Olivia James opened the door to Rocky's knock and regarded him with an expression that was distinctly hostile. Then, seeing Sultan, who had decided Rocky's boots were friendly boots and had stretched himself, purring, across them, she said:

"Oh, there he is. Amelia was wondering if anyone had seen him."

"Does she want him?"

"She's never kept a dog or cat because they get hairs on things, but I suppose she'll take care of him if no one else will. He doesn't like me."

Olivia put out a hand toward the cat and was promptly rewarded with a profane hiss. "See, he swears at me. He always does that to anyone who's mistreated him. I stepped on his tail accidentally, once, and he's never forgiven me for it. He's spoiled, anyway. He expects everybody to love him—whether they like cats or not. Mary Anne might look after him."

"We'll see he don't starve. I want to talk to Mrs. Slack."

"You can't. She isn't well enough to talk to anyone, let alone you."

"Of course, I do intend to put her through a third degree."

"Well, even if you don't, you can't talk to her," Olivia said stubbornly. "Grandfather told her to stay in bed, and I'm going to see she does. She tried to help last night, and she shouldn't have. I won't have her bothered."

"Are you in charge of her case?" Rocky said politely.

"I'm perfectly capable of prescribing for her and most of the other people here. Anyway, Grandfather would tell you just what I have. It's only decent for you to wait awhile to talk to her. She's upset."

"Is she? I would 've thought nothin' would upset her much. And I thought her and Cash didn't get along."

"You see? There you are, suspicious already. Who did like Cash? I didn't, particularly. Neither did Tom Slack."

"I thought they were pals."

"Oh, well"—Olivia shrugged—"Tom talked to Cash and Amelia when he talked to anyone. But it hasn't been so long since he was on the warpath

because Sultan tried to play with his chickens.
Especially that old rooster of his. Sultan found
him rather a rough playmate. Bill—the rooster—
was able to take care of himself. He should be;
he's been around long enough."

"You're gettin' right interestin' info'mation
about the livestock, if nothin' else," Allan murmured.

"I noticed that. Well, never mind about Mrs.
Slack," Rocky said as Olivia scowled at his father.
"What does Tom Slack do for a living?"

"He has about two hundred dollars a year. When
his chickens are laying he sells the eggs, and he
used to be the town bootlegger. I suspect he still
makes enough liquor—if you want to call it that—
for himself. As I remarked to Grandad last night,
everyone in this town is broke. We are."

"Didn't Cash and Junius pay you for those
plates you had made for them?"

"Cash did—cash on the spot." Olivia giggled.
"I didn't say that on purpose. Junius didn't, but
his wife did when he acquired her. Let's see: I
got five dollars out of the Barrys for filling four
teeth for their kids—and lucky to get that. They
live on the La Porte road, and Grandad still de-
livers a new baby for them every year. And Mrs.
Hyphenated-Quinn had some work done out of

the goodness of her heart, and I pulled a tooth for Larry—"

"You did?"

"You needn't look so surprised about it, though I'll admit he never would have let me if it hadn't been abscessed, and he'd let it go—like men always do—until his face was swelled up, and he couldn't stand it. Then he got me up at midnight to tend to it. I practically had to put my knee on his chest to get the thing out." Olivia flexed her strong fingers unconsciously. "June and Cash came to me because I was convenient and cheap. Why?"

"Why? Well, as a matter of fact, I didn't ask you about your practice," Rocky said. "You just started tellin' me you're all broke. What's Mrs. Slack live on?"

"What her husband and father left her—not much more than Tom Slack has. Larry has his store and barely makes expenses. The Barrys and some other families out there trade here. Grandad has a few savings and the remains of a practice and doesn't ever make people pay him. I've got to get back to Amelia. She needs something to eat."

"I reckon," Allan said when Olivia had slammed the door shut, "that's what you'd call a modern female? I wouldn't let her get near none of my teeth.

She'd just as soon yank 'em out as not, and she's got the muscles in her shoulders to do it. I kind of pity that young fellow."

"I guess he's got it comin'." Rocky stirred Sultan gently with the toe of his boot as the cat sprawled in the damp earth and demanded admiration. "I think we'll take a ride out on the La Porte road. Here comes Doctor James. . . . Your granddaughter's been telling me Mrs. Slack's in pretty bad shape, Doctor."

"Amelia? She was perfectly all right an hour ago. Surely Olivia would have called me if she needs attention. Amelia simply overdid a little, and I advised her to be quiet. I was going to take a look at Tom Slack. The man will drink himself into D.T.s one of these days. But perhaps I'd better go in and see how Amelia is, first."

Rocky looked after the doctor as he vanished into the cottage. "I think the lady's an awful liar," he said. "Come on, let's go ridin'."

CHAPTER VI
BLACK WATER

The La Porte Road was fairly level and not so crooked as the one leading to the mountaintop, but it was very narrow and badly in need of repair. Robert Allan looked at it unenthusiastically and spoke briefly on the subject of the superior highways and scenic beauties of Texas as compared with those of California.

"You haven't seen any of the good roads. I reckon," Rocky said, "that what you really mean is that you don't see any reason why we should come out here at all."

"You said yourself that anyone with any sense would light out the other direction to Nevada."

"I was talkin' about Junius, then. He'd stick to civ'lization. But Cash knows the country here and aroun' Downieville, where he could finally land up. He could take care of himself in the woods if he had to. Murdoch says Cash did drive a car but very badly. What surprises me is how he happened to learn at all."

"Did you happen to think you ain't sent out a description of Cash yet?"

"I'll do it from Merton. The telephone service's better down there."

"That sounds to me like a mighty lame excuse."

"Then I won't use it again. I'd just as soon wire as phone. It's apt to be more private in the end."

"Any special reason for keepin' things secret?"

"It never hurts. You know, it's a wonder to me Cash wouldn't take some grub along. But Murdoch, when I was talkin' to him again just before we left, said Cash never bought very much stuff and hadn't bought anything but that coal oil for a week. So what we saw in his place was all he had. He ran a bill with Murdoch and paid up ever' two or three months."

"Ain't that interestin'? I take it you think so, or you wouldn't have that Chessy-cat grin on your face. I think I'll stay down in Merton when we get back there. This business is tryin' to my temper. Where's that road go to?"

"Hunh? Oh, that goes up to Deep Lake."

"Is it?"

"Deep, you mean? Not so very—far's I know. They just lacked imagination when it came to namin' things. There's lakes all over the top of the mountain. They get their water from a bigger one. People just go picnicking up at Deep Lake. That road won't do for a car, but it's only about a quarter of a mile up there."

"Do you figure on goin' very far? Over to this Downieville place?"

"That 'd take too long." Rocky looked at the speedometer. "We've only come about three miles. I sort of wish it hadn't rained."

"You said you couldn't 've seen any tracks in the dust."

"Not any real tracks. I might 've been able to tell other things." Rocky put the brakes on abruptly, and they skidded to a stop in the loose dirt. "I could have told if that car hit a rock because it skidded," he said laconically.

Allan got out of their car and walked around Mrs. Featherstone-Quinn's elderly sedan stand-ing diagonally across the road with its front axle against a large rock.

"Was you lookin' for this?" he said.

"Oh, I was just lookin'. Of course, Cash was a rotten driver, and it would be a bad road to go over at night. And that car has a long wheel base that makes it hard to get aroun' sharp curves. Looks like he tried to take this one too fast, hit that rock and skidded aroun'."

Allan received this statement with a scepti-
cal grunt, more or less justified by something in
Rocky's voice that hinted he was calling attention
only to the obvious.

"The car's been rained on," he said. "It's been
standin' here all night. I reckon he wouldn't have
got much farther along, anyway. The gas tank's
about empty."

"It is?" Rocky came over and stared at the gauge
and then smiled slowly. "It beats hell the foolish
things a man will do when he's excited."

"You can't fill up with gas in the middle of the
night when you're tryin' to get away without anyone knowin' it."

"There's a hundred-gallon drum of gas in the
garage. I noticed it this mornin'. I suppose they
have it partly for the gasoline lamps they use in
the hotel."

"It's a wonder they didn't use some of that to
give that fire a good start."

"Fooling aroun' with gasoline's a risky business.
It didn't need much to start a fire in that house."

"It wouldn't have taken much more to burn
down the whole town," Allan said. "Don't it seem
to you pretty cold-blooded to think someone was
to burn up a town to get rid of a body?"

"It certainly was takin' a big risk. Murdoch
kept talkin' about that. He was madder about the

fire than anything else, said he'd worried about it for years—with so few able-bodied men in town."

Rocky got into the back of the car as he spoke, turning on his flashlight to examine the cushions. "Well, there's nothing in here," he said finally, climbing over into the front seat. He twisted the steering wheel experimentally, touching only its spokes. "The front axle is sprung so bad the car won't steer. I'll have to send someone from Greenleaf to tow it back to town. There's nothing more we can do here. If he went on afoot he took to the woods, an' he'd know how to hide there."

He managed finally to turn his own car and start back toward Slacktown, but when they had reached the rutted track that went up the hill to Deep Lake he stopped again.

"We're goin' up here," he said, when Allan looked at him inquiringly. "Keep your eyes peeled for—well, for anything. In books people are always catchin' their clothes on bushes and leavin' pieces of them where they can be found."

"Obligin' of them," Allan snapped. He did not like to walk, and in his high-heeled boots he made hard work of the quarter mile uphill. Rocky grinned and said:

"Sorry I can't provide you with a horse. That's the trouble with ridin' so much: you get bowlegged and can't walk." He added, before Allan could reply to this insult: "Here it is."

The small lake was so thickly surrounded by trees that its still water looked black and stagnant. The road ran down to a half-circle of jagged rocks, with one immense boulder leading the band. On the other three sides dense forests held the lake imprisoned.

Rocky sighed, sat down on a rock and began to take off his boots. "If it just hadn't rained—then we could 've told if anything had been dragged uphill. Of course, Cash was a lightweight; he could be carried."

"Are you fixin' to dive in there?" Allan said as Rocky pulled his shirt over his head. "It looks mighty cold to me."

"It's colder 'n ice water," Rocky said with a premonitory shiver. "An' I'm no diver, so it probably won't do any good, but as long as we're here I'd better have a try at it. I might be lucky."

"Well, you be careful you don't cut your head to pieces on a rock. You don't know how deep it is."

"Mountain lakes usually drop right off into deep water. I'll wade in first to be safe. Goddam! These rocks are sharp."

He took two cautious steps before the rock shelf under his feet suddenly disappeared, and he plunged into water over his head. He came up, spluttering, shook the water from his eyes and smiled feebly as he saw his father grinning at him sardonically.

"I've a good mind to toss you in—an' see how you—like it," he gasped and submerged again before he swam back to the shore and clambered up to the top of the majordomo boulder.

"It's plenty deep enough for divin' if I don't just do a bellyflop. Well, here goes. . . ."

Three times he touched bottom—rough stones and cold mud—but never for more than an instant. At last, teeth chattering, the veins standing out on forehead and neck, he gave up the attempt.

"There's no use you killin' yourself," Allan said severely. "You'll get yourself a nice case of pneumonia, and then who'll do the detectin' aroun' here?"

"I'll bust a gut if I keep on tryin'. I can't get depth easy enough. Still, he ought to be somewhere right close to the shore. Couldn't be any-place else. I wish I had a towel. You wouldn't like to loan me your shirt?"

"You get your clo'es on. The thing to do is bring up a rowboat an' some grapplin' hooks—if all this hocus-pocus means you think Cash Quinn's body's in this lake."

"It's just a guess. If he was goin' to take the car why didn't he fill up with gas and take some provisions along? Cash would. But it seems more likely he'd— Well, I'm not satisfied."

"You ain't easy to satisfy. Here you got what looks like an open-an'-shut case: one brother kills another one an' makes a getaway. If Cash's body's in there, who killed him? Why'd they want to kill him after he killed Junius? Unless someone killed both of them. If they did, why not put both bodies in the fire? Or up here?"

"I can't tell you that. I may find out something I've got to know, when we get to Merton. It's ten-thirty—"

"Seems to me like it might be ten-thirty tonight—we've been up so long. You ready to go?"

"We might as well. I wish I had a drink; I'm frozen stiff. That idea of yours about the boat is all right," Rocky went on when they were in the car again, "if they have a boat in Slacktown. It 'd be enough of a job gettin' one up here from there, and if we had to bring one from Merton it 'd be easier to get someone to try divin' again. We can get some hooks to use if we locate anything."

"If Cash Quinn's up there in that lake someone else drove that car an' dumped him in there."

"You're sufferin' from a rush of brains to the head, Dad. That's the gen'ral idea. We can't get to Merton much before noon, now. I'll talk to Murdoch first thing. . . ."

Lawrence Murdoch was standing in front of his store, talking to Barnhart and Olivia James. "I'm glad to see Mrs. Slack's so much better you can leave her, Miss James," Rocky said blandly. "Maybe she'll be well enough to talk to later this afternoon. Did your grandfather go to see Tom Slack?"

"Tom's still sleeping it off. He should be as rational as he ever is after a few more hours. And as for Amelia, she's sleeping, too. I only left her to buy some tea."

"Of course." Rocky turned to Murdoch. "Is there any kind of boat in this town?"

"Boat? What do you want a boat for? No, there isn't. You'd have to go over to Gold Lake to find one."

"I was afraid of that. We'd have to get a trailer to bring it here and then pull the thing uphill to the lake. Are you a good diver, Murdoch?"

"I am not. I never could learn to do anything more than fall in."

"Barnhart?"

"Lord, no! I'm getting old, Allan. And I can't even swim very well. Why?"

"Well, I reckon I shouldn't ask any of you to do this job, anyway. I've got a friend who's about as good a diver as I know of. He might come back with us—"

"You didn't ask me," Olivia said. "I've taken a lot of swimming and diving prizes. What is it you want to find? I'll go get my bathing suit—"

"You will not," Rocky said pleasantly. "I may be sufferin' from mistaken ideas of chivalry, but no woman's goin' to do this job."

"But what— Is it—is it a body you're looking for? Oh! Of course, that's not a nice job, but I didn't go through dental college without coming in contact with a good many cadavers— What did you say, Larry?"

Rocky was disappointed when Murdoch refused to repeat his muttered: "Chivalry is wasted on her." Olivia gave him a scornful glance and went on:

"I suppose you're going to be stubborn about it, but it's silly to think that a woman— Well, never mind. You haven't said whose body you're looking for, and where you think you'll find it."

"I'm kind of absent-minded this mornin'."

Barnhart laughed. "I won't ask questions, since I'm very doubtful of receiving any answer. But someone has to break the news to Kitty when she wakes up, and Ivy wants to know if we are to tell her the truth."

"I don't see how you can do anything else. I haven't got time to talk to her now, even if I wanted to wake her up. Tell her what you do know.

An' that her car's about three miles out on the La Porte road. Did she look after it herself?"

"No. She paid me to keep it in repair, and a swell job that was," Murdoch said. "Antiquated old rattletrap. June didn't know a spark plug from a tire. Want me to take a look at it? I can make it run if anyone can."

"It 'll take a towcar to bring it in. Anyway, I want to test the steerin' wheel for fingerprints first. Would you mind comin' over to the garage with me for a minute?"

"Thanks, *I* will come along, too," Olivia said sweetly. "Mr. Barnhart?"

Barnhart grinned and shook his head, even when Rocky said: "Oh, come on. The more the merrier."

"No, Kitty may wake up at any time, and, much as I'd like to avoid it, I should be there to help Ivy talk to her. We'll see you again this afternoon? I hope so. I feel easier when you're around."

The garage stood in a vacant lot between the store and the inn and not, as Murdoch pointed out, "right up against it. I'm really closer to the garage, sleeping in the back of the store, than any of them over there are. There's just two rooms on the garage side of the hotel that are occupied. Junius had one of them."

"You'll have to count him out, even if he was driving the car," Olivia said. "And Mr. Barnhart told us he probably wasn't."

"Well, what do you think?" Rocky asked.

"When I'd had time to think things over I began to be doubtful. At the time I was too upset—though Larry did think I was too calm to be quite feminine—to think clearly. But, of course, I soon remembered that Cash hated to wear his plates and the whole thing began to look suspicious. I intended," Olivia said with the frankness that was alternately irritating and attractive, "to confound you with my bright ideas when you had time to listen to me. But what are we here for?"

Rocky looked about the garage, which was large enough to house three cars, and indicated a heap of rubbish in one corner: wheels, nuts and bolts, two battered fenders, an old radiator, several pieces of sacking and a large assortment of cogs and gears of various kinds.

"Do you know anything about this, Murdoch?"

"That junk heap? Mrs. Featherstone-Quinn let me put the things there. You never can tell when some of it's going to come in handy. Those fenders came off— Sa-ay! There's something missing here! Is that what you wanted to know?"

"I wanted you to see if anything was. What is?"

"A lot of old iron chain. I got it out of the mill and an old blacksmith shop that's fallen down. It wasn't much good—"

"But the sort of thing a man delights in hoarding," Olivia said. "And it might also be just the thing to weight a body you were going to throw in the water. Those kidnappers they lynched in San Jose used chains."

"And the kid's body floated just the same," Rocky said. "How much do you suppose the stuff that was taken would weigh?"

"I don't know," Murdoch said. "But plenty. There was a lot of it, and it's all gone. It was hard work lugging it up here. It looks to me like some pieces of sacking are gone, too."

"Is that all? All right, then. We've got to go. I'll get back as soon as I can, and I want you," Rocky said to Olivia, "to keep away from lakes if you've got any bright ideas. Understand? And, Murdoch, I don't like to ask you, but I think you'd better go out and guard that car. Someone might be comin' along the La Porte road and meddle with it when they couldn't get by. Don't you touch the doors or steering wheel. It's a dull job, but I'll relieve you soon's I can."

In Merton Rocky found the fingerprinting apparatus awaiting him in the small office shared by the township's constable and justice of peace. Dud Williams, constable, wanted to know all the details of what he called "this funny business at Gold Gulch."

"I wish," he sighed, "I wasn't so damn busy here so I could come up an' help you out. But with all the bums 'at's hittin' town right now, I got my hands full."

"That's too bad," Rocky said diplomatically. Dud knew everything that could be known about the handling of bums, hobos and bindle stiffs, but in all other fields he had the delicate touch of an elephant. "I may have to deputize somebody here. I don't expect the Old Guard to move up from Brookdale."

"Too fat," Dud said scornfully. He weighed more than two hundred pounds himself but was built along the lines of a gorilla and loved a fight for its own sake. "Anyhow, who'd keep the crim'nals down in Brookdale from runnin' wild if Cy Rand and Al Sully came up here?" He laughed enjoyably at his own joke.

"Do you know if old Hardpan Reid is still in town, Dud?"

"I think so. You want to see him? Him an' old Cash Quinn was pals, wasn't they? Hardpan was stayin' with his cousin Bert. You know where Bert's cabin is? Over across the river—"

"I've been there. If they call me from Brookdale you just talk pretty to them, Dud, and tell them you don't know nothin'. I'll be seein' you."

Jazz Mitchell was copying train orders when Rocky came into the railroad telegraph office. If you knew anything about railroading you never disturbed an operator when he was doing that kind of work. Rocky nodded, wrote out a telegram and sat down to glance through the letter from Eleanor that Cy Rand had sent up from Brookdale. He had finished reading that before Jazz was done repeating the orders to the train dispatcher and had begun on his official correspondence.

"Well, that's that. I'm done with the old billy goat for a while," Jazz said. "What were you grinning about awhile ago?"

"This letter from Eleanor. She says: 'Nancy is positively disgusting. When we are in the hotel she sits and looks out the window and sighs. I told her husbands and wives do occasionally have to be separated, and that the first time is the worst. But she just looks at me with a dying-calf expression and wonders if Jazz is getting enough to eat. And . . .'"

"Go on."

"Well—'And are you doing your own cooking or eating that terrible food at the Brookdale lunch counters?' Never mind the rest of it."

Jazz, who was dark, slight and wiry, grinned and pulled a crumpled letter from his pocket. "This is the other side of the story, according to Nancy. 'Eleanor acts as if I were the only one who misses her husband, but I noticed when I suggested we stay until Monday or Tuesday she had all sorts of reasons why she must be back in Brookdale before Monday. It seems the Woman's Club meets then and can't get along without her.'"

Rocky laughed. "I'd just as soon they stayed," he said. "I don't exactly like the way this business up at Slacktown is developin', and you know she'd insist on goin' up there once or twice. Send that wire off for me, will you? I'll write Eleanor one, too; I won't have time for a letter today."

Jazz read the telegram addressed to one Pat McCarthy and whistled. "If he finds out all you want to know and wires it back collect, it 'll cost you plenty. Do you know the guy?"

"I've never seen him. He's a private inquiry agent—private dick, to you. Jake Thompson's done business with him for years, and he's always produced. He's one of these south-of-Market boys that have plenty of pull. It's quicker to call on him than the cops when the people you want investigated haven't any official records."

"Ivy Horne, Arthur Barnhart, Kitty Featherstone and Leon Glidden. That's the bunch at the hotel? Oh yes, we've heard plenty about what's happened, and some of it may be true. I know from experience that about half of it isn't."

"I was wishing you could lay off—"

"With a wife running wild through the stores in San Francisco? Well, Nancy's been trying to get me to come down after her. There's a fellow expected in town this afternoon, from relieving the agent at Reno Junction. I was considering getting him to work for me if Sacramento thinks he's heavy enough for the job. I think he is—though they'll burn his shirttail plenty. What did you want me to do?"

"I was thinkin' of deputizin' you. You'd get paid. It's hell tryin' to find a deputy here—for anything but a strong arm job."

"What about your father?"

"I couldn't deputize him, an' Dad's disgusted with what he calls detectin'. He thinks his little boy's lost some of the frank-and-open disposition he used to have. He's over at the house shavin' himself and probably takin' a nap."

"I'd not be much good to you; I couldn't even help you get me out of a mess last October. But if you want me to I'll try to get off . . . Nancy? She'd tell me to stay right here and pay back— Oh, all right."

"I may not need you tonight, but I've got a nasty job for you this afternoon—if you'll come up to Slacktown as soon as you get off shift."

"What is it?"

Rocky told him, and Jazz's mouth twisted wryly. "It sounds like a hell of a pleasant assignment. I've got a weak stomach. All right, I'll be there. The second-trick operator owes me an hour, and I'll try to get him to relieve me at three and get up there early. Is that wire for Eleanor? I'll send it with this one as soon as I can get San Francisco."

"It's close to two now. If you can get off at three we can wait for you. An' you'd better bring a bathin' suit with you," Rocky advised, walking toward the door. "There's a nosy female up there I intend to keep away from the place, but she might manage to sneak up there to watch proceedings. It might embarrass you to be caught in a state of nature. I doubt if it would embarrass her, very much, to catch you that way."

CHAPTER VII
"HE HAD ABOUT TWENTY THOUSAND DOLLARS"

Hardpan Reid had a high, rusty voice. His sentences trailed vaguely off into space as if he did not expect an answer from anyone but himself. Where Cassius Quinn was slight and short, Hardpan was a stooped six feet, but you would never look at one man without thinking of the other. There was the same dried skin and squinted eyes and knotted, scarred hands.

Hardpan wore a sparse fringe of whisker, stained with tobacco juice, and beside him Cash would have been something of a fashion plate. Frayed rope held up Hardpan's shrunken trousers, and four safety pins were needed to keep his faded blue shirt and stained vest together.

He was delighted to talk. He accepted one of Allan's cigars, tucked it ceremoniously into his vest pocket and bit a chunk off his plug of tobacco. Yes, he'd heard about Cash Quinn. The callboy had told them when he came to call Bert out.

Yes, he'd known Cash pretty well, "about as well as anybody. Him and me was over near Tonopah for two-three years. That was—let's see—ten years ago. No, it 'd be nearer six or seven . . ."

"Have any luck there?" Rocky said.

"Not to speak of. I always did say there was gold there if we could 've found it, and I wanted to stay a little longer."

"Cash did strike it rich once or twice, didn't he?"

"Depends on what you mean. He got in a vein of good ore once or twice, but it petered out. Still, he made some money."

"When's the last time you saw him?"

"Me? 'Bout a week ago. Let's see—this is Friday. No, it wasn't that long. It was a Sunday I was over to town and run into him. We talked quite a bit."

"What about?"

"Oh, little bit of everything. Had a drink or two—"

"Did Cash— I suppose he treated you?"

"I wanted to stand treat, but he wouldn't let me," Hardpan said with forlorn dignity. "Cash was like that."

"Gen'rous?"

"I wouldn't go so far's to say that. He never spent no money when he didn't have to, but he'd spend it when he wanted to—like that day."

"Even when he didn't have it to spend?"

"Hunh? Oh, you mean he wasn't supposed to have any money? That was Cash all over," Hardpan said with a cackling laugh. "He was s'posed to 've gambled away all he got his hands on, and he did lose a lot, but he won some of it back. And he did spend a lot when he was younger, but he had enough to get along on."

"I kind of expected he did," Rocky said, without looking at his father. "He told Junius he didn't have to beg meals from him."

"So he didn't. He'd a lot more than Junius's got. He didn't have to live up there, but the way Cash 'd figure it he might as well, as long as he could, and save his own stake."

"Did he ever say so?"

"Not exactly, but I know Cash. He'd pay when he thought he ought to but not if he didn't. Didn't hurt June's wife any to feed Cash; she'd never miss what that cost."

"Of course," Rocky said, "you're only guessin' at this. You know Cash had a little money, but you don't know how much."

"I don't, don't I? I guess I do," Hardpan said indignantly. "Guess I'm about the only one that did. He wouldn't ever let June or anyone up there know it. They'd borrow it away from him—or try to. I'll tell you how I know. I had to have my appendix took out, an' I couldn't pay for it, so he did. That's why I say he'd spend money when he wanted to."

"How long ago was that?"

"Right after we was in Tonopah, when we come back through Reno together. He told me then he had about twenty thousand dollars he wasn't ever goin' to trust to no banks. He didn't like banks."

"That's what I heard. How much do you think he had left last time you saw him?"

"Prob'ly most of it. He'd made money since then, and it didn't take him much to live on. He said t'other day, kind of laughin', that he didn't have to live in Slacktown. Said he could pay board there or go live somewhere else like June was always wantin' to. I wouldn't be tellin' this if he wasn't dead. That's what the callboy said the fire ranger said."

"I don't reckon you know where he kept his money?"

"Do too. Wore a money belt round his waist, right next to him. He wasn't goin' to bury the stuff an' maybe forget where he put it or have someone find it. He used to carry round quite a few twenties, and he got fifties and hundreds at banks when he could. He liked gold, but it was too heavy to carry around. He never seemed to worry about it or be careful about lockin' himself in and things like that. I guess he was so used to havin' it on him he just didn't think about it."

"Did he say anything to you about leavin' Slacktown?"

"He said it 'd been kind of interestin' up there, but he was gettin' tired of it."

"Tired of ringin' bells?" Rocky said.

Hardpan's jaw dropped. "How'd you know that? Not that Cash ever said he'd been doin' that. He just laughed and said it was funny to see folks chasin' out in their nightshirts. He did kind of hint Tom Slack might be behind it. But Cash was always kind of a practical joker. I don't know as he done it, though. He said he guessed June's wife was there to stay, an' maybe he wasn't through prospectin', after all."

"Did he say where he was goin'?"

"No. I got a notion," Hardpan said, "that he thought he might be onto somethin' good. If he was he wouldn't tell me. He'd trust me not to steal money from him, but he wouldn't take no chances tellin' me where he was goin' to stake a claim—because I might get there first."

"What makes you think he knew just where he was goin'?"

"Well—nothin' much. Only he was kind of fingerin' that nugget he had on a pin, and we was talkin' about where he found it, an' then he says:

'Well, there's bigger ones than this if you happen to find them.'"

"I suppose," Rocky said slowly, "that if someone showed you a nugget they'd found somewhere an' told you where, you'd light out for the place first thing?"

"Any of us would. Why, it's just this spring that old Blake found a nugget worth three hundred down around Spring Valley."

"I remember he did. Well, you've helped me out a lot. I reckon you wouldn't—just for takin' your time . . ."

"Don't mention it; wouldn't think of it," Hardpan said, but somehow a five-dollar bill passed from Rocky's hand to his. "You just come back any time you need any help. Glad to talk to you if I'm still here."

"You always pay off ever'body you talk to that way?" Allan asked, climbing into the car.

Rocky smiled sheepishly. "Not by a long shot. But the old fellow hasn't a dime. Bert Reid 'll feed him, but he won't hand out any money. Hardpan 'll probably just get roarin' drunk with it, but it was worth it to me."

"You found you a motive—maybe. But—"

"Well, we'll see," Rocky said quickly. "I've got to get hold of some kind of hooks. We'll wait till three to see if Jazz can get off then an' go back with us. That gives me just about time to make a phone call, long as we're here. . . ."

"Glidden? Leon Glidden? Sure, I know him," Ed Paulman said. Paulman called himself a realtor, was interested in several Reno night clubs and boasted that he knew everyone in the city. "What's Glidden been up to? Is he in trouble?"

"Is he in the habit of gettin' in trouble?"

"No—no, of course not. You've got me wrong, Allan. Naturally, I'm curious—"

"He's stayin' at a hotel where there's been a murder," Rocky said. "And I've got to check up on ever'body, and he happens to be the only one from over your way."

"I suppose you know he hasn't been here for six months? And you know he's a painter? His father was a lawyer—divorce, of course. That didn't keep Glidden's mother from getting a divorce of her own. I think she's dead; the father is. I guess Leon hasn't always had an easy time paying bills. People like him. The only thing I ever heard against him was when some guys called him a gigolo."

"Why a gigolo?"

"Oh, he did have a habit of running around with rich women, not too young, who were taking the cure and wanted a good-looking, young escort. But it's being done all the time."

"Anything else?"

"I don't know . . . Well, he and some fellow got into a row about something at some club, and Glidden broke a bottle over the fellow's head. Of course, they were both soused. Think nothing of it," Paulman said with a jovial ha-ha. "I used to meet him a lot in a shooting gallery here. He's a crack shot, used to go to all these turkey shoots they have."

"Any idea how old he is?"

"Oh, about thirty. He's older than he looks. Went to university here, but I don't think he graduated. Oh, he's a good egg, Allan. You're on the wrong track."

"I'm not on any track at all," Rocky said patiently. "I thought I might as well find out about him while I had time. Thanks a lot."

He stopped to pay the operator for the call. "Was it a good connection?" she asked solicitously.

Rocky grinned. "You ought to know, Goldie."

Goldie shook her peroxided head reproachfully. "Oh, Rocky, you're such a tease!"

"Am I? Well, you let the newspapers tell the news, will you, please?—an' I'll buy you a box of candy next Christmas," Rocky promised. He walked away and left Miss Goldie Thomas staring after him with her mouth formed into an indignant O.

Jazz poised himself on the boulder at the lake's edge and looked at the black water with open distaste. "You say this is plenty deep?"

"After about two steps it was over my head so I couldn't touch bottom. After that I had a hell of a time getting down to the bottom at all."

"O.K. Somewhere near the edge of the lake, you think? Well, we'll see."

Jazz's slim body knifed into the water with only the faintest splashing sound. Rocky admired this performance before he sat down on the rocks beside his father. Allan said:

"There wasn't no fingerprints on that steerin' wheel?"

"Just a smudge or two, like someone 'd wore gloves. The wheel wasn't polished off, which would be the safest thing to do. But the person that drove that car—"

"If it wasn't Cash Quinn himself—"

"If it wasn't Cash . . . But I don't think he'd be apt to be wearin' gloves. . . . Any luck?"

Jazz shook his head, treading water while he got his breath. "Only been down twice. I'll try a little closer in. God, this water is cold!"

"You're tellin' me? I suffered from it this mornin'. . . . I was sayin' the person who drove the car, if it wasn't Cash, had to walk back to the hotel, and the quicker he got there the better for him. So he didn't— Got something?"

"I think so." Jazz's mouth had thinned to a straight line, and his nostrils had a pinched look. "There's something down there that feels damned nasty. Toss me one of those hooks. There seems to be a lot of chain around it, and I think I can get a hook caught in it."

Rocky waded into the water as far as he dared and pushed one of the heavy hooks toward Jazz, holding the end of its chain in one hand. He turned to Allan. "I'll make you a sportin' offer, Dad. Ten dollars that it's Junius Quinn in there." His peculiarly light eyes were suddenly more nearly yellow than brown.

"Junius? But you said—"

"I don't remember sayin' it would be Cash in here—not very lately."

Jazz's black head came into sight again. "You can try it, now," he gasped. "You'll have to pull pretty hard."

He swam away from the thing they were pulling toward the shore and climbed out of the water, bruising his shins on the rocks. Coming over to Rocky he took one look at his discovery, said: "I think I'm going to be sick," and retired behind the nearest clump of bushes.

"It's Junius, all right." Allan looked at his son with unwilling admiration. "I reckon you can strut a little if you want to. Though why, after arguin' a blue streak that it wasn't Cash that got killed, you turn right aroun' an' decide it was—"

"Because I didn't stop thinkin' where I was supposed to stop," Rocky said complacently. Then he grinned apologetically. "Oh well, I admit I'm kind of proud of myself for guessin' right. There's no use us lookin' at this." He reached for the blankets he had carried with him and threw one over Junius Quinn's body.

"He don't look like he was shot. All that chain wrapped aroun' him to keep him down. Somebody," Allan said, "has got a lot of cold nerve to do a job like that."

"An' somebody's pretty damned smart to figure out a setup like this, even if it didn't work. Feel better now?"

"I guess so," Jazz said with a pale smile. "Yes, I'll have a drink. I feel like a fool, doing that."

"Oh, I felt kind of the same way, but it ain't been the first time I've seen things like this," Allan said. "An' we wasn't clawin' aroun' down there in that water."

Jazz took another drink and began to dress. "I've got a slimy taste in my mouth. Did I hear you say this is Junius Quinn?"

"He's all prepared to expound if you give him half a chance," Allan drawled. "Just wants to be urged a little."

"They won't have Mrs. Featherstone-Quinn's car towed in yet, and we can't pass them on that road," Rocky said, sitting down again. "I don't mind gettin' it straight in my own head. It's like this: we find what's left of a body with a few objects we can identify it by, the most important bein' some false teeth. They're Cash's, so we say right away the body must be his.

"But then we get to thinkin' how he never wore those teeth unless he had to, so we begin to think the whole thing looks like it 'd been arranged by Cash to make us think he's dead. We find evidence he'd shaved off his mustache and imperial and maybe trimmed his eyebrows—the thing he'd do if he was makin' a getaway and didn't want to be recognized. So we say the first body was Junius's, an' that he was killed by Cash, and Cash had got away."

"That sounds reasonable," Jazz said.

"That's just what we were supposed to think. But when we found the car one or two things was wrong. In the first place, Cash wouldn't be apt to try to get away in a car. He drove badly, an', besides, his instinct would be to take to the woods. He'd be safer there. And if he had taken the car he'd have filled it up with gas. But there was hardly any in the tank. An' he'd have taken along provisions so he wouldn't have to depend on stores for his meals. He'd had plenty of practice in thinkin' fast in tight spots. And anyone could 've run that car into a rock—to make it look like Cash did it. They wouldn't dare drive much farther because they had to walk back to the hotel."

"Are one of us supposed to ask a question now?" Allan said as Rocky paused.

"You're supposed to ask: 'Why would anyone want to kill Cash?'" Rocky said amiably. "But that's a lot easier question to answer than the first one we had: 'Why would Cash kill Junius?' Just meetin' Cash that first night we was here I wondered if he was as broke as people thought. It's true most prospectors don't keep their hands on any money, but there are always exceptions. You remember how Cash said to Junius that he'd made a livin' for a good many years while Junius never had?"

Allan nodded. "He said Junius could talk about small fortunes—talk was cheap. It strikes me what Junius said about them feedin' him seemed to kind of get under Cash's skin."

"It would. Cash was an awful old bragger. Maybe Junius figured on that. Then Cash told me he thought he'd go prospectin' again and would I like to grubstake him. When I said I knew someone who might he laughed like something amused him. He knew damn well he could get along. He managed to pay his grocery bill an' for those false teeth when Junius didn't pay for his. I thought he might have money hidden where he lived—that's why I tore the place up. But he carried it on him, accordin' to Hardpan Reid. And that money's the only reason I've found for either of the Quinns to be killed."

"It's a good enough reason," Jazz said. "But why all the elaborate stage setting?"

"That's the right name for it. Well, if we thought it was Cash who killed Junius and cleared out we'd want to know why he did it, and right there we'd be stuck. Or we'd hit on some motive that wasn't the right one. But the minute we knew Cash had been killed, too, we'd start diggin' around, and in time we'd hit on the right motive for his death and Junius'.

"That's why I say whoever did this was smart. They figured out what we'd think, up to a certain point. They didn't just say: 'If we plant Junius' belongings in the fire they'll think it's his body,' but went on: 'Only that will look too much like something that's been staged: So they reversed things—planted Cash's belongings and figured we'd think it wasn't him, and that, therefore, he'd killed Junius. Is that plain?"

"I guess so," Jazz sighed. "It's what I'd call involved. I suppose your idea is that Cash was shaved after he was dead, to add to the idea he wasn't—dead, I mean."

"It must 've been done that way. If things had worked out we'd have said Cash killed Junius and got away. When we couldn't find him we'd have to write it off the books. But if Cash was dead, and Cash had money— Well, as far as I know, everybody in Slacktown except maybe Mrs. Featherstone-Quinn could do with a little money."

"Show me anyone who couldn't. She can't have too much."

"I was thinkin'," Allan said slowly, "that the only motive you could 've found for Junius' death— if you wasn't sure Cash killed him, like you was s'posed to be—would point right back at Mrs. Quinn. I reckon she was fond of that wo'thless husband of hers, an' I noticed him lookin' kind of soft and sweet at that lady poet. I reckon they wouldn't have minded if you'd figured it out that way."

"It looks to me like you're still in plenty of trouble," Jazz said. "Is it your idea Junius killed Cash, and then someone killed him? Why?"

"Because he fin'lly found out about Cash's money. He's the most likely one to 've done that. Cash must 've been expectin' to talk to someone at his place late at night. He usually went to bed early, but he hadn't gone at all. Cash wouldn't tell just anyone about his money—he'd kept it a secret too long. Even if he might 've told Tom Slack I can't stretch my imagination to the point of seein' Slack thinking up this layout."

"Well, but if Junius killed Cash to get his money, who found out about that?" Jazz objected.

"I'd like to know. He might 've told his wife or Ivy Horne. He seemed to be on good terms with everyone but Tom Slack. If he lost his head he might have confided in almost anyone."

"And," Allan said, "he might 've stumbled onto somebody else killin' Cash or been put out of the way just because he knew about the money and told someone who killed Cash to get it and then killed Junius, too, to be safe. Or killed him first."

"I think that last idea's the most reas'nable. I'm betting it was Junius that found out about Cash's money, but I doubt if he had the nerve to try to get it himself—by murder. If he told someone about it who did, then he was probably killed first. That don't matter so much. Someone had to kill at least one of them. They couldn't kill each other and dispose of both bodies. That's the main reason for the stage setting: so's we'd think it lay just between the two of them."

"I'm getting a headache," Jazz said peevishly. "You can't prove any of this. You can't even produce a weapon."

"Good old Exhibit A? I've noticed," Rocky said, "that amateur detectives have kind of a tendency to be impatient. Not that patience could ever be called your strong suit, Jazz. I reckon you won't mind bein' classed as amateurs? I think I've about graduated from that class, and I've learned there's no use wastin' energy just chasing my own tail aroun'. I read once that a good detective never waits for things to happen, but sometimes you have to. Or just take one thing at a time—particularly when you've no more help than I have.

"I know I can't prove much of this," he added, "but I've got a start now. I know someone in Slacktown killed one or both the Quinns, an' that Cash carried enough money on him to tempt anyone who wanted money."

"What about the money?" Allan said. "It's got to be somewhere."

"Not where we'll be apt to find it easy. I can search the whole town, but I'll bet I won't find it, and everyone 'll get sore. They'll mind it enough when I have to take their fingerprints. Which is something I'd better be getting at. I didn't much like leaving those things in Cash's room all this time, but it couldn't be helped. Bring that other blanket over here, Dad."

"Doctor James will have a nice time on his hands," Jazz said. "That is, if you're going to let him take a look."

"It 'll save time. I'll have to call the cor'ner right away. He'll be relieved to find he's got somethin' substantial to hold at least one inquest on."

"It's substantial, all right," Allan grunted. "You should 've took them chains off. It 'll take the three of us to carry him. You two take his feet. . . ."

"I wonder," Rocky said, midway in their slow progress down the hill, "if there's any chance of gettin' that James girl to talk?"

"I doubt it. You might try lettin' her pull a tooth for you," Allan said. "That might put her in a good humor."

"I've done a lot of things in the line of public duty—such as playin' bridge with a lot of females once—but I'm damned if any woman dentist is goin' to get a look at my teeth. She knows somethin' about Amelia Slack or something Amelia told her—"

"There's one thing you've forgotten," Jazz said. "How did Junius, or anyone find out about Cash's money? From all you've said about them Cash didn't break down and tell Junius just because his heart was in the right place."

"Well, I said Cash was a bragger, an' Dad thought some of Junius' dirty cracks kind of got under his skin. He did have one or two weaknesses like that," Rocky said evasively, "and they could be worked on by someone who knew them."

CHAPTER VIII
WHY KILL A CAT?

"Kitty wants to see you, Allan. She says she'd—" Glidden stopped abruptly as Rocky opened the car door, and he saw the shapeless, blanket-wrapped bulk inside. He swallowed convulsively. "I didn't know— Murdoch came back with the car and said you'd gone up to some lake. He didn't say why. Is that—"

"Junius Quinn," Rocky said briefly.

"But I thought— Well, never mind. Except for what we're to tell Kitty . . ." Glidden looked toward the inn and beckoned to Barnhart as he appeared in the doorway. "You'd better hear this. He says this—this is Junius. Are you sure there's no danger of Kitty's running out?"

"We're taking him in here to Doctor James," Rocky said. "You wait outside. If she comes out, send her back in. I'll be back in a minute."

The old doctor asked very few questions, told them to put their burden on his operating table

and began putting on a pair of rubber gloves. "I
don't think you gentlemen will care to stay. If
you'll come back this evening I'll be able to tell
you something. Olivia is with Amelia—"

"How is she? Feelin' all right?"

"She isn't as well as I expected, Mr. Allan."
The old man spoke with professional gravity, but
his lined face flushed pinkly, and he fussed with
a case of instruments without looking at Rocky.
"I've recommended that she be very quiet, and
Olivia is looking after her."

"I'll bet she is," Rocky said politely. "Maybe
you'll go with me to talk to her this evenin'?"

"Well, if it isn't too late . . ."

"I hope it won't be." They went back to Barnhart and Glidden, still standing by the car. "I
want to talk to Mrs. Featherstone-Quinn, but I
don't feel like I ought to take the time right now,"
Rocky explained. "Will you tell her I'll be over
soon as I can?"

"But you're to come to dinner, all of you," Glidden said. "I was to tell you that—"

"That's mighty nice of her. It sounds like she's
got over her hysterics."

"She has," Barnhart said. "Kitty may talk like
a fool at times, but she's far from being one. But
she doesn't know what this is all about, and what
are we to tell her?"

"Well— Oh, I'll take time to talk to her, if you—"

"Nonsense!" Barnhart said, "I don't intend to keep you from your job by shirking mine, but what *am* I to tell her? That it was Cash's and not Junius' body we found in the fire?"

"Will that disturb her more than if it was the other way aroun'?"

"I don't know. She thought Junius was dead, anyway, and that Cash had killed him. Now, isn't there a possibility Junius killed Cash? And then someone wiped him out?"

"Why?"

"I don't know," Barnhart said again, warily. "Do you?"

"I wonder if you didn't— Oh well, let it go," Rocky said. "I'll talk to you later. Tell her both of them are dead. We found Junius' body in Deep Lake. Know where that is?"

"N-no."

"Isn't that the one where we picnicked?" Glidden said. "Kitty dragged us uphill to some little lake two or three miles from here; we had to walk from the road."

"That's the one. We found her car a little way past it," Rocky said. "And— But we'll be over pretty soon."

"Where to, now?" Jazz asked.

"The place where Cash lived. Get that fingerprint stuff out of the car, will you? We got to be
scientific, though I don't expect any results from
it."

"There's no place where they have prettier lilacs
than up here," Jazz said, drawing down a branch
loaded with red-tipped, purple blooms. "They
bloom so late, too. I'll have to bring Nancy up
here; she's crazy about lilacs. I like the smell of
them myself."

"Next best to lavender," Rocky said, unlocking
the door.

"I hate to interrupt you gentlemen's aesthet-
ic confidences," Allan drawled, "but *I* smell coal
oil."

"You're right; the place reeks of it." Rocky fum-
bled for his flashlight. The room before them, with
all the shades drawn, was dark in the late afternoon. "Don't take a chance strikin' any matches—"

He stopped, the light directed rigidly toward
one small spot on the floor. When he spoke again
his voice reminded Jazz of thin ice over turbulent
water. "It's a wonder you didn't smell blood, too,
Dad."

He knelt down by the velvet blot of black fur
on the floor, and a little bell tinkled faintly as
he raised the cat's battered head. After an instant
Allan said: "Well, it's only a cat, Son."

Jazz thought: the old man's embarrassed; he'd like to say more, but he don't know how. He was wise enough to say nothing at all, though in five years' friendship he had seen Rocky angry only once—the time that big Swede kicked that skinny little brat of a kid. He thought irrelevantly: I never saw any man hit the ground as hard as that Swede did when Rocky hit him. . . .

"I guess," Rocky said at last, "that we can be glad it wasn't a person that happened to come in here this afternoon. Will you put up the shades? The lamp's broken."

"That's funny," Jazz said, looking at the fragments of heavy, rounded glass and the long, sharp slivers of it that had been the lamp's base and chimney. "I wonder how that happened? "

"A lamp usually does break when it's dropped or gets knocked off a table," Allan said dryly.

"I meant I wondered why anyone was in here, and why the lamp's the only thing that's broken. It is, isn't it? And you locked the place—"

"Almost any kind of key would fit these locks," Rocky said. "That's why I should 've got back here sooner."

"You've been busy ever' minute since early this mornin'," Allan said. "And you tore the place up, lookin' things over. You don't think you missed anything?"

"I don't think so. But there might 've been something here I did see and didn't know was important. Can you see that anything's missin', Dad?"

"I been lookin', and I don't miss anything. I put that poker on the table right where it was handy, didn't I?"

Rocky looked briefly at the crust of blood on the poker's knobbed handle, lifted Sultan's limp body and put it on the bed. He took off the leather collar with its little bell and put it in his pocket.

"I was going to send that poker off to a lab'ratory, but I guess there's no use, now. The cat kept comin' back here. It would be dark in here, so you'd leave the door open a little because you wouldn't dare light a lamp or put up the blinds, and you'd want to hear if anyone was comin'. What do you think was the first thing the cat would do when he got in?"

"No guesswork about that; he'd rub up against your legs," Allan said.

"And that would startle you."

"Not to the point of droppin' a lamp or knockin' it off the table. But it might some people. Then I'd cuss the cat."

"Someone did more than cuss him. As you say, the poker was handy on the table."

"You're arguing whoever did it hated cats, aren't you?" Jazz said. "You'd have to, to kill one like that just because it scared you. If you find someone who has a phobia about cats—"

"It does look like someone didn't have any love for 'em, but as to a phobia . . . I'm not so sure," Rocky said. "Suppose you'd sneaked in here an' didn't intend anyone to know the room had ever been entered, searched, or whatever did happen. Then that cat comes along and is the cause of you breakin' the lamp. It's no good to cart away the pieces. It'll still be missed, and you can't clean up the coal oil that was spilled. It's going to be known, spite of anything you can do, that you've been in here—"

"So he lashed out at the cat with the first thing that came handy?" Jazz shivered. "I don't like that," he admitted. "I can understand hitting at the cat instinctively, but after that—well, he had to finish the job, and that's—that's—"

"The results ain't pretty. But he did have to finish the job—or thought he did. Because while Sultan was a friendly beast he did have a habit of spittin' very vociferously at anyone that 'd ever hurt him."

"That lets the James girl out," Allan said. "He wouldn't ever 've got near her. She let us see he didn't like her. Haven't you no idea at all why it was important to someone to get in here?"

"Just one. Ever'body knew I'd be goin' over this place for fingerprints. Three of them heard me tell Cy Rand over the phone that I wanted the outfit. I warned Murdoch not to plaster his prints over the car—"

"But you didn't expect to find any in here. And you said the driver of the car wore gloves," Jazz said. "Wouldn't he have sense enough to wear them in here, too?"

"Yes, but it's hard to handle things with gloves on, and Cash was shaved in here, you know. I'd hate to do even a rough job of shavin' with gloves on. It's just possible whoever did that had his gloves off and remembered afterward that he'd slipped up an' left his fingerprints somewhere—or was afraid he did. It's hard to be sure about things like that once you let yourself start wondering about 'em. After all, there's quite a few things that must 've been handled."

"The lamp, maybe," Allan suggested.

"Someone turned it out. The base would 've taken a good print. Incidentally, some of that oil probably splashed on the person that broke the lamp. Well, I'll look at the pieces and everything else here. This mornin' I thought I saw a few smudges that might develop into prints. I'll have to take yours, Dad; you've handled some things here. And yours, Jazz." Rocky grinned briefly. "You two don't need to look like that. I don't know why just the suggestion that they have their prints taken makes most people feel their rights as law-abidin' citizens are bein' invaded. It won't hurt you. Go on outside till I'm through, if you want to."

The dining-room table had been extended to its full size again, and Mary Anne showed her sympathy for her mistress by hovering near her as they ate and filling water glasses and coffee cups before they were half-emptied. Kitty Featherstone-Quinn had put on a black, chiffon dinner dress, and her cheeks looked more than ever like those of a pink-enameled doll. But she was very quiet, and her round doll-eyes were red and swollen.

"Just sit anywhere you want to," she said listlessly. "It doesn't matter."

Rocky introduced Jazz: "Gerald Mitchell," and Mrs. Featherstone-Quinn smiled vaguely. "Oh yes. I'm very glad to know you, Mr. . . . Mr. . . ."

"I've heard of you, haven't I?" Glidden said, sitting down next to Jazz. "Last fall—last October, I think it was."

"Perhaps you did," Jazz said ungraciously, "though I didn't know I ever rated the Reno papers."

"Well, naturally, after you and Allan brought in that man-eating Negro who was wanted for murder in two or three states . . ."

Glidden spoke with a friendly smile, but the damage was done. Jazz was still painfully sensitive to any reference, real or fancied, to his having once been the principal suspect in a murder case. Now he made a mental porcupine of himself, putting out warning quills against anyone who dared approach him. Rocky was perfectly familiar with this mood, but he would have been tempted to kick Jazz had he been within kicking distance.

Conversation lagged. Glidden gave up trying to talk to Jazz, and Ivy Horne looked pale and tired. Robert Allan cherished a belief that people came to the table only to eat, and Lawrence Murdoch scowled at his food as if he might have been quarreling with Olivia again.

No one paid a great deal of attention to Barnhart's monologue on the subject of the Wells-Fargo express, but at least, Rocky thought, Barnhart's deep voice was pleasant to listen to, and as long as he kept on talking no one else had to. Then Mrs. Featherstone-Quinn said abruptly:

"Mr. Allan, did you— Oh, I'm sure it's all very interesting, Arthur, but it's really no use, and you'll just wear yourself out. Did you find any fingerprints in Cash's room, Mr. Allan? They said you'd probably look to see if there were any."

"No, ma'am, not one. And that's kind of queer."

"It's decidedly queer," Barnhart said. "You'd think there would have been some of Cash's—and yours."

"Oh, there were one or two of mine, and some blurred prints under them that might have been Cash's. Nothin' else. It's kind of remarkable how well all the furniture is polished up—now. But I'd still like to take all your prints after dinner. I might need them to refer to."

"But why would you ever need to refer to our fingerprints?" Ivy asked.

"Don't be silly," Glidden said. "It's customary. I'll admit the very idea of it makes me feel like I've a rope around my neck. Still, here we are, and here's the—situation. Only I'd like to know if you think any of us had any motive for—well, for doing what—"

"For killing Cassius or Junius? You're being silly now, Leon," Mrs. Featherstone-Quinn said. "There's no use trying to spare my feelings any longer. The lamb was very nice, Mary Anne. Bring in the dessert now."

"Since we've started talkin' about it we might as well finish," Rocky said. "Cash, and probably Junius, too, was killed because he had something aroun' twenty grand in a money belt."

"You—you don't mean Junius had twenty thousand dollars?" Mrs. Featherstone-Quinn said uncertainly.

"No, I meant Cash had it. He carried it in twenty and hundred dollar bills in a money belt he wore next to his hide. Someone found out about it, killed him to get it and killed Junius to be safe."

"Because Junius knew about it?"

"What do you think, Mrs. Featherstone-Quinn?"

"I don't— I'd rather not discuss it here."

"Can you prove that he had the money?" Glidden asked.

"I can't produce anyone who could swear he recently saw Cash's money belt and the money. But we know he had it once, and, if you don't mind, we'll suppose he still had it. If he did is there anyone here that couldn't use that money?"

"No one that I know of," Murdoch said. "I could."

"And I," Ivy said. "But wishing you had money and killing to get it are two different things."

"For ever'body but one person. I don't know if Amelia Slack lives enough in this world to care about money."

"Not for herself," Murdoch said. "But she's wanted for years to erect some sort of gigantic monument over her husband's grave instead of the little bit of one she could afford. I know that's odd when half the time she talks like he was alive. She can't save enough for it out of her income—

and eat, too. But that's all she's ever wanted money for."

"Didn't she blame Cash for her husband's death?"

"Well, when she takes a crazy streak she does say Cash killed him for his mine—which wasn't worth anything. I shouldn't have mentioned it," Murdoch said uneasily. "She doesn't talk like that very often. And she can't drive a car, so she couldn't have taken it out there to the lake."

"I see. What was each one of you doin' this afternoon after I left here an' before I got back?"

"You know what I was doing: sitting out there twiddling my thumbs and watching that car for you."

"I know you were. What about you, Barnhart?"

"I suppose we—Ivy, Leon and I—finished lunch about one o'clock. I tried to take a nap but ended up by reading in my own room. I don't know for how long. I stopped in to see how Kitty was, tried to send Ivy out for some fresh air and when she wouldn't go I sat on the front porch until Murdoch and the garage men came back with the car."

"Haven't you any idea how long you were on the porch?"

"It was about three when he stopped to talk to me, if that helps you," Ivy said. "I'd been with Kitty in her room since we finished lunch. But, of course, she was sleeping, so she can't swear I was there all the time."

"I was only dozing, dear, and every time I woke up you were there. Is it important, Mr. Allan? What happened this afternoon?"

"Somebody got in Cash's room an' killed his cat."

"K-killed—not Sultan?" Mrs. Featherstone-Quinn's eyes filled with tears. "Oh, the poor thing! Cash was so fond of him, and he used to follow him over here. I meant to tell Mary Anne to go look for him and feed him."

"Why kill a cat?" Barnhart said.

"I suppose because he got in the way. That's as good a reason as I know for killin' anything."

"But it seems such senseless cruelty," Ivy said. "How could a cat get in one's way? Oh, I know you're not going to tell, but I—I don't like it."

"None of us do," Rocky said. "Are you fond of cats?"

"Not particularly. I like to watch them, but I've never had one because they expect you to pamper them."

"They demand it. I detest the beasts," Barnhart said, "I suppose because my wife always had two or three around, and there was a marked resemblance between them and her."

"I didn't know you were married."

"I'm not," Barnhart said curtly. "I was. Does it matter?"

"I reckon not. What about you, Glidden?"

"Where was I this afternoon, or do I like cats? No, I sat on one when I was a youngster, and I've never gotten over it. As to my movements this afternoon, I did take a nap—on a couch in the living room. I woke up when Arthur came downstairs feeling like the devil. Went upstairs and—"

"That don't matter. Did you see anyone goin' into Cash's place while you were settin' on the porch, Barnhart?"

"I couldn't see the back of the house, but no one from here was outside then. I saw Miss James go from Mrs. Slack's house to her own. Then Mrs. Slack came out—"

"She did?"

"Yes. I thought she looked rather badly. She walked over to the remains of the fire and looked at them for a while. I got up and walked out to the street so I could see her—I was curious—and she was walking back and forth and looking at the ground. Then she went home. After that, Tom Slack came over to the store and tried to break down the door when he couldn't get in."

"Probably wanted me to give him a drink," Murdoch said. "He'd be wanting one about that time."

"Well, the doctor was just coming over here, and he went over to Slack and apparently made him go home. Then he came on here to see Kitty, and Slack sneaked out of his place and headed for the end of the street. He seemed to disappear down into the canyon."

"He's got a still down there somewhere," Murdoch said. "I suppose that means he'll be drunk again tonight. If I could find where he makes the stuff I'd smash the works. He's a public nuisance."

"Is he dang'rous when he's drunk?" Rocky asked.

"He's always been a surly brute, and he's drunk like a fish as long as I've known him, but he's never tried to hurt anyone."

"You ain't asked me what I was doin' this afternoon, Mr. Sheriff," Mary Anne said unexpectedly. "I guess you ought to know, even if I can't give you any information reverent to the case. I cleaned up the kitchen an' then took a cup of tea to Miss Kitty, but she wouldn't take any nutrition, and she said to have just anything that was on hand for dinner, but I thought I'd whip up a few butterscotch pies."

"I hope it will be convenient for you to do it again," Barnhart said. "You might save me a piece for this evening."

"It's a pleasure, Mr. Barnhart. There's a redundance of it in the kitchen. Well, I didn't get up to my room to lie down a bit till about three o'clock. I guess that's all."

"Thank you, Mary Anne." Rocky pushed his chair back from the table. "Will you excuse me?"

"We're all through eating. I'm going into the office," Mrs. Featherstone-Quinn said. "I'd like to talk to you when you have time, Mr. Allan."

"I'll be there right away. What's that, Murdoch?"

"Any objections to my going down to Greenleaf for the mail and some supplies? That's my job, you know."

"Go right ahead. Could you take Jazz on into Merton? The guy he thought might relieve him hadn't showed up when we left there so he's got to get back."

"Fowler should show up sometime," Jazz said. "He started for Merton, all right. But if he stopped along the road he may not get in tonight or be fit for duty when he does. I can't take a chance; have to report at eight in the morning, as usual. If he turns up tomorrow, I'll lay off."

"I'll be glad to take you on to Merton. It's not far— Say, is there something wrong with me?" Murdoch said truculently. "You look like you smelled something rotten."

Jazz glanced guiltily at Rocky and said with unusual mildness: "I thought I smelled coal oil and wondered where it was."

"Oh, that's it?" Murdoch laughed and sniffed at the cuff of his shirt. "It's on me, all right. Mary Anne came over for a gallon of the stuff before dinner. I gave it to her, though I don't think Mrs. Featherstone-Quinn wants her to use it to start fires with. Well, we'd better be starting, Mitchell, before it gets any later. . . ."

CHAPTER IX
"SHE WAS LOOKING FOR A PIN"

Rocky said: "All right, then, I'll expect you sometime tomorrow mornin'. If you don't want to take
all your jury from here you'd better bring some
fellows with you. . . . What? . . . Well, there's ten
people here, but you won't want some of 'em to
serve. Fix it to suit yourself."

He got up from the telephone, an old-fashioned affair on the wall of the hall that ended at
the dining room. A small room to the left of the
front door was the office Mrs. Featherstone-Quinn
had referred to. There was no desk or any of the
appurtenances of a hotel in the enormous living
room opposite. Another small room, furnished
with a pool table, two slot machines and a radio
bar, opened off the living room and had another
door into the dining room.

Mrs. Featherstone-Quinn was sitting at an old
roll-top desk in the office with an account book

in front of her. She closed it when Rocky came in and cut short his apologies.

"I know you had other things to do, and I don't know that I have anything important to tell you after all. I thought I did until you said you were already certain Cassius had all that money, but if you knew that, the hints I was going to give you won't be any help."

"You did suspect he might not be as broke as he wanted you to think?"

"When Olivia told me Cassius had paid her for those plates of his I began to wonder. I—Junius paid for his this month, and she happened to mention Cash had paid for his in November, when he got them. And they cost quite a lot, even if Olivia's price was very reasonable. Of course, Cassius was always saying he didn't have to live here, but I hadn't paid much attention to him because that's the way he talked, and people like that are always expecting to strike gold and talk about it so much they think they really have.

"But I was rather provoked at the idea he might have been fooling us all along, and I mentioned it to Junius. At first, he just laughed and said Cassius hadn't a thing in the world but a little bit of income from some investments he wasn't allowed to sell—and neither was Junius—when their father died, and they ran right through all the money he left them. But they were pretty young then. Anyway, I think Junius began to wonder, when he'd thought it over, and to try and find out if there was anything to my idea.

"He kept trying to make Cassius angry by saying he was living on my—our charity. He got to going over to see Cassius in the afternoons and evenings, and he hadn't ever done that before. He was always out of sorts when he came back, and when I asked him why he went he said they were 'just talking.' Once he said: 'He's as close mouthed as a clam, but there are ways of making people talk if you're smart enough.' Then he tried to turn it off by saying he'd like to be on better terms with Cassius now that he was getting older, and there were only the two of them left."

"How long had he been doin' that?"

"Going over to see Cassius? Oh, just during the last two weeks. Particularly the last ten days and this last week. I don't know all the times he talked to Cassius because often he must have gone after I'd gone to bed. I suppose you wonder why I was so upset last night."

"Enough happened to upset you, didn't it?"

"Yes, but I don't usually lose my head and have hysterics. When we couldn't find either of them I was certain Junius had gone over to see Cassius, that they'd quarreled, and one of them was hurt.

And all the time that awful fire was threatening
to wipe out the town—and I can't get insurance—
and I felt it was connected with them in some
way or other, but I didn't know how, and I simply couldn't stand the uncertainty. It looks now,
doesn't it, as if my idea was the right one?"

"I don't really think Junius killed Cash, an'
Cash had no reason to kill Junius," Rocky said.
"But it's possible. What do you think?"

"Junius did want money, more than we had. But
I don't believe he'd kill anyone, except in self-defense, and the same thing applies to Cash. The
killing in self-defense, I mean, and Junius wasn't
very brave, and I can't imagine him ever attacking
Cassius. But Mr. Allan, Junius wouldn't wait until
two or three o'clock to go over to see him."

"When the fire broke out has nothin' to do with
that. Someone had to dispose of—had to drive out
to Deep Lake an' walk back before he dared touch
a light to a fire that 'd rouse the town. I don't see
how everything could 've been done in less than
two hours, and three would be more like it."

"Oh, I see. I hadn't thought about that. Mr. Allan, I hope you don't think that—that Junius and
I weren't fond of each other just because we had
separate rooms."

Mrs. Featherstone-Quinn nibbled embarrassed-
ly at a polished thumbnail. Rocky conquered an
impulse toward laughter and said soberly:

"I hadn't given that any thought, ma'am."

"Well, I didn't know. Sometimes people in country communities think twin beds are immoral. I've slept alone so long, and I like to put my hair up on curlers sometimes and plaster my face with cold cream and wear a chin bandage. Oh, I don't mind telling people I do it, but Junius was rather romantic. And he was—yes, he was vain. I guess he gave himself facial massages, and he was very sensitive about his false teeth, so as long as there were extra rooms, we each had one."

"That reminds me to ask you where ever'body sleeps."

"You haven't been upstairs? There are eight rooms. The front and back four are the nicest. Ivy has one back one, and Junius had the other. He'd had it ever since he moved here," Mrs. Featherstone-Quinn said, answering Rocky's unspoken comment. "No one else wanted it, so why should I move him out of it?—even if it is one of the best. Leon and Arthur have the front rooms: Leon on the same side of the hall as Ivy, and Arthur on the left side where Junius' room is. I'm on that side, too, next to Arthur."

"And Mary Anne?"

"There's a room off the kitchen, but when the bell began ringing, and she was so frightened, I let her move in next to me. For the last three nights she's been putting cotton in her ears so she won't hear anything."

"Are any of those rooms connected?"

"Mine and Mary Anne's, and the two like them on the other side of the hall. I don't know why they didn't put connecting doors between all the rooms. Whoever built this place.— But that doesn't matter. Would you like to have Junius' room?"

"If you don't mind."

"N-no. I suppose you want to look through his things. You can. I haven't been in there yet."

"Mrs. Featherstone-Quinn, do you think your husband would 've told you when he found out about Cash's money?"

"You mean *if* he did? Not if he meant to try to steal it, because he knew I happen to be honest. If he just wanted to turn the tables on Cassius by having me charge him for his meals, of course he'd have told me."

"Is there anybody else here he might 've told even if he meant to try to get his hands on some of the money?"

"He'd have to share it then, wouldn't he? If he got it— Oh, I don't know. He liked Olivia James; he liked any pretty girl. He thought very highly of Ivy and Arthur. But he surely wouldn't be foolish enough to think Arthur would encourage him in any plan that was the least little bit dishonest."

"And Miss Horne?"

"I'm not sure. It's always fairly easy to tell what a man's principles are, but you can't be sure whether a woman even has any. I don't know why I say such a thing about Ivy. I've no right to."

"Glidden?"

"Junius didn't like him well enough ever to confide in him. He trusted Doctor James, but you know how saintly and unworldly he is. He and Lawrence Murdoch weren't awfully congenial. He might have trusted Amelia. Of course, he might have told any of them, just to pay Cassius back and make him angry, but in that case he would have told me."

"If he had time to. Well, I won't keep you any longer," Rocky said, rising. "Do you mind if I talk to Mary Anne? Oh yes. Do you wear gloves when you drive?"

"I don't like to, but sometimes I do wear an old cotton pair with holes in about five fingers."

"Which would leave marks as identifyin' as fingerprints. Does anybody aroun' here have any gloves?"

"You should know better than that. Junius did have a pair he wore when he was in the city. I don't think Ivy or the men even wore them on the train. The men certainly didn't, and Ivy hates gloves like I do. I'll see about making up your beds—one for your father, I mean. Junius's wasn't—wasn't slept in. . . ."

By now, Doctor James' report on his post-mortem would be ready, and Rocky did not want to keep the old man waiting. But Barnhart was still smoking and talking to Robert Allan on the front porch. Rocky stopped in the doorway to listen.

"I've always wanted to do some short biographies of some of the almost unknown generals of the Civil War," Barnhart was saying. "Confederates, of course. Men who are associated with lost causes are always more interesting than those who win. Jeb Stuart—there was a personality."

"My mother had an uncle fought under him," Allan said. "When he was a old man he could still tell you what Stuart looked like, an' how his voice sounded. Used to get tears in his eyes, talkin' about him dyin'."

"Well, Thomason did too nearly a perfect job on his life for me to try it. But I'd like to write up Ashby and Van Dorn, Magruder—*El Capitan Colorado*—McLaws, Loring and A. P. Hill. There's a man who persistently eludes you. If I could take him apart and see what made him tick . . ."

"Why don't you? I'd like to read a book about those men."

Barnhart shrugged impatiently. "I can't do the necessary research here. I'd need several years in the South, money to travel—I've only been able to go East once. Oh, if I were younger and prepared to live on crusts I might manage it. But an uncle left me a small house in the city, so—" He looked up, saw Rocky and got out of his chair.

"Can you spare a minute? I'll try to make it brief. I suspected Cash Quinn had some money, though I didn't suppose as much as twenty thousand dollars or that he carried it on him. I thought he might have hidden it where he lived."

"Well, that was my first thought. How did you get wise to Cash?"

"I talked to him a great deal. He told me interesting stories about the town and other places like this. Of course, I hoped to use the material in articles."

"What did he say that gave him away?"

"You probably know. He was always saying he didn't have to live up here, that he could pay his way when he had to. No one thought that meant anything, but there was a malicious gleam in his eye at times that seemed to me to mean it amused him to be treated like a poor relation when he knew he wasn't."

"Yes, Cash would think that was funny and wait aroun' for the right minute to make people feel small by tellin' the truth."

"Then I saw him pay his bill at Murdoch's store one day with two twenty-dollar bills. Murdoch

said Cash had a small income from a few investments that were left from his inheritance—as Junius did."

"Did Junius ever say anything to make you
think he knew Cash wasn't just a poor relation?"

"Not one word. He complained about what he
called Cash's 'sponging' off them. But I thought,
the last week or so, that he was trying to goad
Cash into losing his temper so that he'd betray
himself. However, you've considered all that, I
know. I don't believe you miss many things like
that. I did want to tell you that I wasn't entirely
deceived."

"Did you tell anyone else that?"

"Why should I? It would only have distressed
Kitty, and she's too softhearted to have done anything about it. Leon and Ivy wouldn't have been
interested. But I did want to tell you I talked to
Cash yesterday afternoon in his room, and he
seemed to be amused about something. He kept
telling me stories that were meant to show how
clever he was. He harped on what he called 'skin
games.' Said he'd never been taken in by one in
his life, and that the man or woman who could
play him for a sucker hadn't been born yet."

"Did he mention any particular kind of skin
games?"

"Oh, fake mining stocks, stocks of all kinds, gold bricks, oil wells—the usual things. Then he started to get down that scrapbook of his, but I'd had enough without listening to him read aloud, which he did very badly."

"I don't like to have people read to me, either. Had he ever done that before? What about?"

"Some of the articles he'd pasted in that book. They were mostly about gold rushes, past and present. I didn't pay too much attention because his reading did get on my nerves, and I can find anything of that kind that I want to use in the libraries."

"What you've told me is damn interestin'. I'd like to talk to you again when I've got more time. Do you want to come with me over to the doctor's, Dad?"

Doctor James did not take them into his office but insisted that they sit down in the dining room while he poured whisky for them and, guiltily, for himself.

"We haven't any living room now," he explained. "Olivia took that for her office. She's still at Amelia's, or I wouldn't be doing this. Of course, she's right; whisky is bad for me."

"She seems to be fond of Mrs. Slack," Rocky said.

"Amelia was very good to her when she was a child. Olivia's mother died when she was born, and my son when she was six. Amelia sewed for her, nursed her through measles and chicken-pox. Amelia is very helpful when she sees the need for help. Her queerness is greatly exaggerated. So far as her habit of sometimes speaking of Andrew as if he were alive—well, that only means she doesn't *want* to realize he's dead.

"But you want to know about Junius. I can't fix the time of his death. You know he was killed between the time he went upstairs and about three o'clock in the morning. Earlier than that, of course, because the fire must have started about three, but it's obvious his body was thrown in the lake some time before. He was dead then—no water in his lungs. He'd been struck over the head with the usual blunt instrument of fiction—I've no idea what it was—but that would only have stunned him. After that, he was strangled—throttled is the better term."

"Does it take strong hands to do that?"

"Not when a man is unconscious," the doctor said, looking at his own blunt-tipped fingers. "It's simply a matter of exerting a steady pressure. You can see the marks of thumbs on his throat but whether man's or woman's, large or small, I can't tell you."

"Then there weren't any wounds that would bleed? That was convenient."

"Very. I wouldn't be surprised," James said, "if Cash's lower jaw wasn't deliberately disfigured. That's only a guess, of course. I don't suppose Olivia could have identified it as his if it had been in perfect condition. I don't think I could have."

"I've been wonderin' about that. Seems like it's askin' a little too much of the fire to be responsible for that when he was lyin' on his face. Do you mind if we leave the bodies here till the cor'ner gets through his inquest?"

"No. That office has been used often enough as a morgue. When I first came here I saw enough of violent death. Not," James said, absently pouring a second round of drinks, "that Gold Gulch was not a very well-behaved town, for a mining town. But men would quarrel and shoot it out."

"Was there ever what they call a Boot Hill here?" Allan asked.

"Up on the hill. You won't find any of the wooden grave-markers standing now. But outsiders who died with their boots on were buried there. We used the schoolhouse for trials and inquests. I suppose the coroner can convene his jury there tomorrow."

"I reckon no one's told you yet. Would you be surprised to know Cash carried about twenty thousand dollars on him?"

"Twenty thous— I certainly am surprised to hear that. I knew Cash undoubtedly had a little more money than he wanted people to think. He always managed to buy tobacco and liquor, and he paid Olivia for her work. But twenty thousand dollars! Still, he was a queer, secretive sort of person. His father was very shrewd; perhaps Cash resembled him more than I'd ever thought."

"You can see what a nice motive that makes for him bein' killed."

"Of course," James said placidly. "I'll admit the question of motive had puzzled me a great deal."

"Would you say Junius Quinn was smart?"

"Not half so clever as he thought he was, but he really had brains. But he was also lazy and extravagant. His father gave him a good education. Then when Quinn died Junius went through his part of the estate, except for a few investments. He had work in the city several times, but he always quarreled with his employers. He was a Gold Gulch Quinn, and he couldn't get over it; he was too used to lording it over this town"—the doctor sighed—"when there was a town. I wish I could send Olivia away and help her set up an office in the city. A woman in her profession is enough handicapped. Not that I'd ever have chosen that profession for Olivia. If she had wanted to be a doctor . . . But about Junius. He was no poet, as he so fondly believed, but he was clever enough. Only he didn't have that quality described nowadays as guts."

"I'm not surprised to hear you say that. Well, we won't keep you up any longer. You must be tired. Have you any objections," Rocky said, "to us goin' over to Mrs. Slack's, as long as Miss James is there?"

"None at all." The doctor's faded blue eyes twinkled briefly. "None at all," he repeated. "Just tell Olivia I said it's all right."

"Which is the same as sayin': 'Get in if you can,'" Dad Allan muttered, outside. "Passin' the buck."

Rocky grinned wearily. "He isn't entirely under his granddaughter's thumb, but he prob'ly knows what he says won't cut much ice with her." He let the iron knocker fall against the door of Amelia's cottage. "I'm too tired to fight with determined females, but we might as well make a start at it."

"We? You can count me out on this."

"Oh, it's you again," Olivia said. "Well, you can't see Amelia. She's in bed."

Rocky put his foot in the door before she could close it. "I'm gettin' pretty tired of this. Why don't you want me to talk to Mrs. Slack? Your grandfather said it was all right."

"Oh, Grandad! He doesn't believe very much in women's nerves. He doesn't realize how upset Amelia is. I'm not going to have her disturbed. And if you think you're just going to walk in here," she added, as Rocky put his hand on the door-knob, "let me tell you Amelia isn't in the habit of receiving gentlemen in her bedroom."

Allan laughed shortly. "She's got you there. You cain't bust into a lady's bedroom."

"That's what you think. You're a nuisance," Rocky told the girl blandly. "Suppose I tell you to go in there an' bring Mrs. Slack out? She'll come, won't she, rather than have me come in there?"

"Yes, she will! And I suppose if you're going to be so damned official I'll go and get her out of bed."

"Olivia dear, ask the gentlemen to walk in and sit down. If they don't mind waiting until I'm dressed, I'll talk to them," Amelia Slack said from somewhere in the dark hall behind Olivia. "It won't take me more than fifteen minutes."

"There! You see, you've waked her up, shouting around the way you've been doing."

Rocky reddened resentfully. "I wasn't shoutin', and you know it. You just want to make me feel like a big brute tryin' to bully a defenseless woman an' disturb her rest." He raised his voice. "Mrs. Slack!"

"Yes, Mr. Allan?"

"I don't want to disturb you if you're not feeling well. But you're not in the habit of lying, are you? . . . Shut up!" he said softly to Olivia as she started to speak.

"No," Amelia Slack said gently, "I don't think I ever bother to lie, Mr. Allan."

"Then will you tell me if you're sure you don't know anything that ought to be told right away—for your own sake, or maybe for somebody else's safety."

There was a moment of silence, then: "I'm quite certain that nothing I know will help you," Amelia said. "And that neither I nor anyone else can be in danger, any danger that could be averted by anything I could tell you."

"That's good enough for me. Good night, Mrs. Slack."

"Good night."

"Well, I hope you're satisfied. I'll say it before you can." Rocky turned to Olivia with a provoking smile. "And if it turns out I've been a softhearted sap . . ."

"I don't think it will turn out that you've been softhearted."

"Well, I laid myself open for that one. I did mean to ask her one thing that you may be able to tell me. What was she looking for this afternoon over where the fire was?"

"I didn't know she was outside. But she was probably looking for a pin she lost at the fire last night. It's what Mary Anne would call a momentum," Olivia said, more pleasantly. "A memento from her husband: a large, hand-painted affair that she always wears."

"I noticed that pin. Was she dressed when she came out to help fight fire?"

"Amelia wouldn't ever run outside in her nightie. She was brought up to be a lady. I suppose she didn't fasten the brooch securely. I'm afraid she'll never find it, though Larry said he'd look for it. It probably got kicked into the ashes."

"We might be able to find it for her if it means a lot to her. Tell me, did Junius see much of her?"

"He came to see her almost every day, and he was very nice to her. Polite in the old-fashioned way she likes. So do I. Men have no manners nowadays," Olivia said.

"They don't dare, unless they want to be just something that women wipe their feet on at the front door."

"I'm not going to waste any more time talking to you. It's getting cold out here." Olivia slammed the door shut, opened it again and said maliciously: "If you're burning with zeal why don't you talk to Tom Slack? An unprejudiced observer would say he was more worth your official attention than Amelia."

Rocky muttered: "Will you go jump in the lake?" and Allan shook his head reprovingly.

"You hadn't ought to talk to a lady like that. Was you intendin' to go see Tom Slack? . . . Well, that *is* kind of exasperatin'."

"She's right about it bein' time I got aroun' to seein' Slack, but what 're you goin' to do when he's drunk all the time? Don't step on the chickens," Rocky warned, leading the way through Tom Slack's back yard. "They seem to be in their pen like well-conducted birds, but that old rooster might still be up."

Allan chuckled. "Slack, or his pet? Slack's up, anyhow."

A thick voice bawled: "Come in! Well, why don't you come in an' not knock the house down?"— though by that time Rocky was inside the house. Slack glared at him blearily.

"I thought it 'd be you. Well, I ain't goin' to say nothin' at all. I know my rights, an' I guess I can get a lawyer if I need one."

"What makes you think you do?"

"I guess I know ever'body in this town would like to make me the goat. Except 'Melia. 'Melia's a good woman; 'Melia always stands up for me."

Slack's eyes watered; he drew his dirty shirt sleeve across them. "Only friend I got. 'Cept Cash, and I wouldn't call Cash a friend. Friends loan you money, don't they? Think Cash would loan me any?"

"Maybe he didn't have any to loan you."

"Bet he did. Old tightwad, that's what Cash Quinn was. Tried to let that cat of his kill Bill." Slack looked sentimentally at the rooster nodding sleepily on the back of a chair. "Said Bill crowed too loud in the mornin's. Used to have a won-won'erful tail, Bill did. Look at it now. Cat clawed three-four feathers out of it."

Slack yawned and reached for a bottle half-filled with a muddy-looking liquid. "Have a drink? Good stuff, make it myself. Oh, won't drink with a man, hunh? Well, I'll drink by myself. Used to it."

"I suppose you were drunk all last night?" Rocky said tactlessly.

"Drunk? Who says I was drunk? Never drunk in my life. Always get home by myself."

Allan murmured: "You're wastin' time, Son. Try to catch him when he's sober." But Rocky persisted:

"Was it you that was ringin' that bell at night? Cash seemed to think it was."

"He did? Why, the old . . ." Slack let loose a volley of adjectives that made even Robert Allan blink. "Tryin' to put it on me when it was him that done it. Liked to see people go runnin' around at night tryin' to catch him."

"You're sure of that?"

"Next thing to bein' sure. I knew Cash. You get the hell out of here," Slack said abruptly. "I'm sleepy."

Rocky said: "Pleasant dreams," and closed the door forcefully. "You're right, Dad, there's no use talkin' to him now. By his vocabulary he must 've been a mule skinner in his young days."

"Is it important, any more, who rang that bell?"

"I don't think so. I thought I might get him started talkin' by mentioning it. I don't doubt Cash did the whole thing for a joke; I always thought he did." Rocky sighed. "Lord, I'm tired. You go on to bed, Dad. I'm going to take some fingerprints, mainly to show some authority, and then talk to Mary Anne. After that, seems to me I'm entitled to call it a day."

CHAPTER X
SCRAPBOOK

Mary Anne was "just wrenching out a few tea towels, Mr. Sheriff. You set down there and be comfortable. Miss Kitty said I was to talk to you. Like a piece of pie?"

"I don't mind. It's mighty good pie."

"I don't know of any better," Mary Anne agreed. "I expect Mr. Barnhart will be in for a piece before long. Only you ain't like him: his freight increases constantly, but you don't get fat."

She went back to the tea towels. Rocky said, eating the pie he did not particularly want:

"You're pretty fond of Mrs. Featherstone-Quinn, aren't you, Mary Anne?"

"I guess I've got good reason to be. She took me in nearly twenty years ago when I was about starving. Gave me a job, and I've been with her ever since. When Mr. Featherstone was alive the emollient wasn't anything to talk about, but when he died she begin to pay me good wages."

"What kind of man was Mr. Featherstone?"

"He was stingy and very egocentric."

"Self-centered, you mean?"

"Yes, but I meant queer. Don't know why she married him 'less it was to take care of him. He was fussy about what he ate and was always having gastronomy. One of these men that always tells the same antidotes over and over again. He was kind of good-looking, but Miss Kitty was real pretty herself—just like a little doll. He worked for one of the newspapers, though he wasn't a reporter, and that's how Miss Kitty got a job when he died. Because while he left her some money it wouldn't last forever."

"Did she know Mr. Barnhart then?"

"Not as well as she did later. I think he was a professor in them days. He was a friend of Mr. Featherstone's. He was married then, and him and his wife used to come to dinner. I guess they got divorced pretty soon after Mr. Featherstone's demise. He quit being a professor, I guess, just about the same time. It was after Miss Kitty moved to the domicile on Russian Hill that he got to dropping in a lot."

"And how long has she known the other two?"

"Mr. Glidden came to the New Year's party with some man that paints—that's how we met him. He came back quite a lot till we came up here. I guess she's known Miss Ivy going on five years. She ain't as young as you might think—Miss Ivy. She must be around thirty, though she don't look any different than the first day I seen her. There was always a lot of people around, eating and drinking. Enough to put Miss Kitty in the poorhouse. That wouldn't have happened when Mr. Featherstone was alive. But she liked it. She always likes to look after people, and then some of them goes and labels her."

"Labels? Oh. Who libels Mrs. Featherstone-Quinn?"

"People that ain't got nothing better to do than talk gossip which I ain't going to repeat," Mary Anne said definitely. "And it wasn't none of these people, or for a long time. That old-maid sister of Mr. Featherstone's— Well, never mind about that."

"What did you think of Mr. Quinn?"

Mary Anne sniffed. "Another one she was too good for. Oh, he was always real nice to her, and I got nothing pacific against him. Miss Kitty would have got over her allusions about him, but she'd have made the best of it. She just wanted to look after him, so they got married. I hope she don't go and spend a whole lot of money on his obsequious. She needs to hold on to what she's got—she worked hard enough for it."

"You've no idea how interestin' you are, Mary Anne," Rocky said sincerely. "You like all these people?"

"I never knew a nicer gentleman than Mr. Barnhart. Miss Ivy and Mr. Glidden are all right. Mr. Glidden used to kind of stare at me. Maybe because he's a painter, and I know I'm bazaar-looking. Miss Ivy's always been nice to me, and I know she's real fond of Miss Kitty—which she ought to be. She can't help being kind of temper'mental; she's a poet. It's too bad, like Miss Kitty says, that them two don't fall in love. Miss Kitty's tried to throw them together, but maybe she's too ostensible about it."

Rocky laughed. "Maybe she is. Well, you'll be wanting to go to bed. Not frightened any more of ghosts, are you?"

"I guess they ought to be satisfied. I ain't scared, as long's I lock my door and keep cotton in my ears."

"Have all the rooms upstairs got keys?"

"I guess so. Nobody but me uses one. They're all the same, anyway."

"Probably every house in town has the same kind of locks," Rocky muttered. "Oh yes. Do you always use coal oil to start fires with?"

Mary Anne's guilty start set her long, red earrings vibrating. "I'll bet Mr. Murdoch told you that. Miss Kitty does think it's dangerous, but the wood's green, and I just got tired of it tonight and went and got some coal oil. It's bad enough having to cook with wood—though I must say nothing fries chicken like a wood fire."

"No, I reckon not. Well, you be careful of the stuff and don't spill any more, or you might set yourself on fire. Good night, Mary Anne."

Leon Glidden was just starting up the stairway to the second floor when Rocky came back into the hall. He said: "Everybody's gone to bed. I'm not sleepy, myself. Come in and have a drink?"

"Oh, a mod'rate-sized one. Did my dad come upstairs?"

"Fifteen minutes ago. He and Barnhart sat and talked about cavalry raids, and Kitty tried to talk art to me. I like Kitty, but her artistic patter gets me down," Glidden said, rinsing out glasses at the washstand. "Say when. And Ivy's sensitive soul is a little depressed—by events and having to have her fingerprints taken."

"I know she didn't like it."

"I suppose no one ever does. Like the room?"

Rocky laughed but made no attempt to hide his interest in the room's furnishings. "It's my business to be nosy. I wanted to see if there's anything here that would be a good thing to hit a man over the head with."

Glidden choked on his whisky. "Well," he said, when he had done coughing, "you might give me a little warning before you spring a thing like that. Look around. I don't think there are any lethal weapons here."

"I cert'nly don't see any. Mind if I take a look?" Rocky asked, indicating the easel standing near the front window.

"Go ahead, if you think you can stand it."

To Rocky's untutored eye the picture seemed to be composed of haphazard blobs and whorls of color: green, blazing yellows, violent blues. He winced unconsciously and backed away from the easel. Ten feet distant from it he decided that the thing was a landscape, after all: trees in shadow and a sunny, sloping hill.

"It does look better from a distance," Glidden agreed. "Like it?"

"That don't look to me like those paintings of yours they sold in Merton."

"It isn't. I'd always admired William Keith and tried to copy his style. Did it very badly, of course. I've had no real training. If I could get to New York—or Paris . . . One's as remote as the other, for me."

"I liked those sagebrush pictures. So did my wife, which means a lot more."

"I didn't know you were married. Neither," Glidden said with a slight grin, "do Ivy nor Olivia James."

Rocky reddened but refused to rise to the bait. "Well, she—Eleanor—says a lot of the things I like are just plain tripe. Maybe she'd like this."

"And you don't?" Glidden smiled as Rocky shook his head regretfully. "I don't know that I do, either. I was trying to go modern in a big way, with apologies to Cézanne and company."

"Is this what you call impressionism?"

"Oh, call this work of art anything you want to. Creative distortion, I suppose. You distort the thing you paint to express the emotion it arouses in you. Funny emotions some painters must have. Or you distort the drawing of it to fit what you think is your actual knowledge of it. A good many moderns think things are made up of squares and cubes and triangles."

"Now I see why you've got so many funny peaks stickin' up in this picture. I wondered why they were there. Seems to me there's a few curves in the world."

"I don't believe you'd care for Cubism. My fiancée goes in for that—"

"I didn't know," Rocky said, mimicking Glidden's tone of a moment ago, "that you're engaged. Does Miss Horne?"

"You've been listening to Kitty. Women were matchmakers ever. Of course Ivy knows. She knows Marjorie, and Kitty doesn't. We haven't announced it because her family isn't particularly enthusiastic about the financial situation. Neither am I. But Kitty's a talker so I haven't told her. She goes right on trying to throw Ivy and me at each other's heads. It never occurs to her to try to promote a match between Ivy and Barnhart, whom she likes far better than she ever has me."

"Maybe Mrs. Featherstone-Quinn thinks of Barnhart as too old for Miss Horne."

"Well, I suppose he's past forty-five, but Ivy's thirty, as she'd tell you without hesitation if you asked her. If you want a really authoritative lecture on theories of painting, talk to Ivy. Or Kitty. Ivy, for preference. Kitty doesn't really know what it's all about, but I think Ivy must have been raised in San Francisco's art galleries—such as they are."

"Funny place to raise a kid."

"Oh, you heard her say she was precocious. Barnhart told me she was brought up by an old souse of a father—one of these fellows that know a little bit about everything. He wrote. He probably would have been good at it if he could have stayed sober. Barnhart knew him."

"You don't talk like I thought artists did," Rocky said thoughtfully.

Glidden laughed. "I'm only a second-rate daub-
er. The average workman has fewer theories about
his work than the person who looks at it. I'd like
to do portraits, but I've made a mess of every one
I ever tried. What does your wife look like?"

"Hunh? Oh, she's tall and has red hair."

"Admirable," Glidden said dryly. "From your
description I'd be able to recognize her anywhere."

"I'm neither a poet or an artist," Rocky retorted. "She's damned good-lookin.' Her hair's kind
of an orange-red, and she's never cut it. Gray eyes.
That's the best I can do for you, and why did you
want to know, anyway?"

"Vulgar curiosity. I suppose you know you're
'damned good-looking' yourself, and I wondered
if you'd married some washed-out little mouse."

Rocky's ears turned red, and Glidden grinned
at his discomfort. "Seriously, if I were a portrait
painter I'd like to do yours. Collar-ad face with
pussycat eyes. You've watched a cat sit and stare
at you blandly and wondered what the hell it was
thinking about you and everything else? . . . All
right, we'll cut the personalities. No doubt you've
suffered enough from Kitty's habit of making very
personal remarks."

"I have," Rocky said with some feeling.

"Only I do warn you, Allan, that I'm not fooled
by your—shall we call it amiability? I'd damn well

like to know what you're thinking about me and all of us, and I know you're not telling. Amelia Slack's another one I'd like to paint. It 'd be the devil of a job to get her eyes right, to make it clear they were seeing things no one else could see and— Hell! That reminds me . . ."

Glidden got up and opened the door of a closet, found the scorched and blackened pajama jacket he had worn the night before. "This is hers, isn't it?" he said, holding out a china brooch painted with a woman's simpering face and powdered head.

"When I saw her she had on a pin like that, though I didn't get close enough to her to get a good look at the face on it. Olivia James says she lost one at the fire. Is that where you found it?"

"Barnhart found it; he just happened to kick it with his foot. He asked me if it was worth keeping. Ivy said she thought it was Mrs. Slack's so I put it in my pocket. Doctor James had taken her home by that time. I described it to Kitty this evening, and she said it must be Mrs. Slack's. You give it to her when you see her. None of us seemed to think of it when Barnhart said he saw her looking for something this afternoon. Well, you look to me like you needed some sleep, and I know I've talked you to death."

"I've never got anywhere without talkin' to people. But I think I will go to bed. I've still got to look over Junius Quinn's things. By the way, did you bring any gloves with you?"

"Gloves?" Glidden raised his eyebrows. "I didn't think gloves were necessary in Slacktown, and I never wear them, anyway. Neither does Barnhart, if you're curious. Good night."

Junius, Rocky decided, had tried to make his room look like a place where poetry was written. There were several pieces of fine old mahogany, one of them a tall secretary. Its top shelves held neatly arranged volumes of the poets and a dog-eared rhyming dictionary.

On either side of the desk was a diagonal line of photographs: Robert Frost, Vachel Lindsay, Tennyson, Browning, Shelley, Stephen Vincent Benét. Busts of Homer and Dante were in possession of the mantel, with a clock between them and a cloisonné bowl and a large brass vase on either side.

Rocky lifted a vase carefully, testing its weight. The thing was heavy, curving from a slender neck to a round-bellied base. He carried it to the table and sprayed it with metallic powder, but there were no prints except those of his own fingertips.

He put the vase back on the mantel and opened the secretary, finding tidy piles of papers in

pigeonholes and a long quill pen in an empty ink-
stand. A small scrapbook held newspaper clippings of Junius' printed poems, beginning with
those written at the tender age of eleven.

"And I almost think he did better than that
later on," Rocky muttered. "He never did get over
writin' about the beautiful spring. 'Lines to My
Father'":

> Oh, stern and hardy pioneer,
> Whose wisdom was that of a seer;
> Who faltered not when duty called,
> By danger never was appalled.
> And since thou hast been called by God
> And rest beneath thy native sod . . .

Rocky grimaced and closed the book. "Old man
Quinn didn't quite deserve that, but they have to
have somethin' to fill up the local newspapers."

He took up a scratch-pad with a few inane sin-
gles written on its first page. On an inside sheet
he found the title "Birthday Ode" and six labori-
ous lines:

> May's child and fair as May
> Are you. I praise the day,
> After the long and lonely years,
> That Fate sent you to dry my tears,

To teach me to love Life again
And sing it as a sweet refrain. . . .

Rocky laughed, then looked slightly ashamed of himself. He tore the paper from the pad and tucked it into his pocket, looking wistfully at the bed which tried, with the aid of a gaily colored fringed cover and a dozen pillows, to be an Oriental divan.

An old Japanese screen hid washstand and bureau, the latter covered with a collection of small bottles and brushes that were testimony of Junius Quinn's vanity. There was even, Rocky discovered, some sort of reducing belt hanging in the closet, along with two expensive and little-worn suits. The bureau drawers were well filled with shirts and underwear, most of which bore the labels of San Francisco's best men's shops, but there were no gloves in the bureau drawers or anywhere else in the room.

A small table near the bed held Chinese cups and teapot, an old-fashioned spirit lamp and small teakettle. Rocky had a sudden picture of Junius serving tea to any of the hotel's guests who would drink it with him while he discussed his wasted talents.

He took the pillows off the bed, stacked them in a chair and then noticed a small wastepaper basket by the secretary. There was a torn blotter in it and several crumpled sheets of paper. Only one of them showed anything more than the first lines of poems, with haphazard designs scribbled along the margins. But on one page Junius had started to draw a map—at least, something that more nearly resembled a map than anything else.

A tall tree had been sketched in one corner of the page, and a round hump in its center was labeled "White Stone." A series of short lines leading to the hump seemed to indicate a trail. On the left side of the page several inches had been shaded with pencil and the word Canyon printed underneath. Then, apparently, the paper had been crumpled up and tossed into the basket.

Rocky smoothed it out, put it in his pocket and again looked longingly at the bed. But instead of getting into it he took Cash's scrapbook from the table where he had laid it. He turned its pages rapidly, finding that the clippings answered Barnhart's general description of them. He skimmed through them hastily, unfolding one that had not yet been pasted in the book. After an instant he whistled and read it carefully through.

SIOUX JUNCTION (ARIZ.) MAY 18. Today another story of gold came from the mysterious Superstition Mountains to revive legends of unfound riches.

This story concerned the reported discovery of a ten-pound nugget and several smaller nuggets thought to be worth nearly $7000.

The nuggets are supposed to have been brought in by Edward Weldon and Albert Green, both of Tucson. It was Weldon who, in April 1934, brought out of the mountains several pieces of almost pure gold which government assayers at Denver later said were dental gold.

Weldon and Green refused to divulge the present whereabouts of the gold nuggets but hinted they had been sent to a United States mint. Weldon stated that he did not believe they had found any mine but only some free pieces of gold in an arroyo bed, probably broken off years ago from an exposed ledge.

Rocky slowly refolded the clipping and put it with Junius' unfinished map. He thought: well, there it is. All I want to know to be dead certain I'm right. But no proof, of course. Oh well, let it go till tomorrow. . . .

Presently, washing his hands, he found himself staring at his own face in the mirror above the

washstand. Some impulse made him lean forward
and look at it closely. He had his pet vanities, but
he was more apt to look at his waistline than his
face. Not that it ran in the family to get fat, but
there was no use letting a thing like that sneak up
on you. The face in the mirror still looked as if
laughter came very easily to its owner. Glidden's
"collar-ad face" was an exaggeration, and the eyes
looked more brown than yellow. But the pupils
sometimes did contract like a cat's—

Abruptly, the face was his own again. Rocky
turned a rich red and moved hastily away from the
mirror. "Must be Junius' influence hangin' around
the room," he muttered. "Eleanor 'd probably call
me Narcissus if she caught me gawkin' at myself
like that."

He blew out the flame of the lamp and got into
bed. It was a comfortable bed, and he had been
wanting to go to sleep for the last two hours, but
he lay there and wondered if he had been lucky
until now. At this moment there was nothing before him but a wall that had one little chink in
it—and that too small for light to filter through.

He hadn't even the beginning of a case, so far
as tangible proof went, against any one of ten persons. And neither had any of them been eliminat-
ed, even though instinct said: "Mary Anne couldn't
have done it. Or Mrs. Featherstone-Quinn." But

once you began that way you were apt to work through your entire list.

Tom Slack would make a splendid picture of a murderer, but he could hardly be called clever, even when he was sober. Glidden, Barnhart and Ivy Horne had brains; so did Olivia James—and probably plenty of cold nerve besides. The same thing went for the old doctor, though his frail physique was a point in his favor.

Murder begets murder. . . . But nothing led him to suppose anyone was in danger because he possessed any information dangerous to a murderer. Whatever Amelia Slack knew must tell against her, not someone else. There was no other reason why Olivia should try to keep him from talking to her.

This backwoods police system with its inadequate force of sheriff's deputies—or force of inadequate deputies—was enough to run a man ragged, Rocky thought. He had to have some sleep. He would limit himself to three hours and then get up and, for safety's sake, go outside and spend the rest of the night patrolling the town.

Afterward he thought that for several hours he must have slept very soundly, but finally he began to dream. It seemed that he was sitting at Junius Quinn's desk, trying to write a birthday ode to Eleanor. He tried to use the ornamental quill pen, but there was no ink, and neither was there any rhyme for Eleanor.

When he tried to write down the first line of his poem he could not remember it, and suddenly he was standing on the platform in the old schoolhouse. Some kind of program was being given, and he was supposed to recite a poem he could not remember.

He fidgeted from one foot to another, staring down at a vague audience, and then it came to him that the poem was Poe's "Bells." He began: "Bells, bells, bells, bells, bells . . ." His voice went on and on without stopping, repeating the one word until bells seemed to be swaying slowly in the air before him. Abruptly the scene faded. He sat up, wide-awake, but the bell went on ringing.

CHAPTER XI
"I RANG THE BELL FOR HER"

Already there was a sound of voices in the hall and the noise of doors opening and closing. Rocky did not wait to light the lamp. He was stepping, barefooted, into his shoes, tieing the laces around them, when Barnhart said, outside his door:

"Allan! Allan! Are you awake? Did you hear—"

"I heard it. Come in, the door isn't locked. Oh, you aren't dressed yet?"

"No, but I'll go out this way if you—"

"I'm ready," Rocky said, buttoning his leather jacket over his naked chest. "If you want to go that way, come on. When did it start?"

"I don't know. Everyone's getting up. Glidden said he was going to put some clothes on before he came out. Your father—"

"I'm dressed," Allan said briefly. "Hell's bells!"

Barnhart laughed rather jerkily. "I think so, too. I thought this was all over now that— Kitty,

you go back in your room and stay there. We don't
need you."

Rocky stopped, halfway down the stairs and
looked up at Mrs. Featherstone-Quinn's head,
knobbed with round curlers.

"You stay where you are, ma'am," he said hastily.
"You an' Miss Horne. It's nothing serious."

He had thought that the bell would stop ringing before they were outside, but still the sound
went on. Each note echoed through the still night
and died slowly before the bell tolled again. Rocky
found himself counting mechanically as he ran toward the schoolhouse: "One—two—three—"

Behind him Barnhart was swearing because he
had lost a bedroom slipper in the dust, and Glidden had just banged the door of the inn shut.
Lawrence Murdoch said: "Well, here we are again.
Yes, it woke me up." And then: "We don't need
you, Olivia. Oh well, if you're afraid of missing
something . . ."

Rocky spoke without thinking: "Six—seven,"
and his father grunted:

"Don't waste your breath, Son. Maybe we're
goin' to catch the crazy bastard this time."

"He'll have to—run like hell to—get away. But
I don't—understand—"

Rocky stopped. The door to the schoolhouse
was open, and Tom Slack stood under the old bell,

dirty hands grasping the frayed rope. His lips moved laboriously as he counted: "Forty-three—forty-four—forty-five." At forty-five he let the rope swing free and stood looking up at the bell, muttering soundlessly.

Something had kept any of them from speaking until the man had done counting. But now Barnhart said: "So it was you, after all? But why—"

Rocky motioned him to be silent. He said: "Slack! Slack! Tom!"

The rusted bell was motionless now, though the rope still quivered a little. Slack looked at them as if he had not known before that they were there. He was very drunk; his feet scraped uncertainly along the floor as he moved toward the steps. He said:

"No one else left to do it. I did it. Used to always be somebody to ring the bell soon as anyone died. No one left to do it now."

Rocky drew a long breath. "Why ring it fo'ty-five times?" he said.

He hoped that he was wrong, but he thought he knew what Slack's answer would be. After trying to focus his bleared eyes upon them Slack said:

"'Melia was forty-five. 'Melia's dead. So I rang the bell for her. She'd want me to."

"He's talking rot," Glidden said uncertainly. "How can he know, unless he killed her himself? He's so drunk he—"

"Me? Me kill 'Melia!" Slack's voice died to a throaty growl. He lowered his head between his shoulders and leaped toward Glidden. Rocky swung in front of him and said quietly:

"You don't want to do that. Tell us about it, and we'll—"

"I heard what he said! Me kill 'Melia! Went over to see her. Lonesome. Wanted to talk to her. Why'd you let her get killed?" Slack demanded. "Why didn't you take care of her? You—why, I'll take you apart—"

Rocky hit him once, full on the point of his whiskered chin. "Prop him up against the wall," he said to Murdoch. "I didn't hit him very hard, but I can't be bothered with him now. I'm goin' to Amelia Slack's place."

"Her light's still burnin'," Allan muttered. Murdoch said:

"It would be. She hasn't let it go out since I can remember. Olivia, why don't you—"

"I won't," Olivia said. "If what Tom said is true I'm going in." She shouldered her way past Robert Allan, entered the house just behind Rocky. "She—she never would lock that door. Not that we're in the habit of locking doors, but she left hers open in case—in case Andrew came home."

They stopped in the doorway of the prim, spotless living room. After an instant Olivia said huskily: "But she won't wait for him any longer." Then, as if ashamed of her lapse into sentiment, she turned on Rocky angrily: "Well, I hope you're satisfied! Going to sleep instead of looking after her!"

"Don't be a damned fool," Murdoch said harshly. "How did any of us know she might be killed? You certainly did your best to keep everyone away from her."

"Would you," Rocky inquired softly, "mind postponin' this cat fight till some other time? I know you both feel bad about Mrs. Slack, but I'm most to blame for what happened. Now, Miss James, you go over an' wake your grandfather—"

"He's awake," Olivia said sullenly. "I told him he might catch cold if he came out."

"All right. Trot over, an' send him back here. And you stay home. . . . Oh yes, you will! I'll put you out pers'nally if you come back. Go on!"

Olivia caught her lower lip between her teeth as Murdoch looked at her and grinned unsympathetically. "All right," she said finally. "If you want to get along without my help, you can—now and forever! I'm going." She glanced toward Amelia Slack, surprisingly burst into tears and ran for the door.

"Which is goin' to make things difficult," Rocky murmured. "But I can't have her hanging around."

He looked at Barnhart and Glidden. Barnhart was shivering in his silk robe, and Glidden's face had a pasty look under the brick-red of his burned skin. He started to light a cigarette, shrugged apologetically and put it back in his pocket. Barnhart said:

"She looks as if she'd been sitting there, embroidering. You wouldn't know, if it wasn't for her face—"

"People who 've been choked to death don't usually look pretty," Rocky said. "Someone has kind of a fondness for that method. Well, guns make a noise."

"You mean Junius was strangled? No one told us that."

"I'd forgotten you didn't know. There's no use you two stayin' here, Barnhart. You can't help any. An' Mrs. Featherstone-Quinn will be wonderin' what's keeping you so long."

"I suppose she will. If you're sure we can't help here . . ."

"How can we?" Glidden said impatiently. "He's right; we'd better get back to the women. He wants to get rid of us, anyway. Come on."

"It's twelve thirty-five," Rocky said. "Earlier 'n I thought. Seemed to me I'd been asleep hours. It was about ten-thirty when I went to bed."

"An' twelve-twenty when I got out in the hall where I could see my watch," Allan said.

Rocky stood looking down at Amelia Slack. She sat in the shabby rocking chair, a piece of heavy, cream-colored linen in her lap. She had been embroidering it with colored wool, working a design of impossibly pink and yellow roses and green leaves. The needle was on the floor, with a strand of yellow wool trailing from it, but there was a single, bright drop of blood on her right forefinger.

"Pricked herself and dropped the needle when someone got his hands aroun' her neck," Rocky said. "From behind, probably. She wouldn't be able to put up much of a fight. Murdoch, you ought to know if it's true Mrs. Slack always stayed up late."

"Oh, it's true. I guess she never did go to bed before midnight, and I've come back to town later than that—one or two o'clock—and seen her through the side window, still sitting here."

"Did she— How long 've you known her?"

"Twenty-eight years. I was born here, you know."

"Did she ever wander aroun' at night?"

"Once in a while she took a streak and went outside and walked up and down the streets or down in the graveyard. But she wouldn't have had a spell like that last night. You could usually tell quite awhile before, if she was working up to a spell like that. I came over every morning to bring milk so I saw her Thursday morning, and she was unusually—well, wide-awake. Not so vague nor even a little wild, like she was now and then."

"Miss James said the kitchen was the only room she could 've seen Cash's place from."

"It is. Of course, she might have gone into the kitchen for something, but she always sat in here until she went to bed. Last night was a dark night, anyway. Even if she didn't pull the shade down in the window where the light is, she couldn't see anything from there—unless she just happened to be standing there and trying to see out."

"These side windows look out on the school-house, and I suppose her chair was always right here next to them?"

"Always. You see she has an old rug under it so the carpet wouldn't get worn."

"And what about this fancywork— Oh, come in, Doctor. We've been waitin' for you."

"I met Tom Slack outside," James said. He looked down at Amelia, his pale lips tightly compressed. "He wanted to come in. I gathered you had to hit him pretty hard. I persuaded him to go home instead of coming in here to fight you."

"He's pretty drunk, isn't he?"

"I've seen him more so," James said judicially. "Tom's states of intoxication are many and varied. He's ready to go to sleep now, but I'd say it was very likely he did want to talk to Amelia at the time he claims he did."

"He's taken streaks like that before, then?"

"Oh yes. At a certain stage he becomes sentimental and wants to talk to someone. Amelia was the only person he was fond of. He knew she sat up very late. I've told her to lock her door so that he wouldn't be able to bother her, but his being Andrew Slack's brother made her very patient with him. She was always able to handle him without any difficulty."

The doctor opened his bag and bent over Amelia's body. Murdoch said:

"You were going to ask about her fancywork? She's made things for years; she never read, and her housework wasn't enough to keep her busy. That thing she was working on looks like another of those chair tidies. She did lots of other things, too."

"It looks to me like she didn't know she had anything to be afraid of. Otherwise she wouldn't just have sat here and gone on working, and no one could have sneaked into the room, the way she was setting."

"Sometimes she was pretty vague," Murdoch said. "But she certainly had sense enough that if she knew she was in danger she wouldn't just sit there placidly and let herself be killed. I never heard her say she wished she was dead. Did you, Doc?"

"N-no. No, not for many years. She did say that, when her husband was killed, but in time she seemed content to go on living. Well," James said, straightening his thin shoulders, "this seems—appropriate: death in a ghost town, death of a ghost." He walked over to the window and blew out the flame of the small lamp on its sill. "That's all Amelia has been for twenty-five years. And now the lamp's blown out. I'm afraid I'm sentimental enough to wish her death might have been a little different. It doesn't really matter. What you want to know is how long she's been dead."

"If you wouldn't mind makin' a guess," Rocky said.

"It isn't as much of a guess as it often is. Because she hasn't been dead very long. It's a quarter of one. I'd stake my reputation she died not longer than an hour ago—and probably later than that."

"About eleven forty-five or a little later, then? Well, if anyone was watchin' for my light to go out, I went to bed about ten-thirty. If it wasn't anyone in the hotel, I was safe in there with everyone else so it didn't matter. But wouldn't she think it was funny for someone to come to see her at midnight?"

"Well, of course it depends on who it was," Murdoch said. "Anyone she knew . . ."

"Olivia used to come in to see her at any hour," James said. "She left what money she had to you two, Lawrence."

"To the two of us? But I thought—Olivia—"

James smiled briefly. "I imagine Olivia did, too—if she ever thought about it. Amelia had very little, but she never considered touching her principal. One of her old-fashioned notions. She did make arrangements for a large tombstone to be erected over Andrew's grave when she died—if she died before she managed to do it herself. She told Olivia she'd left her some money. She didn't tell her that she left it to the two of you if you marry."

"Now I'm in the doghouse again," Murdoch said unhappily. "Olivia will blame me just for existing because if I didn't, Amelia wouldn't have wanted us to get married."

"It can't be helped; she did want it. She believed in marriage and not in careers for women. The only times Olivia was ever angry with her was when she refused to admit Olivia is a dentist. But that's not important. Is there anything more I can do for you, Mr. Allan?"

"Nothing I know of. You'd better go home an' get you some sleep. Suppose we put her on that couch. . . . No, the cor'ner won't mind. If you'll help me, Murdoch . . ."

"I can stay here tonight if you want someone," Murdoch offered. "If you have to go back to the inn . . ."

"Well— Yes, you might stay. I'm goin' to look over the house first. Did she do all this fancywork for herself?"

"She worked so rapidly that she had far more than she had any use for. She filled a hope chest for Olivia," James said. "Olivia always said it was Amelia who had hope, not her. We—I was over here earlier in the evening—tried to get Amelia to go back to bed, but she said she was tired of bed. I asked her to lock both front and back doors tonight, and she promised me she would. Olivia wanted to stay with her, but she wouldn't let her."

"Do you think there was any reason behind that?"

"You mean any reason why she wanted to be alone tonight? I certainly never thought of that at the time. She always preferred being alone, and she wasn't ill. There's only the one bedroom here. Olivia offered to sleep on the couch."

"Well, she may 've locked her front door—I'll look at the back one in a minute—an' then opened it to let someone in. There's a key in the door. I guess that's all, Doctor."

"Then I'll— I believe that handkerchief you just picked up is Olivia's. If it is initialed . . ."

Rocky looked at the exquisitely worked *J* in the corner of the handkerchief. "It is. Did Mrs. Slack do that?"

"Oh yes. Shall I return it to Olivia? She's always losing handkerchiefs." Doctor James picked up his brown bag. "In the morning I'll make a more thorough examination—anything you want. Good night."

"Good night," Rocky said. "Dad, will you go over an' get that fingerprint outfit and the records of prints? I left them on the table of the room I slept in. Then you go to bed if you want to. I'll be here quite awhile."

It was nearly three o'clock before Rocky came back to the inn, leaving Lawrence Murdoch on guard in Amelia Slack's house. He was relieved to find that everyone had gone to bed—everyone but Robert Allan. He was sitting in Junius Quinn's most comfortable chair, smoking.

"Never could go back to sleep once I've got up," he said. "I thought maybe there 'd be somethin' you wanted me to do."

"You didn't by any chance think we could talk?" Rocky asked. "Oh, I'm willing to. I was dead for sleep once but not any more. What happened when you got back here after you brought that stuff to me? You said they were still up."

"The womenfolks was takin' on—well, Mrs. Quinn was—about poor Amelia. The Horne woman looked all in. After all, Mrs. Slack can't have meant much to her or the others that 're just visitin'."

"I wonder if they ever talked to her."

"Some. They mentioned it. I reckon Barnhart was best acquainted with her. He's a great hand to talk to people: gets 'em started an' listens to what they've got to say. Mrs. Quinn used to run in to try to cheer her up, she said." Allan grinned briefly. "I can pretty near hear her doin' it, but I don't reckon Mrs. Slack ever listened very much. Mary Anne—"

"Then she did fin'lly wake up?"

"She had cotton stuck in her ears, but she fin'lly thought she heard people runnin' aroun' in the hall. She says all these murders has been done by the ghost of some bad man that got himself stuck up on Boot Hill and 's had it in for the town ever since."

"It 'd simplify things to accept that the'ry, but I'm afraid the cor'ner or the voters of this county don't believe in ghosts that much. Anything more?"

"Oh, they was all wantin' to know the why of it. Why should she get killed? Then Barnhart per- suaded the women to go to bed. What did Mrs. Slack know that made someone kill her?"

"You tell me. Probably nothing she knew she knew. Because I do think she was tellin' the truth last time we talked to her—far 's she knew the truth. Of course, she may 've wanted to think things over. And Olivia James kept me away from her, and ever'body knew it. That was partly my fault for being too easygoin'. But people knew I hadn't talked to her yet, and that I cert'nly would this mornin'."

"Well then, what about the James girl? She was with Mrs. Slack off an' on all day. You thought she was keeping you away because she thought Mrs. Slack might incriminate herself. Won't someone be afraid Mrs. Slack told her ever'thing she knew?"

"It's a possibility. I suppose I'd better camp on her doorstep the rest of the night. I doubt if Mrs. Slack would tell her anything she didn't want known. She must 've known Olivia's kind of im- pulsive an' would like to have a finger in things— by settin' everyone right, if she could. I think she'd speak right out against anyone here but her grandad and maybe Murdoch. But neither of them would harm her."

"The old one wouldn't. It ain't entirely impossible the young one mightn't, is it?"

"Nothing's impossible." Rocky sat down at the secretary, pulled a scratch-pad toward him, penciled a few notes and then threw the paper in the wastebasket.

"That ought to help a lot," his father said. "What you goin' to do?"

"I thought I said I'd prob'ly camp out on the James doorstep. If I do you can leave your door open an' see that everybody here stays in their rooms. There's nothing else for me to do," Rocky said. "There weren't any fingerprints that mattered. Some in the other part of the house that I think must be Olivia James's. I haven't taken hers yet. None on any chair where a visitor would 've set. The house was spick-and-span all over—nothing out of place. I went through a desk in her bedroom, but she never got any letters. There was just a couple her husband wrote her before they were married."

"Well," Allan said, "you got no fingerprints and no weapons, except somebody's hands—an' a poker."

"That was used to kill a cat. We can't prove it killed Cash Quinn."

"N-no. Well then, are you goin' to do anything at all?"

"I could arrest Tom Slack. What do you think about that?"

"Might make a good impression an' keep him sober for the first time in years. Would that be your reason for doin' it?"

"If I did? But I'm not going to. I b'lieve his story, though I haven't really heard it yet. He might have killed Amelia Slack when he was crazy-drunk though even that seems doubtful. But the first killings weren't planned by anyone who was half cockeyed.

"Everything's happened at night," Rocky went on. "So, of course, everyone just says they were in bed, asleep. So far no one's come forth with any stories about hearin' strange noises or seein' some dark figure wanderin' aroun' in the middle of the night. Maybe Amelia Slack could 've told some such story, but she wasn't in any hurry about it, and now it's too late. I was thinking that the way I put my question to her last night I almost left it up to her to decide whether she knew anything important or not. What I should have done was to fire questions at her like she was on the witness stand."

"Well, no one likes to drag a lady out of bed."

"That's got nothin' to do with it."

"Ain't it? I was goin' to say: what puzzles me is how whoever killed her found out she might

know somethin'. If they'd known that, when the
two men was killed they wouldn't have wasted a
whole day, takin' a chance she might talk. Maybe
it was when the James girl rode herd on her all day
that they begun to get suspicious."

"That must 've had something to do with it.
But there's a better reason than that." Rocky felt
in his pocket, found the china brooch Glidden had
given him and put it on the table. "You remember
at dinner Barnhart spoke about Mrs. Slack havin'
been over to the fire this afternoon to look for
somethin'? An' Olivia said Mrs. Slack had lost this
brooch at the fire."

"Well, what if she did?"

"But s'pose she didn't? Suppose she'd been over
at the old Quinn house before the fire and lost it
then and not later?"

"What reason would she have for goin' over
there?"

"I don't know. I'm only guessin' about the whole
thing. Olivia told Murdoch about the brooch—
and, I suppose, her grandfather. Everyone at the
table here heard what Barnhart said. Barnhart
found the pin while they were fightin' fire. Glidden and Miss Horne was with him, and Glidden
put the thing in his pocket. He spoke to Mrs.
Featherstone-Quinn about it, and she said it must
be Mrs. Slack's."

"So that ever'body knew she'd lost it? But how'd they know she didn't really lose it at the fire?—if she didn't."

"Someone might 've noticed she turned up without it. If she was in the Quinn house she must 've walked in thick dust, and whoever set the place afire could see footprints without knowing, then, whose they were. That's another wild guess, but I know you could tell I'd been there, after I'd walked aroun' in the vacant rooms over at Cash's place. Of course, I've got to find out if she was wearin' that brooch all day Thursday, but I'll gamble she was, an' anyone who saw her would know she hadn't lost it before the night of the fire. I'm hoping I'll get some help from Olivia James."

"If you can make her talk to you," Allan said with an unsympathetic grin. "She ain't feelin' kindly toward you just now. You oughtn't to talk to a woman the way you've done to her, but I admit she's been a damn nuisance."

"She'll talk—if I have to stick her in jail for not doin' it. Yeah, I know they don't ever do that to a woman down home—*you* say."

"Mind tellin' me what was in them notes you began to make?"

"I did start to jot some down—but what the hell! I'm not apt to forget what I want to know: why folks talked about Mrs. Featherstone-Quinn once; when her birthday is—things like that; when Barnhart and his wife separated; where Junius Quinn's gloves went to—they probably burned up in the fire—if Junius ever asked Glidden to draw him a map—"

"That 'll do," Allan said irritably. "If that's the best you got to work on—"

"Those things may be important. But there's one thing to remember, Dad. The murderer knows things an innocent man don't. He knows some things we don't and probably never can—without him tellin' them to us. But he also knows some things we know, that innocent people don't. Right now it looks like the only way we'll catch him is never to forget the details he's supposed not to know. Maybe, when we least expect it, he'll give himself away. And maybe not. Now, I reckon I'll go out and protect Miss Olivia James."

CHAPTER XII
DETECTION PLUS DENTISTRY

"So I tried the back door to see if it was locked, too"—Rocky stopped to light a cigarette, went on—"and was lookin' aroun' for the best place to camp down till daylight when the door opened, and there was the doctor with a sawed-off shotgun in his hand. He smiled in that saintly sort of way of his and told me to go back to bed. He said it 'd occurred to him someone might think Olivia knew too much, so he'd pretended to go to bed an' then got up an' got his gun. Patted it affect'nately and said he'd often helped enforce law 'n order in the town with it, and he guessed he could look after Olivia now."

"Then you did get some sleep, after all?" Murdoch said.

"An hour or two. But that girl's got to talk—for her own safety."

"That's what I told her, but she's still mad. It's a long time since anyone told Olivia where to head in."

VIRGINIA RATH

"Why don't you?" Rocky said interestedly.

"Think it would do any good? In a pig's eye! I've considered trying to pull the cave-man stunt. They eat it up when it's Clark Gable socking some dame," Murdoch said gloomily. "But I never even get started with Olivia. She's sore at me, too. Says if I hadn't made a pest of myself wanting to marry her and raving about it to Amelia, Amelia wouldn't have made that crazy will. So it's all my fault."

"How much money did Mrs. Slack have?"

"Maybe about five thousand dollars in securities. You couldn't get that much for them if you sold them. I suppose we could. I think Amelia's father tied the stuff up till she was thirty—Andrew Slack had the name of being impractical—and by that time she was sensible enough not to touch it. Well, it's a good deal of money to Olivia or me," Murdoch admitted. "But about getting her to talk—I got her grandfather to promise to lay down the law. I doubt if she knows anything worth telling. She just wants you to think she does."

"That's all right, but it's dang'rous if someone else believes she knows too much. I've got to talk to her so's I can announce she hasn't been able to tell me anything. Well, the county newspapermen an' all the sightseers are gone."

"I did a good day's business: beer, cheese and crackers, candy bars. Someone might as well profit from people's curiosity. So many came up 'just for the ride.'"

"An' to dig aroun' in the fire to try to find a bone or two for a souvenir," Rocky said disgustedly, "and listen to the inquests."

"If they expected to hear anything there they must have been badly disappointed. I've always heard about the way Sloane dashes through one, but this was my first experience seeing it."

"Lorenzo is a swell guy," Rocky said. "He can cut through red tape like nobody's business. Not bein' a doctor, he hasn't much professional int'rest in cases like this, though he'd always be willing to steal some business from the Merton undertaker. But he don't try to tell me how to handle a case, and I reckon Freddie Haynes—the D.A.—is so busy 'lectioneering that he just figures on givin' me plenty of rope to hang myself with."

"You missed quite a bit of the inquests," Murdoch remarked.

Rocky said: "I was busy over at the hotel," without explaining that he had taken the opportunity to search the bedrooms at the inn while their occupants were in the old schoolhouse. The search had been wasted effort; he had expected that it would be. He had not had time to go through the Jameses' house, and Murdoch's store and living quarters had been locked.

"Do you believe Tom's story?" Murdoch asked abruptly.

"Do you?"

"Yes, but I know Tom. A lot of the half-wits that came up here seemed to expect you to arrest him right away."

"Oh, that 'd be foolish," Rocky said mildly. "He told the same story at the inquest as he had before: wanted to talk to Amelia, went in and saw right away she was dead. He swears he didn't move her or disturb anything. I think he thinks he's tellin' the truth about that, and I hope his mem'ry is to be trusted. By the way, you said you saw Mrs. Slack Thursday?"

"The day of the fire? Sure, I saw her morning and afternoon."

"Did you notice if she was wearin' that painted china pin of hers?"

Murdoch frowned. "You'd better ask Olivia. I'm sure she was because she always did, and if she hadn't been I'd have noticed it was missing."

"I've never asked anyone much about what happened that day."

"It was one of our usual, eventful days here— which means that nothing happened. We ate and talked to each other. Glidden did some painting at the end of the street; Barnhart was over as Cash's place for a while—"

"Was Mrs. Slack inside all day?"

"She was digging around in the garden for a while in the afternoon. I can see people going back and forth from here. Business," Murdoch said with a wry smile, "is not good enough to keep me occupied, but I have to be here. I usually sit out here; it's stuffy inside and smells of everything on earth. Well, Mrs. Featherstone-Quinn and Miss Horne paid Amelia an afternoon call. I think she asked them in to have tea. That's one reason I insisted Amelia wasn't getting one of her queer spells: she was unusually sociable. Barnhart and Glidden both stopped to talk to her, and Olivia ran in and out, and the doctor was there for a little while. That what you want to know?"

"Exactly what I want to know. What about Mary Anne?"

"She doesn't seem to be very fond of fresh air. Oh yes, she was outside once. I saw her go over to Amelia's just after dinner with some kind of dish in her hand. Mrs. Featherstone-Quinn was always sending her things to eat."

"What time is it? Two o'clock. Then I haven't time to set aroun' any longer. I've got to talk to Miss James." But Rocky continued to sit on the store steps, and Murdoch said in Mae Westian accents:

"Not scared, are you? Got anything else to do?"

"Plenty. The constable down in Merton's arrested some guy and wants me to look him over. He seems to have a car that don't belong to him. It answers the description of one that was stolen from over at Indian River, though the license plates aren't the same. I hope," Rocky said, "that Dud hasn't run in some perfectly law-abiding citizen."

"What about your deputies doing some work?"

"I inherited two well-meanin' and very fat old guys at Brookdale. I had a good, husky deputy in Merton, but he didn't have much sense. He's in the hospital after goin' down to the Jungle without a gun to arrest a couple of tough guys that 'd robbed a freight down in Stockton. Jazz Mitchell is still waitin' for his relief. The fellow evidently fell by the wayside between Reno Junction an' Merton. I can't ask Jazz to stay up all night when he's got to go to work at eight in the mornin'. I'll have to go to Merton, anyway, pretty soon."

"I was going to say I'd be glad to help you out up here if there's anything I can do, but I forget I'm in it with everyone else. I suppose you couldn't set one of us on guard?"

"I could if I needed to," Rocky said pleasantly. "You'd be the one I'd pick if I had to have help. I did, didn't I?—last night. But you can look out for yourself. Doctor James will watch out for Olivia, an' Dad and I can cover the hotel."

"And Tom?"

"He'll have to take his chances. I don't think he's in any danger. I told him, since he was sober this mornin', not to forget to lock his place up tonight." Rocky stood up, stamping out the stub of his cigarette. "Well, I can't put it of any longer. When is Miss James' birthday?"

"You fly around from one thing to another so there's no keeping up with you," Murdoch complained. "It was the fifteenth of this month. I paid ten dollars for a bottle of perfume, and she said she'd rather have had a new sterilizer or some kind of gadget for her office. What's the use?"

Rocky laughed and crossed the street through the red dust to the James house. Doctor James answered his knock and looked at him with an apologetic smile.

"I've been talking to Olivia," he said. "I tried to be very stern and grandfatherly, but when I told her she must talk, for her own sake, she pooh-poohed the idea that she might be in danger. She firmly believes she could handle anyone who tried to molest her, and she probably could, if she wasn't taken by surprise. She says she still won't talk to you, but I think she will—if you're tactful."

Rocky sighed. "Tactful? I'll make a good start at it by askin' you how you can be tactful to a girl like her?"

"I don't know. She doesn't respond very readily. You have to be tactful without seeming to be."

"Where is she?"

"In her office. The first door to the left. She wouldn't be acting so badly if she wasn't very much upset by Amelia's death. I didn't hesitate to tell her she was probably partly responsible for what happened."

"Well, I've done a lot of unpleasant things in the line of duty, but this can head the list."

Rocky went into the house and knocked on Olivia's office door. A sulky voice said:

"Grandad? If you want to lecture me some more you might as well not come in. I—"

"It's not your grandfather."

"Oh, it's you! Well, I don't want to talk to you. I said I wouldn't and I still—"

"You'll see me profess'nally, won't you?" Rocky hoped his voice sounded as woebegone as he meant it to be. "I've got a tooth botherin' me. I kept puttin' off having it tended to—"

"Where have I heard that before? Well"—a key grated in the lock, and Olivia opened the door— "I suppose I have to put you out of your misery. Come in."

Rocky tried to assume the expression of a man suffering from toothache and thought he probably did rather well as soon as he saw the drill dangling over the dentist's chair. God knew what the girl might do to his teeth once he let her get a look into his mouth. He didn't like the professional gleam in her eyes as she looked him over. She was wearing a starched white uniform, and it didn't seem quite so amusing as usual to think that she was a dentist, especially when she said briefly: "Sit down," and began to wash her hands.

He sat down, reluctantly, and she swung the chair back so that his feet were off the floor. He began to understand why bugs kick so violently when they are turned over on their back and can't get up. Her hands, fastening a towel about his neck, were white and square and strong as a man's. Very likely she would never have any trouble subduing troublesome patients.

"Which tooth is it?—if you know. People think they do when they don't."

"That's funny. Why don't they?"

"Nerves. A bad nerve that really belongs to one tooth can make you think it's another tooth that's hurting. Come on, which one is it?"

Rocky hastily selected a tooth he thought he could do without if it came to the worst. "'At one 'ack 'ere," he said thickly.

"H-hmm. This one?" Olivia reached for some sort of unpleasant-looking instrument and tapped on the tooth with its handle. Rocky restrained an impulse to grit his teeth; the process sent cold chills up his spine. "That hurt?"

"Arh-uh."

"I was afraid it would. It's in very bad condition. You should have had it attended to a long time ago. I'll try to save it, but it will probably have to come out."

Rocky looked at her uneasily. He had been to a dentist in San Francisco only three months ago, and the man had said his teeth were all right. But that was three months ago, and Olivia must know something about her profession. She didn't look like she was joking. She was frowning with exactly the look doctors and dentists have when they are going to say: "This will hurt a little." She reached for the drill and said:

"Open up!"

Put a white uniform on a woman and a drill in her hand, and she suddenly stopped being just an obstreperous female. Her "open up!" sounded just like Eleanor when she had a thermometer in her hand and intended to take someone's temperature whether they wanted her to or not. Rocky found himself meekly opening his mouth again. Olivia stepped on the treadle of the drilling machine, an old-fashioned one that worked without electricity. Then, abruptly, she walked across the room, sat down and began to laugh.

"You win," she said finally. "It's worth giving in to have seen the look on your face when I said that tooth might have to come out."

Rocky got hastily out of the chair with the idea of not giving her a chance to change her mind. "Then there's nothing wrong with it?"

"You know damn well there isn't. Your teeth are perfect. It was a treat to look at them."

"I didn't think there was anything wrong, but how could I be sure? There's somethin' about the atmosphere of a dentist's office. I'd rather take a lickin' than go to any—to a dentist."

"And going to a woman dentist is at least twice as bad," Olivia said mockingly. "The worse patients the dentists at the California infirmary have are the big, hulking football players who aren't supposed to have a nerve in their bodies. I thought I'd just let you sweat for a while. You did."

"All right, we're even," Rocky said affably. "You see, I wasn't any too certain you might not pull that tooth just to show me you could."

Olivia grinned. "You don't know how lucky you were. This morning, Mrs. Hurst, who's the noisiest female in Greenleaf and was among the thrill seekers present, thought she might be able

to pump me for a few details. That's one reason I
didn't fall for your story, though I wouldn't take
a chance you might be telling the truth. Anyway,
Mrs. Hurst came in to have her teeth looked at,
and I pulled one of them before she knew what
was happening to her."

Rocky looked at her and shook his head. "The
female of the species . . ."

"It needed pulling. I could have done it with
my fingers. Out it came, and I collected three dollars from her and sent her on her way, for once in
her life slightly dazed and unable to talk. Well,
your sacrifice shall not have been in vain. What
do you want to know?"

"What do you know?"

"About Amelia? Well, I suppose the first thing
is why I didn't want you to talk to her. I was
afraid if you did you'd suspect her—maybe arrest
her. She was so—so impractical. She'd have told
you everything."

"Do you think so?"

"I'm certain she didn't know who killed Cash or
Junius, or she would have told you. What reason
would she have had not to tell you that?"

"Suppose she meant to try to get her hands on
that money? It's still floatin' aroun' somewhere,
you know."

"Nonsense! Amelia as a blackmailer is just—funny," Olivia said, but she frowned, as if at a disturbing new idea.

"Well, let that go. What would she have told me that would 've made me suspect her?"

"That she didn't like Cash."

"I knew that."

"You never heard her say it. But, more important, she would have told you, if you'd asked her the right questions—and I suppose you would have—that Thursday night she suddenly decided to go over to see Cash. She got over to the house, but one of the shades wasn't pulled down, so she saw that Junius was with him, and she didn't go in."

"What did she want to see Cash for?"

"She was going to ask him to lend her five hundred dollars—for that tombstone for Andrew's grave."

"What made her think Cash had money?"

"Junius had talked to her about it. Asked her if she didn't think perhaps Cash had been fooling all of them. She didn't tell me if Junius gave her any proof to back up his idea. From what Junius said to her, and what she remembered for herself she didn't think the idea an unreasonable one, though she'd never thought of it before."

"Did she watch those two before she went back home?"

"Only for a minute. I asked her if they seemed to be quarreling, and she said they weren't, that Cash was talking, looking as if something amused him, but that Junius didn't look amused."

"Well, now we do know Junius was with Cash that night," Rocky said. "But her knowin' that was no reason for her to be killed. What did she do after that?"

"She gave up the idea of seeing Cash then and went back and sat and embroidered, as she always did. She didn't know how long after that she went to the kitchen for a drink. She didn't carry a lamp with her; she knew her way about in the dark. She was standing by the window and looking over toward Cash's room. It was very dark that night, but she was used to seeing things in the dark. She thought she could make out some moving figure. There was something queer about its shape. Afterward she thought it might have been a man carrying something. Cash's body, of course.

"The fence between her house and Cash's is close to her kitchen, and whoever it was she saw—if she did see anyone—walked right along the fence. Well, she was curious, for once. She went back through her house to the front door and stood on the porch, trying to see through the dark. She still thought she could see someone moving down the street to the old Quinn house. Do you think she did see that?"

"I don't know," Rocky said slowly. "If she hadn't been killed I might 've thought the story sounded like something she'd made up to cover up some guilty knowledge."

"That was just what I was afraid of. I even—I even doubted it myself. But I've remembered times when Amelia seemed to see—to see I don't know how to express it," Olivia said impatiently. "Sometimes she seemed to see more than other people could. I don't mean in a physical sense. Goodness knows, I'm not given to believing things like that. They haven't any scientific basis."

"But they do happen."

"Y-yes. People say they do. I can almost believe, now, that she really did see someone moving near the fence, and that when she stood on her porch—though it seems physically impossible that she could have seen even a vague shape go into the Quinn house—something other than her eyes made her see it. The important thing is that she thought she did. But all she did then was to go back and sit down again."

"What time was this?"

"She never knew what time it was. It was just like her to start over to see Cash without stopping to think whether he'd already be in bed."

"Well, if Junius was with him it was after ten."

"Whatever time it was, she sat there and worked for a while longer—she didn't know how long. She did say she hadn't been sitting there very long after she came back from the front porch before she thought she heard a car drive away. She wondered about it, but she thought it might be Larry going somewhere, and she was busy thinking about other things.

"Wondering what anyone could be doing over at the old Quinn house. She said that finally she felt she was 'called on' to go over there. So she went. She wasn't at all frightened, and all she took was a few matches because she didn't have a flashlight. She went in the front door, went through all the rooms and out to the kitchen. By that time she had just one match left, and she lighted it. Before it went out she'd seen Cash, lying there dead."

Sometimes the tone in which only a dozen commonplace words were uttered was enough to give you a living picture of something you hadn't witnessed. Rocky could see Amelia Slack standing in a bare room, the match burning low in her fingers, Cash's dead face blotted out by the darkness. The old house would have creaked and sighed in its sleep, the lilacs whispered in the wind. Then suddenly Amelia Slack must have been afraid.

She had been, Olivia said. For she had heard someone coming very quietly around to the back of the house, someone who brushed against the lilacs, stumbled a little and muttered incoherently. Amelia turned and went back through the house, moving with quiet and fearful haste. Afterward she wished that she had stayed there in the kitchen until the door opened. But at the moment she felt that when that door opened it would be death that confronted her.

"And she was right," Olivia said, "though she apologized for having been fanciful. But her first instinct was right. You see, afterward she thought it over and was afraid Junius had killed Cash. She'd been afraid there might be trouble if Cash did have some money. But now we're almost certain that it couldn't have been Junius who came back to set fire to the house, aren't we?"

"Yes. She'd already heard the car drive away, and Junius must have been in that—dead."

"Oh, of course. Then she must have sat there in her own house a long time before she went over to the Quinn place. But she wouldn't have realized whether it was half an hour or two hours. She didn't run to tell anyone what she'd seen because she was fond of Junius and not at all fond of Cash.

She thought it was a terrible thing to have happened, but she wanted Junius to have time to get
away. I suppose it's hard for you to understand
the way she had of just standing aside and letting
things take their course.

"Usually," Olivia added. "She made that will,
but she was fond of me and thought I should marry Larry, and she liked him, too. Well, she didn't
give the alarm. She went and lay down without
undressing. She was shaking all over. She still had
that feeling that something, something deadly
dangerous had been at the door of the old house
before she got away. It was when she was calm-
er that she began to think of Junius having been
with Cash and decided he must have killed him. I
suppose that's what she would do."

"There's still a chance she was right. Did she
get a good look at Cash before the light went out?"

"It was the way he looked that helped to fright-
en her. His face was—was terrible. Bloody. She
recognized him, because she'd known him so long,
but afterward she was sure his mustaches had been
gone. And she thought the room had smelled of
coal oil. After the fire she was certain it had."

"I suppose the place was thick with dust?"

"She didn't mention that, but of course it would
be. Why— Oh, you mean her footprints would

have been there for anyone to see? We—we never thought of that."

"Someone had to strike a match to light that fire. He'd see someone had been there; he may 've even heard her slipping away. She dropped her last match right there, too. But he wouldn't be sure who'd been there, except, probably, that it was a woman—from the size of the footprints. Then she lost that brooch of hers—"

"You knew that she didn't lose it at the fire? She'd noticed that it was gone just before I ran in to rouse her after we'd seen the fire."

"It probably dropped off somewhere near the front gate," Rocky said, "or it wouldn't 've been found. Barnhart found it while they was fightin' the fire. That showed she'd been over near the Quinn house."

"You mean that's what it meant to some one person? But can't you eliminate some people because they couldn't have known the brooch was lost, or where it had been found?"

Rocky shook his head. "Everyone had a chance to know it was lost. Some people knew it was found; others could 've seen it was missin' and where she looked for it. She was wearin' it Thursday afternoon, wasn't she?"

"Of course. She was never without it. You want me to go on? Of course, I lied—or at least I didn't tell you she wasn't asleep when I came in to tell her about the fire. That worried me, finding her awake and fully dressed. I thought it would look bad if you knew about it."

"But after she knew Junius was dead, too, why didn't she tell me what she knew?"

"I persuaded her not to," Olivia said defiantly. "I told her you wouldn't believe her. And she said: 'Well, do you believe me, dear?' But I got her to promise to wait until tomorrow—today, that is."

"Then you knew, before we did, that it was Cash's body we found in the fire?"

"Oh no. Amelia didn't tell me all this until late afternoon, when you were up at the lake. I hadn't told her very much until then—she really wasn't feeling very well. But she insisted on getting up then. It must have been while I ran home to find some scraps of wool for her so she could finish the piece of work she was doing that she slipped outside to look for her brooch. All I knew then was that she hadn't been to bed before the fire. But when I told her you'd decided it was Junius' body we'd found in the fire, as we thought you had, and that it was Cash who'd run away, she told me I was wrong."

"Well, if she told you the whole truth she really didn't have anything def'nite to tell," Rocky admitted. "But at that, someone must 've been settin' on the anxious seat all day."

"And I played into their hands by keeping you away from her," Olivia said bitterly. "Oh yes, I did. We didn't think of her footprints in the dust or about the brooch."

"Well, I knew about that, but it didn't mean anything till too late to do any good. I should 've guarded her."

"You would have if you'd heard what she had to say?"

"Yes, I would," Rocky said reluctantly. "I might not have believed her story, but I wouldn't have taken any chances. Do you think she wanted to think things over?"

"Y-yes. I don't think she actually knew one thing more than she told me. And I think she believed she was telling you the truth last night when she said she didn't know anything that would help you and that nothing she knew could be any danger to her. She wouldn't let me stay with her. I wish I hadn't let her have her own way. I think she did have a feeling that she'd—oh, this sounds so silly!—that she'd know the person she'd come so near to meeting that night, that she'd have some feeling that would tell her when he was near her again. She said: 'I should have known that wasn't Junius.

I wouldn't have felt that way about him even if he had killed a man.' Of course, you wouldn't have paid any attention to just a—a psychic feeling."

"It might have influenced me. I've heard some of the older Quinns had a gamblin' streak in them. Do you think Amelia inherited any of that?"

"You wouldn't think so, would you? I don't know. She never had any occasion, all her life long, to show if she would gamble on anything. I don't think she was as—as cautious as—Junius, for instance."

"No, I doubt if she valued her own comfort as much as he did. I suppose ever'body here knew about what you call these psychic feelings of hers?"

"Oh, they must. Mrs. Hyphenated-Quinn does, and she always tells everything she knows. All of us here knew Amelia was like that. I remember when I was a little girl— Well, that doesn't matter. She won't ever accuse anyone now."

CHAPTER XIII
"A FAIRLY LARGE GOLD NUGGET"

"Have you a cigarette? Yes, we can smoke in here as long as the window's up. What now?" Olivia said. "I mean, what do you do now?"

"You look out for yourself. I'll tell the whole town you don't know anything important, but someone might think I'm lyin'."

"I'm not in any danger. I'd have been put out of the way with Amelia if I'd been considered dangerous."

"Maybe, but there's no use bein' foolish. Have you got a gun?"

"A very nice one. I can shoot it, too. And I won't hesitate to, if it's necessary. You should have a gun strapped on your hip."

"I never carry one unless I think I've got to have it. I don't like," Rocky said, "to get to dependin' on one. I've known officers who do, and sometimes they shoot when they don't need to. I never killed a man yet by hitting him."

Olivia laughed. "Tell that to Tom Slack. That was the swellest uppercut you used on him. Larry's been admiring it— What's the matter?"

Rocky looked out the window and then sat down again. "I thought I heard someone out there, but I guess it was just the wind in the lilac bushes. Well, to go back to you—I think you're safe in the daytime, but there's no sense wandering aroun' by yourself. We'll look out for you tonight. Now, about this other business—"

"What other business?"

"I guess I forgot to mention it. I wanted to ask if you have any gold in here."

"Dental gold, you mean? No, it's too expensive for me to keep on hand when I might never need it."

"Damn! There's another swell idea blown to pieces. Didn't you ever have any?"

"Never. I haven't had to make any crowns or in-lays—worse luck. I'd like to try my hand at a few."

Rocky grinned. "If I ever do get a bad tooth I'll give you a chance at it," he promised.

"Greater love hath no man. But why does my not having any gold here blow your swell idea into bits?"

"Well, I haven't talked this over with anybody, but I don't mind tellin' you. Cash had money no one knew about for a long time. If he was killed for his money someone had to find out first that he had it. Question: how did they?"

"I've wondered."

"Junius cert'nly suspected Cash had this money and was tryin' to find out if he did. Lots of things prove that. Junius said Cash was closemouthed but could be made to talk—if you were smart enough to know how. Which seems to suggest that Junius, after tryin' just to make Cash mad enough to talk, had some other scheme in mind. Is that reas'nable?"

"So far, very good." There was a look of suppressed excitement in Olivia's face, but she said calmly: "What kind of scheme?"

"Any kind of scheme like that has to be based on the weaknesses of the guy you're workin' on. Cash liked to brag, and he was crazy about gold. Playin' on the first one didn't work. But if you told any desert rat like him that you could tell him where to find gold he'd listen to you. If he was as shrewd as Cash he wouldn't believe you, without proof. The best proof to offer him would be a hunk of gold supposed to come from some vein or ledge that you'd just happened to stumble on. And which Junius couldn't work because he didn't know enough about minin'. Did he?"

"Surprisingly little for a man who'd lived most of his life up here. He was short on practical knowledge, and mining is too much like work."

"Well, figure out that 'd be his story, and he'd offer from the generosity of his heart to draw Cash a map of the place where he found the stuff an' sell it to him for as much money as he could get out of him. Junius was practicin' drawing what looked like a map for locatin' buried treasure. Was he out of town lately?"

"Not— Yes, he was. Over a week ago—I don't know the exact day—he went off to the woods one afternoon. He said he wanted to commune with nature, but that was such an unusual happening that it made an impression on me."

"I imagine he did take most of his exercise settin' on the porch. Well, that may 've been the day he claimed to 've stumbled on a pay streak. He couldn't claim he found more 'n one nugget—not a pocket, because he could 've cleaned that out himself. I still think he tried to work that scheme, but I don't know what he offered Cash for bait."

"I do!" Olivia said triumphantly. "I never would have if you hadn't explained, but now I can tell you. About two months ago a great-uncle of mine died and left me some old-fashioned jewelry I wouldn't be caught dead wearing. One thing was a fairly large gold nugget, made into a pin. I wrenched it off the setting and thought, since gold brings so much now, I'd sell it the next time I went to the city. I took the things over to show to Amelia; I thought she might admire some of them. Junius happened to be there, so he knew I had the nugget."

"Did he know where you kept the things?"

"Of course he did. He knew this house as well as I do. All he'd have to do was to watch his time and take the thing."

"It was taken?"

"Yes! Oh, I know how you feel. It's fascinating, isn't it, when things work out so nicely? I noticed the nugget was gone about a week ago. Probably just after or before Junius took his walk in the woods. I was pretty mad, but I wasn't going to hurl accusations right and left. I suspected Tom Slack, but Grandfather looked his place over one night when he was dead to the world but couldn't find it. So I gave the thing up."

"Did Slack know you had the nugget?"

"Not unless Amelia told him about it, and I don't think it would have occurred to her to do that. But he'd been suspected of taking things from the store, though he'd have said he was just 'borrowing.' The main thing is that Cash didn't know I had that nugget. I didn't show the things to anyone but Grandfather and Amelia and Junius, and I hardly ever talked to Cash. Neither did Amelia."

"I wonder what became of that nugget. I suppose either Cash or Junius had it. In that case, it's probably gone for good."

"It was rather a clever scheme, wasn't it? Of course, it might sound foolish to someone who didn't know Cash. But just the rumor of gold is usually enough for an old prospector, though he seems to have been shrewder than any of us thought."

"Smart enough that he didn't swallow the bait," Rocky said. "Of course, he nibbled at it. He told an old pal of his he might be onto a good prospect. He said to me even a 'greenhorn' might happen to find gold."

"I'll bet he tried to find the place where Junius was supposed to have found that nugget," Olivia broke in. "Cash always spent a lot of time in the woods and canyons."

"I don't doubt he did go prowling aroun' to see what he could find. But he read the newspapers, and he kept a scrapbook full of clippings. Some of them told about fellows who'd salted mines with dental gold. That's where I got that idea. I doubt if he'd have paid out any money for a pig in a poke, though he couldn't resist listenin' to Junius. Junius may 've picked out a likely-looking place to show him, if he wanted to see where that nugget was supposed to 've come from. A few months ago some old prospector found a big nugget near Brookdale, so the notion wasn't so far-fetched."

"What makes you so certain the scheme didn't work?"

"Partly a clipping from a newspaper a few days ago, referrin' to some fellow that salted a mine once. Also the fact that on Thursday Cash was braggin' to

Barnhart how he'd never fallen for a skin game in his life. He was right proud of himself that afternoon, Barnhart says, an' kept tellin' how smart he was. Since he said to me the day before that he might go prospectin' again, I reckon it wasn't till Thursday that he fin'lly made up his mind Junius was playin' him for a sucker."

"And then?"

"What do you think? Mrs. Slack said Cash was talkin' like he was amused, but Junius didn't look like he was."

"Cash would love to tell Junius how smart he was and to laugh at him because his scheme didn't work."

"I reckon that's what he did. But after that I'll bet Cash's other weakness cropped up. He'd got started to braggin', so he went right on with it and told Junius he did have more money than anyone here would ever have."

"You think he hadn't admitted, yet, that he did have money? No, of course he wouldn't," Olivia said quickly. "He'd have played the game of trying to get what Junius wanted to sell for nothing, would have insisted he didn't have a red cent." She sighed. "Wouldn't it be nice if you could prove all this?"

"Wouldn't it! What interests me now, since I've got this figured out to my own satisfaction, is whether the scheme was all Junius' own idea."

"Oh, I'm sure he could have thought of it. He was always thinking up money-making projects, though he never quite got around to putting them into operation."

"I reckon he had brains enough to think out a thing like that by himself. But it's also perfectly possible he had help. As soon as he did find out Cash had this money he probably went runnin' to tell someone about it. It seems to me he'd have been more likely to do that if there was someone who'd known all along what he was tryin' to do. Someone who didn't want to kill Cash just on the off-chance he had money and was usin' Junius to find out what he wanted to know."

"Y-yes, that does seem more reasonable. It's a horrible idea," Olivia said, shivering involuntarily, "to think that Junius brought about his own death without knowing he was doing it. You don't think he killed Cash?"

"I don't think so, but that's only an opinion, based on what I've heard about him and saw for myself—an' everything in gen'ral."

"Very illuminating," Olivia said dryly. "Anything more?"

"Not that I think of now. It's gettin' late, and I've got to drive down to Merton. You've been a lot of help—"

"Once I made up my mind to be? Well, I'll admit I'm glad to be rid of my guilty secrets. You know, someone has that money."

"You don't have any ideas where it might be hid, do you?"

"I wish I had. I'd go looking for it," Olivia said, "and then hide it again. It would be bad to be caught with it, I suppose? It makes me mad to think of its going to Mrs. Hyphenated-Quinn if it's ever found."

"You don't know it would go to her. If Cash was killed first, all right. Junius' widow would inherit."

"But if Junius was killed first, she has no claim on the money? Then Amelia would have inherited if Junius was killed first, as Cash's next of kin?"

"Yes. I wonder if she realized that?"

"Why—I don't know. She didn't mention it to me if she did. Well, I hate to think of the money's going to some of the distant Quinn cousins. I don't even know where they are, now."

"Don't you get ideas in your head," Rocky said sternly. "I told you not to wander off by yourself. I've searched the rooms at the hotel—"

"Don't you think you had a hell of a nerve? Maybe you'd like to search this house."

"I can get a search warrant if I have to, you know. But I won't waste time here. I'll drop in this evenin' to see if everything's all right. . . ."

Rocky whispered: "Get some sleep, now, Dad," closed the door softly and turned on his flashlight. The upper hall was still and dark, all the bedroom doors closed. He looked at them thoughtfully. He'd told everybody in the hotel to lock their doors that night, and Mary Anne had scurried around and found keys for them. You couldn't very well wake people up at one-thirty just to ask if they were all right.

Very quietly he tried all the doors and found them locked. He'd said, when he saw that the keys would fit any lock, that it would be best to leave them in the doors. But without a light on the other side of a key-hole it wasn't possible to tell if everyone had obeyed his instructions.

Near the head of the stairway he stopped, hesitating. Robert Allan had been on guard since ten-thirty, sitting in his room with the door open. But Rocky thought that if he sat down he would be in danger of going to sleep. He was wide awake as long as he kept moving, but the sight of a bed made his eyes ache. Since he intended to see if everything was all right at the Jameses' before morning he might as well go over there now. The fresh air would be good for him

He'd gone over to speak a private and extra word of warning to the old doctor just after everyone here had gone up to bed. Olivia was in her bedroom, but she called out:

"Don't you worry about me. I have my own gun, and Grandad broke down and admitted he had Old Blunderbuss out last night. No one with any sense would risk coming up against that cannon."

She should be perfectly safe. He had told the bare essentials of her story at the dinner table and said he was disappointed that she hadn't known anything important. But there was always the danger that someone might not believe him. At least one person would know he'd omitted a good many details. Of course, no one with any sense would expect him to tell everything he knew. And if Olivia had been able to tell him the murderer's name he would have acted by now. But there was always that possibility that someone might think she knew something—not enough to prove conclusively who the murderer was but enough to make her dangerous to him.

"Of course," Rocky muttered, pushing open the door into the kitchen, "her story may be a lie from beginnin' to end or have just enough truth in it to sound convincin'. I wonder if Mary Anne *did* lock this back door."

Mary Anne had not failed in her duty, though the door was not locked but bolted on the inside. A trap door led to a flight of stairs into the cellar built under the hill. Mary Anne had put a heavy chair over the trap, and Mrs. Featherstone-Quinn had locked the cellar's outside door just after dinner.

Two enormous sandwiches, oozing mayonnaise and mustard, had been placed on the kitchen table with a thermos bottle beside them. On a scrap of brown paper Mary Anne had scribbled: "In case you get hungary." Pouring out steaming black coffee Rocky made up his mind that Mary Anne should have a very substantial tip whenever he was able to leave Slacktown for good and all.

He made certain the door into the dining room was open and sat down, alert for any sound from the front part of the house. He turned off his flashlight; it was easier to hear things in the dark. Easier to think, too. . . .

Down in Merton, Jazz was in one of his nervously irritable moods because he hadn't been able to locate the operator he'd counted on to relieve him. There had been a letter from Eleanor, unimportant except for its: "What is happening up there that keeps you too busy to write to me? Don't say it's only car thieves, because I know better. You aren't in the newspapers yet, but I have hopes of getting news of you with my morning coffee."

And Dud Williams was very proud of himself because he'd managed to arrest a man who was driving a stolen car. The youngest and least fat of the Brookdale deputies was indignant because Rocky said he couldn't spare time to "come look at" a hobo who had evidently been killed falling off a freight near Indian River. Well, what the hell! Let the coroner and Al Sully look out for that. . . .

Then back here just before supper Mrs. Featherstone Quinn had been in her office, frowning as she looked at the stubs in her checkbook and compared them with a yellow bank statement.

"I can't make my balance agree with theirs," she said. "And just now— Well, I'll probably never make anything of this place now. Even if I had the heart to try, I'm certain as soon as this gets in the newspapers what reservations I did have will be canceled, and, after all, you can hardly blame people for feeling that way—can you? Why is it so long getting into the papers?"

"They depend on local correspondents, ma'am. Since the inquest was put off a day they didn't have anything much to wire the papers until today. If what they send out sounds important to them in the city we'll have some reporters up here tomorrow."

"I wonder if the publicity might be any advantage? Oh, I know that sounds horrid, but I have this place on my hands, and I may want to get rid of it because I put my money into it, and I'm getting too fat and lazy to want to go back to work. Did you want anything in particular, Mr. Allan?"

"Here's something Mr. Quinn was writin' on. It's a birthday ode for someone who was born this month."

"He must have been writing it for me." Mrs. Featherstone-Quinn's round chin jerked a little as she took the paper. "My birthday is the thirtieth. Olivia had one this month, but since he didn't finish it— And she'd laugh at a thing like that. I never did. He used to celebrate anniversaries and special occasions by writing poems about them. I thought it was an awfully sweet idea. I guess dinner is ready by now; Mary Anne was a little late tonight."

There was nothing worth remembering about the first part of their talking at the dinner table—or was there? Rocky frowned, pouring the last of the coffee into his cup. Barnhart had said he hoped Kitty hadn't stayed in the hotel all day, that she needed to get outside for a while.

"I was outside this afternoon," Mrs. Featherstone-Quinn said. "I walked down to the end of the street and watched Leon painting."

"She didn't like the picture," Glidden remarked cheerfully.

"I always like your pictures, Leon, though I haven't really gotten used to really modern art yet. But I'm sure this one will be very sweet. Ivy, you aren't eating anything. Don't you feel well?"

"That's the penalty for almost always having a very unpoetic appetite," Ivy said with a pale smile. She managed tonight to look more than ever like one of the nine Muses. She was wearing a misty white dress with wide, trailing sleeves and a white ribbon bound around her dark hair. Barnhart said abruptly:

"How do you manage always to look the part, Ivy? I never look like a distinguished historian—which I'm not. But I can see you with a lyre in one hand, intoning poetry—"

"I hope not with a harp in her hands and nice, feathery wings floating behind her," Glidden said flippantly. Mrs. Featherstone-Quinn frowned at him.

"Don't talk like that, Leon. I really don't like it. There are times for joking and times when it's best not to, but very few men ever seem to realize that."

"You might have heard me elocute when I was younger, Arthur," Ivy said hastily. "You knew Father. Didn't you ever come to his little at-homes to hear me? Well, he'd have borrowed money from you if you had. I'm perfectly all right, Kitty—just tired."

"We're all tired, what's left of us," Murdoch said tactlessly. "Our permanent population's reduced—Sorry, I didn't mean to bring that up. I was just thinking it's getting to the point where there's no excuse for a store in this place."

Rocky got up abruptly: he shouldn't have sat so long over Mary Anne's sandwiches and coffee. He passed through the dining room, went through the blackness of the lower hall. Mrs. Featherstone-Quinn had given him one of two keys to the front door. The other was on a small table in the hall "in case of fire."

It was, Mrs. Featherstone-Quinn said, the first time they'd locked the place, and as almost any key would fit the front door it seemed rather a waste of time to bother doing it, but she supposed they must be businesslike, and perhaps everyone would feel better if the front door was locked—but for her part, if she felt nervous, which she didn't, she'd push the bureau in front of her door.

She was probably right, Rocky thought, but he locked the door again and put the key in his pocket. Drifting clouds blotted out the stars tonight; the dark seemed a tangible thing that fought to get past the white circle of light in front of him. A shy wind ruffled the lilacs in front of the old James house; under his feet the thick dust stirred with a dry whisper of protest. The light wavered suddenly and blinked out.

Rocky shrugged philosophically and put the flashlight in his pocket. He'd known the batteries were getting weak, but he had fresh ones at the hotel, and he could get along without a light just now. He didn't want to wake Olivia.

He felt his way along the side of the house until he touched the ledge of Olivia's bedroom window. She had made a face and said she couldn't sleep without air when he'd told her to leave her window closed. Probably she had opened it from the top, for he thought he heard her sigh and the bed springs creaking a little as she turned in her sleep. But the window was high off the ground, and as far as he could reach his fingers met nothing but smooth glass.

It was difficult, without a light, to pick his way through Tom Slack's littered back yard. He was afraid of stumbling into the chicken pen, and he did walk into a heap of empty tin cans. Cautiously he shoved them aside with one foot and heard one roll against the wire netting of the pen. The chickens made a sleepy, twittering sound, there was a rustling of feathers, one or two anxious chirps and then quiet again.

Tom Slack had also obeyed orders and locked his door, but he very obviously was sleeping. Rocky shook his head as he listened to Tom's stertorous gurglings on the other side of the door. He suspected the man had gone into retirement with another bottle of home-brew to make up for having been cold-sober for half a day. Probably nothing short of an earthquake would wake him, but he'd have to take his chances since it seemed impossible for him to stay sober.

Rocky turned, kicked another tin can against the chicken pen and managed to get out of the back yard without any further mishap. But going around to the front of the house he stumbled over one of the timbers that propped up the porch. Swearing under his breath he limped into the street and sat down on the schoolhouse steps, rubbing a twisted ankle.

The strain was not a bad one, but his foot ached, and he lighted a cigarette and sat still. He would

probably have to go to Brookdale tomorrow. Presum-
ably, he was done questioning these people, but so
long as Cash's money belt wasn't found he had an excuse for keeping the town under observation. It might
be worth while to look through the deserted houses. There were hundreds of possible hiding places in
them. Jazz might be able to come up tomorrow. . . .

CHAPTER XIV
A BELL WHISPERS

Thinking of Jazz reminded him of the kitten and Jazz's idea that whoever killed Sultan hated cats. The kitten belonged to Mary Anne. It was a round, soft thing with a ridiculous spike of tail. It had followed her into the dining room when she brought in the dessert and promptly tried to climb Barnhart's leg.

Barnhart could certainly not be blamed for saying: "Damn!" and picking the kitten up by the back of its neck. But he straightened the blue ribbon about its neck, even patted it perfunctorily when it squalled.

"Is this yours, Mary Anne? You should file down its claws; they're like needle-points. Where did it come from?"

"I don't rightly know, Mr. Barnhart. I guess its mother just up and left it. It come crying around the door, so I took it in. I'm very fond of felines."

"You take it, then. I'm not."

"Cute little devil," Glidden said, pushing his chair back from the table. "I don't care for dessert, Mary Anne. Let me see the animal. So hygienic: cat hairs after dinner. Nice purr he has. Is it a he?"

"I'm sure I hope so, but I wouldn't know, Mr. Glidden," Mary Anne said primly. "I guess it's one of Sultan's prodigy. It's got an affectionate disposition like he had."

"Well, time will tell," Glidden said mischievously. "About the sex, I mean. Though if the cat crop was dependent on Sultan's activities . . ."

"Leon! You're really very naughty tonight. What is it, Mary Anne? . . . Oh yes, you can keep it. I know there are mice in the kitchen, and perhaps he'll be a good mouser. Was a sweet thing, so it was," Mrs. Featherstone-Quinn said. "Such an innocent little baby face. If their eyes would only stay blue."

"I wonder if Mr. Allan's eyes were blue when he was born," Glidden murmured.

Robert Allan looked at him suspiciously. "Most babies' eyes are blue when they're born," he drawled. "His was always the same color for a long time. His mother had hazel eyes an' light hair. Why?"

"No reason at all. Anyone else want to cuddle the baby? Leave my ear alone, cannibal!"

"Do put him down, Leon!" Mrs. Feather-stone-Quinn said impatiently. "As you just said cats are unhygienic animals. At least, I was taught they were, and Mr. Featherstone always said so."

"I'll certainly collaborate that, Miss Kitty. Never would let us have one around."

"I didn't know you wanted one, Mary Anne. We never had any mice in San Francisco, and this one mustn't get bad habits like jumping on the table, which he looks like he wanted to do right now."

"He probably would like to taste the butter," Ivy said. "Give him back to Mary Anne, Leon. You're making Kitty nervous—and me, too."

"Nervous? Why?"

"Oh, I don't know. Yes, I do, too. When Mr. Allan told us what had happened to Sultan I thought of that story of Poe's."

"About the black cat?" Rocky said. "Where the fellow kills his wife an' puts her body in the wall, but just about the time he's satisfied the police ever' thing's all right the cat manages to get in there and yowls?"

"That's the one. It's a horrible thing. Gave me nightmares when I was a child."

"You hadn't ought to been readin' stuff like that when you was so young," Allan said severely.

"I suppose not, but no one censored my reading. Probably if they had I'd have read the books on the sly."

Rocky grinned at his father. "What was that book you caught me readin', Dad, the time you set me to copyin' one of the worst 'begat' chapters in the Old Testament to take my mind off it?"

"It may 've been that copy of Boccaccio's stories one of my mother's Virginia uncles—the one 'at read Greek—brought back from Europe before the war. Well, that was kind of foolish. I reckon you already knew ever'thing you could learn from that book, bein' brought up on a ranch and all, even if it wasn't expurgated. It may 've just been *Madame Bovary,* though. Your mother always kept that Boccaccio hid pretty well."

"Madame Bovary? Boccaccio?" Ivy said faintly. Barnhart laughed.

"Even in the sticks they know how to read, Ivy."

"We got what we call a lib'ary at home," Allan said stiffly. "Not a modern one, I reckon, because it's all filled up with books. Readin's just a habit; you almost got to get it when you're young. We don't have none of this here modern slop, but our books does to read. Rocky," he added rather apologetically, "always did have kind of funny tastes in readin' matter: this fellow Browning and things like that."

Ivy Horne looked at Rocky and smiled. "My apologies," she said with one of her graceful gestures. "I thought it would be Edgar A. Guest or Robert W. Service."

"I think Edgar A. Guest's very nice," Mrs. Featherstone-Quinn said. "Leon—"

"Yes, dear. I'll give up my little playmate. He's very interesting, or else it's the maternal instinct coming out in me. His pretty blue bow is coming undone. You fix it, Ivy."

"It looks to me as if he'd been trying to chew on it." Ivy retied the ribbon and adjusted the bow, behind the kitten's left ear. "There. Give him to Mary Anne. Yes, I'll take coffee, please."

"If it's too strong I'll delete it for you, Miss Ivy. Is that all, Miss Kitty?"

"That's all. I don't care about Browning," Mrs. Featherstone-Quinn said, steering the conversation back into literary waters. "He's too obscure, and I'm not at all intellectual, and I certainly don't like those stories of Poe's like the one you were talking about or that terrible one about the teeth. You know . . . this girl was dying or something, and she had such lovely teeth that he got sort of obsessed with them or something like that and then went and got them after she was dead and buried—only it seems to me she'd been buried before she was really dead, though that may have been in another story. Well, that's not pleasant, and I'm sure I don't know why we talk about such things at dinner, but then, it seems to me most literature—what people call literature, nowadays especially—isn't very pleasant. . . ."

It wasn't until they were sitting on the hotel porch after dinner that Rocky had a chance to ask Barnhart and Glidden the questions he didn't want Mrs. Featherstone-Quinn to hear. She had gone into the kitchen, and Ivy Horne was upstairs. Murdoch had returned to the store.

"Say that again!" Glidden requested. "Did Junius ever ask me to draw a map for him? What kind of a map? He didn't, anyway. He only suggested a few signed landscapes would look well on the living-room walls."

"He had kind of a nerve, didn't he?"

"Oh, he happened to find out Kitty had made me a very special rate," Glidden said frankly. "I guess he thought she wasn't charging enough, but she knew what I could afford. I promised to advertise the place: in Reno, when I go over there after I leave here, and in San Francisco, if I decide to go back there. Not that it's going to need any advertising after this."

"She isn't charging any of us what she should," Barnhart said. "But we're her first guests, and we would have done all we could to recommend the place to others. Why a map, Allan?"

"Junius started to draw one himself but didn't finish it. I thought maybe he'd gone to someone who *could* draw to get it done."

"Oh! He asked me one day—I've forgotten when—if I had a copy of *Treasure Island*. You remember the map in it? The one that shows the location of the pirate treasure?"

"I remember. You've known Mrs. Featherstone-Quinn a long time, haven't you, Barnhart?"

"I first met her a good many years ago," Barnhart said warily. "I didn't know her very well until after Featherstone died."

"What kind of guy was he?"

"He was all right. One of these fussy men who wants to be babied. No one ever thought he was really sick, but he proved we were all wrong, even if he had to die to do it."

"You wouldn't like to tell me," Rocky said bluntly, "why people talked about her once? Libeled her?—labeled, in Mary Anne's words."

"I would not! Has that damned woman been talking? Oh, I know she doesn't mean any harm by it but of all the damned rot— Excuse me. I think I'll stroll down the street and back before I go to bed."

"Well, you certainly got under his skin," Glidden commented. "I never heard him flare up like that before. Ivy, you tell us. Has Kitty a skeleton in the family closet?"

"Do you think I'd tell you if she had?" Ivy came out and sat down in one of the porch chairs. "You're too curious, Leon. And it wasn't nice of you to tease Kitty tonight."

"You know she loves to be teased. It makes her feel coquettish. Probably she was, in her youth."

"She didn't love it tonight. Neither of us likes to be reminded of Sultan, and even that kitten— Well, considering what's happened, she has a right to a little consideration."

"I was only trying to take her mind off her troubles," Glidden said lightly. "You know I like Kitty, and I know just how good she's been to all of us. But I can't pretend to grieve for Cash. Anyone who carries wads of fifty- and hundred-dollar bills around on him is asking to be killed. I'm sorry about Junius, on Kitty's account, but she'll probably be just as well off without him when she's had time to get over this."

"Well, even when you really do like people you want to know all about them."

"Naturally."

"Not naturally at all. Because if what you learn amuses you, you always tell it. I pity—"

"My wife," Glidden finished. "You've said that before. Never mind. Marjorie doesn't understand me, and I don't want her to. But Arthur was quite snappy."

"Then he must have had some reason to be. He may laugh at his friends sometimes, but he doesn't tell tales on them."

"We appear," Glidden said pleasantly, "to be all rather out of sorts."

Rocky stood up and stamped his cigarette into the dust. He seemed, he thought, to have a tendency tonight to sit still and try to digest all the conversations he'd listened to this evening. The time hadn't been wasted. Sitting there he'd recalled words that he'd hardly heard when they were uttered. One previously disregarded sentence might solve this case. But just now he was supposed to be guarding Olivia James. . . .

He stopped, one foot still on the bottom step, startled to immobility by the whisper of sound in the schoolhouse behind him. It was as if some fleshless hand had touched the bell rope lightly in passing, so that the old bell shivered and replied to its ghostly bellman with an echo of harsh clangor.

The fancy passed. Some living person had come toward the half-open door of the schoolhouse, had brushed against the rope and set the bell to swaying for just an instant. Rocky turned quietly back toward the schoolhouse. The movement was instinctive; that it might be dangerous did not occur to him.

Afterward he remembered that he was annoyed because he had no light and must somehow locate the person in the schoolhouse without one. As he opened the door he was thinking that he must not brush against the bell rope and almost at once felt it against his cheek. He reached quickly for its frayed end, but it slipped between his fingers, and again he heard the bell's harsh whisper.

He stood still in the little vestibule, renewing in his mind a picture of the schoolroom. There were the rows of desks, the platform with the teacher's desk. Nowhere for anyone to hide, and he stood in the only exit from the place. The windows were high in the walls. Whoever was in that room couldn't get away, even if it was impossible now to hide his own presence there.

He moved a cautious step or two into the schoolroom, fumbling in his pocket for matches. "There's no use you tryin' to get away," he said softly. "There's no way out of here except where I am, and I know you're here."

The match flared briefly and went out. The box fell from Rocky's fingers as he dropped face down on the floor. A burning sensation spread along his right shoulder; he thought foolishly that it was strange that should come first and the roar of the gun and rank smell of powder afterward. He remembered the White Queen and the finger that had bled before she pricked it. Eleanor was always quoting from *Through the Looking Glass,* and she—

Deliberately he set his teeth in his lower lip, and the dizziness passed. The only thing to do was stay still and play possum. There was nothing heroic about lying flat on your face with splinters digging into it, but he'd be a fool to try anything else until he was certain he was alone in the schoolroom.

Perhaps his assailant had shot and run. He didn't know; the roar of the gun had filled his ears for an instant. Then when he dropped to the floor he'd thought only that he must lie limp and still and almost without breathing. In those few minutes the person who'd shot him could easily have escaped. If he'd stayed to be certain he'd made a thorough job of it, it was going to be just too bad, Rocky decided impersonally.

He thought, almost dreamily: here I am, probably the best shot in the county, and I never have a gun on me when I need one. Blunder in here, give away my position by talking, even light a match—and that only showed him where to shoot. If he wants to blaze away in the dark, I can't stop him. Still, that might wake someone up. One shot didn't. Tom Slack's dead to the world, and the other houses are too far down the street. I didn't think anyone had a gun. Dad will call me all kinds of a fool. . . .

He got dizzily to his knees, blood running down chest and back. It seemed he must choose between bleeding to death while he played safe or being finished off because he didn't. The last would at least be quicker. But nothing stopped his unsteady progress toward the door.

His groping fingers found the edge of the doorway into the vestibule, and he stood leaning against it. He remembered that he'd walked two or three steps into the room, toward the right. Someone must have been standing just to the left of the doorway and so been able to shoot from behind him. The bullet had gone into his shoulder from the back and too far down for him to try to bandage it.

He knew he must get to Doctor James as quickly as possible, but he wanted, more than anything, to relax his grip on the door and lie down again. Perhaps that was the way a man felt when he'd fought snow and storm for hours and was finally overcome by the desire for sleep. Snow would be cool and soft to lie in and ease the burning pain in his shoulder. . . .

He jerked himself erect and walked waveringly across the vestibule. The old bell rope swung against his cheek. It seemed to him like a rope flung to a drowning man. He didn't have to try to reach the doctor's house; all he had to do was pull that rope. And then sit there waiting for someone to come to him.

He flung the rope aside. "Be damned if I do," he muttered and stumbled down the steps into the street. One, two, three houses—black hulks in surrounding blackness. The next one would be the Jameses' house, but it was like the mountains that sometimes looked so close to you and then were farther and farther away if you started to walk toward them.

Everything seemed to be trying to hold him back: the deep dust under his feet, the lilac bushes along the fences that caught at his clothes. Somehow, he reached the porch and the front door, pounded on it weakly. He went to his knees again, but he went on hammering against the door until the pounding noise merged with that inside his head. Abruptly, something snapped, and the hammering stopped. . . .

Sunlight struck warmly against his eyelids, but he didn't want to open them. There was a brassy taste in his mouth, and his shoulder throbbed painfully. Soon enough he'd have to sit up and take an interest in things, make explanations and listen to them.

But it was very odd. He certainly was in bed, and the bed must be in a room, so why should there be a faint scent of lavender near him? No one here used lavender water—Olivia James didn't wear any sort of perfume. But the fragrance persisted, seemed to move a little. Someone was sitting by the bed, and all he had to do was open his eyes . . .

He murmured instead: "I couldn't be delirious, I reckon," put out his hand and touched soft hair that clung to his fingers. "It feels like red hair. If it isn't I'll be sure I'm out of my head."

"All you have to do, to see what color it is, is to open your eyes, you silly idiot," Eleanor said. But she held his hand tightly against her cheek as she went on: "You see? I can't leave you for even three or four days without something happening to you. If you'd written me what was happening I'd have come back sooner."

"And I wouldn't have got shot? I don't see the logic of that."

"I don't have to be logical; I don't even want to be. What on earth happened to you, darling? I got Jazz to bring me up here as soon as the train got in. We nearly broke our necks getting here, and then I find you all bandages—"

"Why didn't you wake me up? What time is it now?"

"It's nearly ten. Of course I didn't wake you; the doctor intended you should sleep. He found you on his doorstep, b-bleeding to d-death . . ."

"You haven't kissed me yet," Rocky said tactfully.

"How could I when you didn't wake up? There!" Eleanor laughed shakily. "One would never guess, from the way I'm acting, that I'd ever been a nurse. What you need is quiet and rest."

"Sounds familiar, but it don't happen to be what I want. I've got one good arm. You don't call that hyg'enic little peck on the forehead a kiss, do you? . . ."

"There was nothing hygienic about *that* kiss," Eleanor said breathlessly. "I'm glad you're feeling so well, and I'm never going away again, but I'm afraid you're running a temperature."

Rocky grinned. "That's a new name for it. All right, if it 'll make you happy to stick a thermometer in my mouth. Someone's coming."

"Your father and the doctor," Eleanor said, opening the door. "Yes, he finally woke up."

"An' about time. Don't seem to me you get any sense as you get older," Allan snapped. "Wanderin' aroun' town with no gun an' a dead flashlight an' all. No wonder you got yourself shot up. Teach you a good lesson, maybe."

Rocky looked at his father thoughtfully. He must have been pretty badly scared last night, or he wouldn't be in such a bad humor this morning. Doctor James said hastily:

"It was quite a shock, finding you there on the porch. Olivia and I couldn't imagine what had happened. I sent her to wake Lawrence, and you insisted that we bring you over here, though I could have slept on a couch in the office."

"Did I? I don't know exactly why."

"Don't you remember anything at all after you managed to rouse us?"

Rocky frowned. "Not much. I remember you digging aroun' in my shoulder and fin'lly sayin': 'Here it is.'"

"The bullet, I meant. I thought you were unconscious then. Well, you walked over here with Larry's and your father's aid, and we put you to bed. You're doing quite nicely, though. It's a clean wound, but you'd lost a good deal of blood. You'd better go back to sleep when you've had a light breakfast. Oh, I wouldn't try to sit up," the doctor said soothingly. "You'll be much better—"

"He's very stubborn," Eleanor said as Rocky set his teeth and pulled himself up against the pillows. "Let me fix those. Better?"

"That's fine. I can't think lyin' down, and there's some things I want to get straight. I couldn't sleep till I do."

"We-ell, in that case— What do you want to know?" the doctor asked.

"Did it occur to any of you to look in the old schoolhouse?"

Allan snorted. "Did it occur to us? We ain't complete nitwits. There was a trail leadin' right back to it: drops of blood in the dust. We put two 'n two together, an' exercisin' all our wonderful powers of deduction, we deduced you got shot in there. Only we ain't quite decided, yet, what you—an' someone else—was doin' in there."

"I went in because there was someone else there. It's an awful disappointment to me," Rocky said, "that you ain't figured out what that person was in there for. I was countin' on you, Dad."

Allan smiled reluctantly. "I reckon you ain't hurt very bad. Only reason I could think of for someone prowlin' aroun' the place was because they'd hid that money there an' wanted to get it back. But I don't know. Once it was put there, seems to me it was a safe place for it."

"It was. But I reckon when you've killed someone to get hold of twenty grand you might get kind of nervous about it. If the money was hid there someone must 've been plenty nervous while the inquests was goin' on. An' Tom Slack had been there the night before. Just to ring the bell, he said, but the place was next door to him, an' he might just happen to get prowling aroun'. But I imagine it was mostly nervousness."

"I can understand that," Eleanor said. "When I have to leave money in the house I hide it half a dozen times before I'm satisfied. And even then I keep thinking of better hiding places and wondering if one of the first ones might not have been the best, after all."

"We all do that," Doctor James said. "But to risk hiding money in a deserted building . . ."

"Safer 'n to hide it in one that's occupied," Rocky said. "And a lot less risk than keepin' it on you or in your own room—or house. Well, I don't know if that's why someone was in the schoolhouse, but it's the only reason I can think of. Did you search the place, Dad?"

"No use tryin' to do a good job in the dark. Murdoch found a key that 'd lock the door. I was goin' over there pretty quick if you said to. I did find one funny thing. It was lyin' on the floor in front of the platform. Kind of glistened when the light fell on it."

Rocky looked at the dull gleam of the nugget in Allan's brown palm. "So they even wanted that, too?"

"You ever seen this before?"

"No."

"But I have," James said uneasily. "It belonged to Olivia. A brother of mine had it set in a pin. She called it atrocious, and she—"

"She told me about that," Rocky said. "You get her to tell you what it was probably used for. I supposed she had. It seems pretty certain either Cash or Junius was carryin' it when they were killed, so it was probably taken along with Cash's money belt, put in that an' fell out."

"What I want to know," Allan said, "is how you happened to catch that fellow in there?"

Rocky told him. "If it was someone from here, I'll take the blame," he added. "No one could 've sneaked out when you were on guard, and that was too early, anyway. He wouldn't have been apt to still be outside when I got out. Someone could 've sneaked out of here while I was in the kitchen, though I thought I'd hear if anyone tried to. But when I left here I went over to your place, Doctor, and someone could have got out of here then and to the schoolhouse. If it wasn't someone from here, there was nothin' to stop 'em goin' where they wanted to.

"Of course, chance played a pretty big part in things. If I hadn't bumped my ankle against that timber by Slack's front porch and set down on the schoolhouse steps nothin' would 've happened.

I'd have gone back to the doctor's house again and left the way clear. I suppose the fellow in the schoolhouse was walkin' out very careful and saw the light of my cigarette. Then he hit the bell rope, dodgin' back, an' I heard the bell an' went in after him."

Allan muttered something that sounded like: "Damn fool!" Then: "You should 've had more sense," he said.

"I didn't start out with a bum light; it went dead on me outside. If I came back here for a gun and light, that gave him time to get away. I never thought about anyone here havin' a gun. Of course, I was a damned fool to speak and then try to light a match to locate him."

"You didn't see him?" James asked.

"He shot the minute the match flared up, and I reckon I was facin' the wrong way to see him. I was shot from the back, wasn't I? It was either mighty good or very lucky shootin', even if he did just get me in the shoulder."

"It's a wonder to me he didn't—" Allan stopped, with a quick glance toward Eleanor. She said:

"Didn't stay to finish his job? That had occurred to me, Father."

"The idea he might still be there gave me a few unpleasant minutes," Rocky said candidly. "But he evidently shot an' ran away. That kept me from followin' him, and to get away without bein' seen was the most important thing. Now, you tell me what you know, Dad."

"Nothin' It seems like we was all sound asleep till Miss James come runnin' here for me. Hadn't heard a thing; hadn't saw nothin'. I went to Slack's place and couldn't rouse him. He's got a hell of a hangover this mornin', and it looks genuwine to me."

"It is," James said. "I saw him this morning. You might like to know that, being in a penitent mood, he admits Cash persuaded him to hide in the cellar here and ring a cowbell to scare Mary Anne one night. Not that I suppose it's important."

"No, but you like to have things cleared up. I thought Cash was behind this monkey-business that got us up here in the first place, though we knew he couldn't 've rung that cowbell in the cellar." Rocky moved restlessly and closed his eyes for an instant.

"You've talked long enough," the doctor said quickly. "I mean it this time. You enforce my orders, Mrs. Allan. I'll come back this afternoon."

Rocky let Eleanor feed him soft-boiled eggs, which he detested, but it seemed they were Mary Anne's notion of the proper food for invalids. "Is Jazz still here?" he asked.

"Walking around and gnawing his fingernails. Of course, he doesn't, really, but he gives that impression. You know Jazz. His relief man showed up last night so he was able to drive me up here. Nancy didn't come with us, and when he telephoned from here she told him to stay as long as he was needed. I call that noble. He wants to do something, but he doesn't know what."

"Set him to searchin' the vacant houses for that money. It won't do any good, but it'll keep him out of trouble. An' speakin' of trouble, you keep an eye on Dad."

"Why?"

"He's pretty mad. I know the signs. He's put on his best boots: the ones with fancy designs aroun' the tops. That means he's ready to go gunnin' for someone, an' he's cert'nly got a gun in his suitcase—if not on him. Soothe him down as much as you can."

"I'll try. Anything else?"

"You'll have to phone to Brookdale. Not to Merton. I don't want Dud Williams chargin' up here to help out. If he calls tell him Jazz is lookin' after things. You circulate aroun' an' get acquainted."

"With pleasure." Eleanor put the tray on the table and pulled down the window shades. "Who," she said innocently, "is the handsome amazon who was playing Florence Nightingale when I got here?"

"Was she? Olivia James, I suppose. She's a dentist. I'll tell you about that sometime. I reckon she helped the old man out."

"I wondered, because of the way she said: '*Mrs. Allan!*' when your father introduced me. Didn't she know I existed?"

"Hell! I supposed she did," Rocky said uncomfortably. "What of it?"

"Oh nothing. She'll probably get over it. You do blush so beautifully," Eleanor said sweetly. "Go to sleep, precious. I was only teasing."

CHAPTER XV
MR. MCCARTHY INVESTIGATES

The sun had moved on to the front of the house. Eleanor raised the window shades quietly and turned to find Rocky looking at her with the peculiar, unwinking gaze that meant he was barely conscious of seeing her. Then he smiled and said:

"I'm hungry. What time is it?"

"After two o'clock. I brought your lunch up. Somehow I have an idea you've been awake quite awhile. Why didn't you call me?"

"I was thinkin'."

Eleanor sighed. "I was afraid of that. Wait, let me help you if you're going to sit up. . . ."

Rocky looked over the contents of the tray Eleanor put on his knees. "Thank God, this is a little more fillin' than that breakfast. Any objections to me thinkin'?"

"The habit is growing on you," Eleanor said, holding the tray steady. "This habit of going into a trance for an hour or two, where I can't get at you. My feminine possessiveness resents it, so it's probably very good for me. Do you feel better?"

"Like settin' up—in a chair—when I get through with this."

"Oh no."

"Oh yes. I don't feel I possess any authority when I'm flat on my back and wearin' mainly a lot of bandage. An' I want to talk to some people."

"And some people say you're henpecked."

"They've got a hell of a nerve!"

"I think so, too. They have the idea I always get my own way. It makes me pretty damn mad. I wouldn't mind if it were true, but it's not fair for people to say I do when I don't—if you happen really to want something different. Well, I suppose it won't hurt you to sit up. For some reason or other you don't seem to be feverish."

"What do you think of the people here? Met all of them? I reckon you'll have to cut up this meat for me."

"I've met everyone, and they all seem to be very nice. Obviously, one of them must not be."

"More than likely two of them aren't."

"Two? You think—"

"It seems to me several things have always pointed to it not bein' a one-man job. Did you manage to get all the details of the case?"

"I think so. From your father and Jazz and Mr. Barnhart. He's nice. I don't care so much for Leon Glidden. He's a trifle flip if you ask me. Olivia told Doctor James what you thought was Junius' scheme for getting some of his brother's money. He told me about it; she wouldn't."

"How do you know she wouldn't. Did you ask her?"

"N-no. But we aren't exactly kindred spirits. Too much alike, I suppose," Eleanor said.

"You are not—like her, I mean. That girl's been a nuisance ever since this thing began. I reckon you'll laugh at this . . ." Rocky described his interview with Olivia in her office, and Eleanor did laugh.

"Serves you right," she said heartlessly. "A woman can be just as good a dentist as a man."

"You'd have been pretty sore if she'd pulled that tooth. And I don't notice you goin' to any woman dentists."

"But my dentist is such a handsome young man. I feel sorry for Mr. Murdoch; I like him. He and Olivia were having words about something when I came by the store awhile ago. His nose twitches when he's angry. Probably they were talking about Mrs. Slack's will. Doctor James told me about that. He's a sweet old thing. He couldn't be mixed up in this."

Rocky started to shrug and thought better of it. "He's crazy about Olivia an' worried because she's stuck up here with no money to get a start somewheres else. Has the doctor got that bullet he took out of me?"

"Yes. Mr. Murdoch wants to talk to you."

"What about?"

"I'll let him tell it. I suppose you're going to insist on seeing him. And I've got something here for you: a night letter from Mr. McCarthy."

"When 'd it come?" Rocky said suspiciously.

"About three o'clock this morning. Jazz stopped to see if there were any telegrams for you, and I brought this with me. I knew you'd insist on reading it this morning, and I didn't think you should."

"So you read it yourself," Rocky suggested, "to see if it was important."

"Don't beat me! What was I supposed to do? When I got here you were in no state to—"

"All right: suppose you read it to me now."

"Mr. McCarthy's conversational tone is really quite remarkable. Most people are so self-conscious in telegrams."

Eleanor drew a chair closer to the bed, began: "'Re. your inquiries—Very little information Glidden, who's lived here about six months. Came from Reno, exhibited paintings, sold one or two.

Shared studio on Russian Hill with two other painters. All of them broke. Went Featherstone party, met Horne and Barnhart there. Seen a good deal with Marjorie White, student Arts and Crafts. Respectable family; father works for P. G. & E. Naturally not rich. Glidden well liked; supposed to have talent but needs training'.

"There should be a parenthesis here," Eleanor said. "He says: 'Posed as collector of landscapes, looking for Glidden, interested in local talent. Talked to man he roomed with.' Then he goes on: 'Good deal of information on Kitty Featherstone. Wrote sob-sister column for *Bulletin* fifteen years. Forty-five now. Came out here from Indiana, married Featherstone when twenty-five; he died five years later. Worked for *Chronicle,* left her about five grand. Died of acute indigestion, but old-maid sister claimed arsenic.'"

Eleanor stopped. "I don't believe that," she said. "I simply can't see Mrs. Featherstone-Quinn dosing a husband with arsenic."

"It's been done. Go on."

"'Kitty said wanted body exhumed, but authorities figured sister half-cracked, as always stirring up trouble. Brother didn't leave her anything, and she didn't like Kitty. Doctor in charge insisted all right. Lot of talk, but people forgot about it. Kitty took studio on Russian Hill; belonged to semiartistic group: writers, reporters, artists. Her attraction probably that she fed them. Half-breed Chinese cook been with her eighteen years. No information on cook, except devoted to Kitty and didn't like Featherstone. No scandal about Kitty last fifteen years.

"'Barnhart forty-six. Had job in history department, University of California, until 1912. Resigned job, and wife divorced him same year. Grounds: cruelty. Threatened to name Kitty in suit but didn't. I talked Featherstone's sister: she thinks the worst. Everyone else says nothing to it. Couldn't contact Barnhart's ex-wife; lives down South. Seems to have been flighty and extravagant. Barnhart no income but writing. Gets good reviews but never been best seller. Belongs to Richmond Gun Club; crack shot. Name never linked with any woman but Featherstone.

"'Knew Ivy Horne's father myself. Ex-newspaper man; plenty brains but always drunk. Wife died when Ivy small. Horne always one jump ahead of bill collectors. Girl has small allowance from Horne's family in East. Writes few articles for papers; very little sale for poetry. Belonged Kitty's crowd; otherwise name not coupled with Barnhart or Glidden. Has small apartment in Chinatown. Unable find out anything re. private life—if any.

Hope this helps out. Will dig around some more if you say so.'"

"I never saw Pat McCarthy, but somehow I don't imagine he'd be very convincin' as a collector of paintings. He cert'nly does get aroun'."

"And that's all you have to say?"

"Well, what should I say, honey? You read it yourself. Barnhart's a good shot—but so's Glidden. Some people thought maybe Mrs. Featherstone-Quinn poisoned her husband—"

"Poisoners usually repeat themselves."

"Yes. She an' Barnhart may 've lived together, for all anybody knows, but there was nothin' to prevent them marryin' any time in the last fifteen years. There's really not much new in that wire."

"Then you know everything you need to know?"

"You wouldn't get sarcastic with a sick man, would you? I know everything I'm apt to get to know. There's one thing bothers me."

"Only one?"

"Oh, lots more than that. But if I didn't have that china brooch of Amelia Slack's— Of course, Glidden would turn it over to me, but I wish he hadn't. If someone had just found it an' kept it . . ."

"Oh, do talk sense!" Eleanor said with pardonable exasperation. "You mean this china brooch on the table? Yes, it's still here. Do you want it? Well, what do you want?"

VIRGINIA RATH

"A shave," Rocky said reflectively. "I s'pose I can't manage with one hand—"

"I'll shave you. I've always wanted to try it—it looks so easy."

"Honey, I love you, and I might even consider dyin' for you, but I will not let you shave me. An' Dad uses an old-fashioned razor and kind of a slashing technique. I reckon you'd better find Jazz and have him play barber. I want to talk to him an' have him go to Merton before it gets any later."

"I suppose you'd better do that before you talk to the reporters. They have cameras—"

"Reporters." Rocky sat up, wincing as he jolted his shoulders. "Are there some reporters up here?"

"I wanted to break it to you gently. They came on the same train with Nancy and me. They've been taking pictures and trying to talk to people. They arrived about ten—it took them awhile to find out how to get here. I've talked to them as tactfully as possible, and your father has glowered at them so persistently that they've given up trying to interview him. In a perfectly nice way they are very persistent."

"I thought maybe we'd have another day of grace."

"One of them said they'd begun to think, in the city, that when a murder case broke up here in your bailiwick it was usually worth investigating. Are you going to talk to them? We've tried to give them the idea that you're at death's door."

"Oh, I've got to talk to them. You tell Dad not to let them use the telephone. Then they'll have to go to Merton to send off their stories. But I'd like to talk to Jazz first, an' meanwhile you might tell Murdoch to come over when he can."

"You understand," Jazz said, "that this is at your own risk? No, I don't expect to mutilate you, if you'll hold still. That was a swell job you handed me this morning."

"Did you do it?"

"Your father and I did; looked through every house in this town. The dust of ages is ground into my hands. We didn't find anything. I have a sneaking idea you didn't think we would, but it kept us both out of mischief."

Rocky smiled soapily. "What queer ideas you have, Grandmamma. Didn't you find anything in the schoolhouse?"

"No distinct footprints. The dust was all tramped up. I suppose because the inquests were held in there. But we did notice one thing. The blackboard is nailed to the wall, but the wooden frame around it is rotting, and all the nails there are pretty loose. On the bottom right-hand side you could pry them out with your fingers. Your father said it looked to him like someone might have pried them out with a knife and then stuck them back in.

"Well, when you got them out, you could get your hand between the wall and the blackboard. Do you think that money belt would be flat enough to go back there?"

"I don't see why not. When the nails was stuck back in that would hold it, even if just the board itself wouldn't."

"If I killed somebody to get twenty grand I'd hate like hell to let it out of my hands or hide it in a place like that."

"It was as convenient as any house on that side of the street and closest to Amelia's. I don't think it was hid there the night Cash was killed, because of the risk of the fire. Also, it wasn't till the next day that ever'one knew I knew Cash had had that money. How's Nancy bearin' up?"

"I talked to her again. She's cleaning house. And I thought I'd kept everything in perfect order, even if I did forget to wash the milk bottles. Shoot out your upper lip, will you? Nancy says for me to stay here as long as you need me."

"Well, you can start to Merton soon's you finish this. For God's sake, don't let those reporters follow you aroun' town, or wherever you have to go. I want you to— Is that someone comin'?"

"Seems to be. I call that a pretty damned good job for an amateur," Jazz said, surveying his work proudly. "Shall I tell 'em to come in?"

"I suppose you'll have to."

"I brought Mr. Murdoch with me," Eleanor said. "The reporters are clamoring outside."

"They'll have to wait a minute. Get me a pencil and some paper, will you, honey?" Rocky scribbled a few lines on the scratch-pad Eleanor handed him, tore off the top sheet and gave it to Jazz. "There's what I want from Merton."

Jazz read his instructions, swallowed convulsively and said: "For the love of—of Pete! Suppose I can't get—what you want? Or the kind you want?"

"Try some of the farms out aroun' Monte Verde if you can't get it in Merton. I'm dependin' on you. You don't need to hurry back. Nine o'clock will be early enough."

"You're sure you— Oh, all right. I'm going," Jazz said. "You'd better feel his pulse, Eleanor. I don't think he's as well as he looks."

He went out, Murdoch staring after him with frank curiosity before he said: "I won't take much of your time. Mrs. Allan's got that bullet the doctor got out of your shoulder. I had a look at it, and it—well, it worries me."

"Why? Let's see the thing."

"Because I think it came from my gun. It's a .38 Smith and Wesson hammerless."

"That's a nice gun. Small enough to carry aroun' without bein' noticed much."

"That's why I got it. I drove stage a couple of winters and carried it with me then. I've had it in the cashdrawer at the store—"

"And you're going to tell me it ain't there any more."

"Well, it isn't. I know that's just what I'd be expected to say—"

"It's nothing to get excited about. It don't matter much what kind of gun I got shot with. It is a good thing to know someone still has a gun. It hasn't turned up yet?"

"No. The minute Doctor James showed me that bullet I got suspicious and went and looked for my gun. The last time I'm certain I saw it was this Wednesday. Glidden and I got to talking guns, and I showed him this one. He said Barnhart would like to see it. I understand both of them are good shots. So am I," Murdoch added.

"An' Miss James?"

"We-ell—yes. She could always," Murdoch said gloomily, "shoot better, swim better and catch more fish than I can. When we go hunting, *she* never gets buck fever. Well, Glidden said he didn't have a gun with him."

"He didn't have one in his luggage or suitcase. Neither did Barnhart. Or anyone else. And nobody but Mrs. Featherstone-Quinn had any gloves."

"Gloves? I wouldn't know about that. I was going to say anyone could help himself to that gun. There's plenty of times when I'm out of the store without locking it, or in the bedroom or kitchen in back."

"I know. Well, I wouldn't worry about it," Rocky said. "We'll know what to guard against, anyway."

"Could I keep an eye on Olivia tonight? Without telling her anything about it. She thinks she can take better care of herself than I could."

"I've no objections. But I think if anyone had wanted her out of the way they'd have made a try at it last night. I guess I'd better get up an' see those reporters now."

"Don't you think," Eleanor said, when Murdoch had left, "that you'd better stay in bed and look very sick? You're pale enough, goodness knows. If you lie there and talk in a weak little voice they won't ask you half so many questions. They're really very gentlemanly—for reporters."

"I always said you were smart, honey. All right." Rocky slid down into the bed again, pulled the covers up to his chin and assumed an expression of patient suffering. "Will that do?"

Eleanor giggled. "Perfectly."

"You might stand by an' keep your fingers on my pulse and look very much like a nurse. Maybe pullin' the shades down would give a better sickroom atmosphere."

"I'm sorry we haven't any flowers. Hold that look, and I'll go and bring in the Press."

The two newspaper men were, as Eleanor said, persistently nice and nicely persistent. They wouldn't ask to talk to him very long; very nice of him to see them; hoped he'd feel like a longer interview tomorrow. Did he expect to make an arrest in the next twenty-four hours? Well, of course, under the circumstances . . . No clues? No one under suspicion? Oh, but that was hardly possible, was it? . . . Well, yes. Of course everyone would be. Any idea who shot him? Hadn't seen his assailant? Too bad . . . How about a picture? Oh yes, Mrs. Allan, we want you in it. Just stay right where you are and look worried, but as if you were thankful it wasn't any worse. That's swell. Flash! . . .

"You can get the details of the case from anyone here," Rocky said, closing his eyes. "Probably you already have. I'm sorry I don't feel like talkin' any more. Tomorrow, maybe . . ." He waited until

Eleanor ushered the men out, then sat up and kicked off the covers. "Well, that's over, and we may 've fooled them for a while. Where's ever'body right now?"

"Just sitting and talking—or not talking. Olivia James came over with her grandfather—"

"I want to see them. I want to see ever'one else, too."

"Everybody?"

"All of them. You'll have to lace these boots. I wish I had some other clothes up here."

"And I wish you had some sense," Eleanor said, as Rocky sat down rather dizzily on the edge of the bed. "Oh, I'll lace your old boots! I don't mind that."

"If I had that very elegant, brocaded bathrobe you gave me I'd put it on an' look just like a detective in a movie. You could scare me up a pipe somewhere. I'll be all right, settin' down. How do I get a shirt on over these bandages?"

"I'll slit the sleeve. Oh dear, and I paid four dollars for this shirt. Well, it can't be helped. Here: put your good arm into this sleeve. . . . There!" Eleanor said finally. "Stagger across to that chair, tough guy, and let me tuck a blanket around you. Oh yes, you look much more like a wounded hero that way. Now, shall I bring the fair Olivia up to you?"

"I'll take a drink, first. There's some whisky on the bureau. Be sure those reporters ain't aroun' before you bring the Jameses up—an' you stay here an' listen. . . ."

Olivia came in with her grandfather, sat down on the window seat and smiled at Rocky maliciously. "So-o! I was to be so very careful, and then you go wandering around without a gun or even a light."

"Unfortunately, flashlight batteries don't last forever," Eleanor said in a patiently instructive voice. "They usually go dead when you least expect it. The perversity of inanimate objects, I suppose."

"That couldn't have happened at a worse time," Rocky said hastily. "Anyway, I reckon we can say you're safe."

"I always told you I was."

"You can hardly blame us for taking precautions, my dear," her grandfather said disapprovingly. "Though I envy you your lack of nerves. I sat up, but she went to bed and slept."

"After I told you not to, and you promised— Oh, all right. But you're not going to do it again. If anyone has to sit up tonight, I'll do it. I do wish you'd set Larry's mind at ease. I'm getting tired of his dashing out of the store with a worried look every time I come out of the house. Of course,"

Olivia said reflectively, "if anything happened to me he'd lose what little chance he has of getting his half of Amelia's money."

James said: "Olivia! Don't let me hear any more talk like that! I'm surprised at you."

"Perhaps he doesn't want any harm to come to you for quite unselfish reasons. Men in love are seldom completely rational," Eleanor said sweetly.

Olivia muttered: "You should know," but James frowned at her forbiddingly.

"We mustn't waste Mr. Allan's time. You shouldn't be sitting up. Why did you want to see us?"

"Give that pin to Miss James, Eleanor. Is that the one Mrs. Slack always wore?"

"Why—yes, of course it is. Didn't you see it on her?"

"Not close enough to see it was anything but a brooch painted with a face. Not near enough to get a look at the face."

"Well, it's certainly Amelia's. I should know. What made you think it might not be hers?"

"I wanted to be sure. What else was there in that jew'lry your uncle gave you, besides that nugget?"

Olivia sat very still, turning the brooch over in her strong, white fingers. "Are you just guessing again? Of course, I did say there were some things

I thought Amelia might admire. Yes, there was a pin very much like this. The woman's face on it was different: she wasn't smiling, and she had a rose in her hair. You couldn't possibly confuse the two brooches."

"Where is yours?"

"I'll try to find it for you. I suppose there's no hurry about it? I've forgotten where I put the things."

"She hasn't forgotten," James said. "And she lies very badly. She said she intended giving that brooch to Mary Anne."

"I thought she might like it and a pair of terrible garnet earrings, so I did give them to her," Olivia said unwillingly. "I certainly didn't want them. I've never seen her wear them, but she said they were 'elegant.' But I did not show that nugget to anyone but Grandfather, Junius and Amelia. I was telling the truth when I told you that."

"Dad found the nugget in the schoolhouse," Rocky said absently. "You can have it back in a day or two."

"I'm in no hurry for it. But why were you so anxious there should be another brooch like Amelia's?"

"I had hers before she was killed, so no one could 've used that for an excuse to get to see her. It would 've made such a plausible one. . . . That's all I wanted to ask you," Rocky said abruptly. "I won't keep you any longer. Would you ask Barnhart an' Glidden to come up here?"

"You run down and tell them, child," James said. "I'm going to stay here."

"Why should I go when you're going to stay?"

"Because I tell you to. And if that isn't reason enough, because Mr. Allan doesn't want you here. He probably would rather I went, too, but it's time I asserted myself—both as a grandfather and professionally. I'll give you not more than an hour, Mr. Allan, and then you're going to lie down again. Run along, Olivia."

Olivia went, slamming the door. James shook his head regretfully. "She has an excellent professional manner, and she really is a goodhearted child, but sometimes she acts like a spoiled baby."

"I suppose I shouldn't have been so—so ritzy toward her," Eleanor said. "But she got under my skin. Rocky will tell you there's only one person who's allowed to criticize my husband, and I'm *it.*"

The doctor laughed and opened his old brown bag. "It was very good for her. Will you get me a glass of water, my dear? Thank you. Here, drink this, Mr. Allan. And remember, not more than an hour. . . ."

CHAPTER XVI
"HE COULDN'T KEEP A SECRET"

Barnhart finished reading Pat McCarthy's telegram and flung it angrily toward Glidden. "So he dug that up?" he said. "I know you had to investigate, but it seems to me about time people forgot that old scandal. Lilian Featherstone was nothing but a malicious troublemaker. She didn't get along with her brother, and she hated Kitty because he married her. You know that if they'd thought there was anything to her accusation the police would have investigated."

"It's a wonder they didn't, anyway."

"Oh, Miss Featherstone didn't dare make any formal charge to the police. So they didn't have to pay any attention to her. It wasn't the first time she'd started stories like that. She had insisted some woman who lived near her had deliberately neglected her stepchildren so that they died. I think she even suggested the woman had fed the children diphtheria germs. And she thought another woman had managed to hasten the death of an elderly father. Naturally, she wasn't popular with her neighbors, and no one but a few half-wits would pay any attention to a woman like that."

"And the rest of it?"

"You mean about Kitty and me? Miss Featherstone was at dinner one night when my wife and I were. Every time I spoke to Kitty the old girl glowered at me. If a man and woman so much as said how-do-you-do to each other she thought they were at least considering adultery. She had that kind of mind."

"Pleasant sort of person. What did your wife say?" Rocky asked.

"Oh—that. We should never have married. I can't think of any two persons less suited to each other than we were. She didn't fit into a faculty circle, even if I was only an humble assistant. But when I decided to give up what was at least a fixed income and try my hand at writing—well, she went into hysterics, and when that didn't work she packed up and left. She did threaten to name Kitty in the suit, but when I said I'd fight if she did I heard no more about it. That was sheer spitefulness and the result of talking to Lilian Featherstone."

"So you resigned from the university?"

"I wasn't kicked out, if that's what you're hinting at," Barnhart said. "There wasn't any scandal connected with my divorce. Remember, Mr. McCarthy talked to Lilian Featherstone. Yes, I resigned. My wife had an income of her own—as much as I had. I lived on my savings, such as they were, until my first book was published. Then, of course, my fortune was made," Barnhart said satirically. "At least, I managed to live from one royalty check to another. It's better than trying to pound a few elementary facts of American history into the thick heads of college students."

"I think he treated me quite well," Glidden said, handing the telegram to Eleanor. "So we're all broke? Well, that's no lie. But I hope this McCarthy hasn't been buzzing around Marjorie's family. They aren't too well pleased with me as it is. But it's as good a character as I could expect."

"I reckon," Rocky said blandly, "that you haven't broke any bottles over anybody's head down in the city."

"Any bott— Oh, you've been talking to someone in Reno. You wouldn't hold that boyish escapade against me, would you? I was drunk. So was the fellow I hit. I'll tell you what he called me, sometime. What other spicy items did you dig up?"

"Nothin' in particular. Should there 've been some more? The fellow I talked to did say he used to see you a lot in a shootin' gall'ry."

"I wonder who— Oh yes. Well, I plead guilty to that and also to being a pretty fair shot."

"There's too many of you aroun' that are. One in particular," Rocky said with a rueful look at his bandaged shoulder. "Though hittin' me may 've been just luck. Barnhart, do you know anything more about Mary Anne than McCarthy was able to find out—which was nothin' at all."

"She's never talked about what she was doing before Kitty took her in: picked her up out of the gutter like you would a stray dog and took her home. And kept her, in spite of Featherstone's objections. She has good reason to be devoted to Kitty. I don't even know how old she is. Around forty, I suppose. I've sometimes wondered if Mary Anne knows the exact year of her birth, herself."

"I suppose both of you were sleepin' soundly all night long? . . . I thought you would be. I guess that's all, then."

"Sorry you're laid up," Barnhart said politely. "I hope you—" He broke off, looking at the cloison-né bowl on the mantel. "So that's where that went to? I might have guessed he'd manage to bring it up here to decorate his sanctum."

"Junius, you mean? What made you wonder where it was?"

"Because I sent it to Kitty for her birthday last month, and naturally I wondered why it wasn't downstairs. But if Junius happened to like it he'd simply have brought it up here. Well, there's nothing criminal about that, is there?" Barnhart said impatiently as Rocky still sat looking at the mantel.

"Junius glomming onto it, or you giving Mrs. Featherstone-Quinn a birthday present last month? Neither one—far's I can see. Will you ask Miss Horne if she minds comin' up here?"

"I think he wants us to go," Glidden said, grinning. He added: "You're right, Allan, she *is* damned good-looking," and closed the door hastily.

"Who?" Eleanor said.

"You. He wanted to know what you looked like."

"Oh! I imagine Mr. Glidden never fails to notice in detail what every woman he meets looks like."

"Most young men—most men do," Doctor James said. "There's an expression: 'You pay your money, and you take your choice.'"

"Between those two, you mean?" Rocky asked. The doctor nodded. "Then you think one of them did it?"

"Who else— Oh, of course," James said with an apologetic smile, "I'm always forgetting that everyone in this town doesn't live here, and that we're all under suspicion."

"I'll take Mr. Glidden if I have to choose. I like Mr. Barnhart, and I'm sure his wife was a cat," Eleanor said. "Yes, my love, I know that's no proof he isn't a murderer. But if Mr. Glidden goes around hitting people over the head with bottles I think I'm justified in thinking he can't have a very amiable disposition—"

She stopped as Ivy Horne came in, watched her drop languidly into a chair. Since their brief encounter Eleanor felt fairly well acquainted with Olivia James. And Mrs. Featherstone-Quinn had not only figuratively but actually clasped her to a well-upholstered bosom as soon as she set foot in the inn. After allowing Kitty Featherstone-Quinn to talk to you an hour by the clock it was hard not to think you knew her intimately. Of course, people like that, who appeared to have no reserves, were apt to deceive you. The volume of their talk was so overwhelming that it stupefied you, and you very nearly forgot that it might possibly be all sound and fury, "signifying nothing."

But Ivy Horne had so far completely eluded her. Not purposely, Eleanor realized. Everyone had finished breakfast before she left Rocky and went downstairs, where Mary Anne insisted on bringing her coffee and French toast while Mrs. Featherstone-Quinn "cheered her up." But Ivy had gone upstairs. "Making the beds and straightening up the rooms. So thoughtful of her when we're so upset, and someone must keep an eye on these reporters. And it must have been a dreadful shock to you. Your husband is such a nice young man, and I wish I had a son like him. . . ."

Eleanor smiled, remembering Allan's description of Ivy. "That lady poet that looks kind of soulful. She talks to you about these fool modern painters and poets that can't write anything that rhymes. She all the time flutters her hands aroun'. I reckon she was rightly named; there's something kind of droopy and clinging about her."

That was good as far as it went, but Ivy's look of frailty was deceptive. It was possible she was a trifle undernourished, but there was strength and endurance in the long lines of her body. And even while she looked like a pale martyr prepared to face the Inquisition without recanting, she was saying practically:

"We're rid of the reporters since Kitty refused to let them have a room here. Since Mrs. Allan is here, she could say she had none vacant. They did talk of coming back here tonight, but they've gone down to Merton to the telegraph office. Your father, Mr. Allan, insisted the telephone be kept open for official calls."

"Trust Dad. So they've left?"

"A few minutes ago. They said they'd be back. They wanted to know if I wouldn't like to write a poem for them."

"What 'd you say?"

"As Mary Anne would put it, that I would not prostrate my Muse. That," Ivy said with a bleak smile, "is not exactly the truth. I've seen the time when I'd sell it for a—well, let's set a high value on it and say a fur coat. But they wanted some masterpiece on 'an appropriate subject', and I don't feel up to writing poetry dealing with murder."

"You don't look very well, Miss Horne," the doctor said. "Are you still having headaches?"

"Off and on. This is getting me down. I've always known the correct pose for all situations that confronted me. Maybe there's one for this, but it seems to elude me. Oh, I don't pretend any grief for Cassius, but I'm fond of Kitty, and Junius was always very nice to me."

"That's what I wanted to talk to you about," Rocky said. "You don't mind me not beatin' aroun' the bush? The doctor's holdin' a stop watch on me. Did Junius think he was in love with you?"

"He— W-what makes you ask that?"

"It occurred to sev'ral people. Dad remarked on it; so did Cash. Just the way he looked at you. And he had the reputation of bein' susceptible."

"He was. There was really nothing to it. I— You won't misunderstand when I say Kitty isn't exactly a romantic figure? Well, I write poetry, and I look like I do. That was enough for Junius. He—it wasn't so awfully obvious, was it? I mean, you didn't think that I—"

"You didn't appear to be encouragin' him," Rocky said bluntly. "He just acted like he admired you. Did he write po'try to you?"

"Y-yes. He— Yes, several times. Have you seen any of his poetry? Then you can imagine—"

"I can. Did you know he was writin' an ode for your birthday?"

"He didn't—well, he did say he would have a little offering to lay before me then."

"When?"

"Why, the thirtieth of this month. Didn't you know? Then how— Had he already started to write it?"

"He had a few lines done."

Ivy fingered the stiff folds of her brocaded Chinese jacket. "I'd—I'd hoped he hadn't started the thing."

"Why?"

"Well, you see, you did find it."

"Let's go at it another way if you don't want to answer that. Who does the bedroom work here?"

"Mary Anne's too busy to do anything but her own room. Kitty does most of it, but I help her—do my own room."

"But you didn't look after Junius's room—this one here?"

"No, Kitty always did that. She said she was the only one who could dust his desk without disturbing things. She never did disturb anything," Ivy said quickly.

"She's a very unusual woman then. Did Junius ever ask you to run away with him?"

"He did not!"

"Sure of that? You deny it so loudly . . ."

"But he didn't. Oh, what's the use," Ivy said wearily. "He made me no dishonorable proposals—that *is* the truth. But one evening he began to talk about his wasted life, and how long he'd waited for the one woman, only to have her appear when it was too late. He was in honor bound to Kitty, et cetera, et cetera. He meant no disloyalty to her, also et cetera. But if he were only free we could hie ourselves away to the flowering wilderness with a jug of wine and a loaf of bread. I suppose I'd have had to furnish those while he contributed the book of verse.

"I was furious," Ivy added. "We were alone on the front porch, and someone might come out any minute. It was so silly, but Kitty would have been hurt by it. People do weird things; she married Junius when Arthur Barnhart— Well, that was the end of it. I snubbed Junius so badly that the next day he decided to renounce me. No word of what he suffered would ever again cross his lips if I would only not deprive him of the boon of my friendship."

"He might 've confided in you," Rocky said slowly.

"But he did. In one respect he was a true genius: he adored talking about himself. Or is that being only masculine?"

Rocky smiled briefly. "You can discuss that with my wife sometime. I meant he might have discussed more important things than his pers'nality with you."

Ivy put her hand to her throat. For once there was no studied grace but only genuine fright in her gesture. "I— you'll have to tell me what you mean."

"Suppose he found out, after trying quite awhile, that Cash had this money. He'd want to tell someone about it; he very likely already had spoken of the possibility that Cash had it an' his scheme for gettin' some of it. He may even have come back here from killin' Cash, wantin' help—"

"And I talked to him and then killed him!" Ivy sprang to her feet. "Do you think I'm going to incriminate myself?"

"No one's askin' you to do that."

"Following your argument, if I told you Junius had ever confided in me I certainly would be making a very dangerous admission."

"Nothing you say here can be held against you if you deny it later. Please set down again, an' let me finish. We're pretty sure of one thing: that Thursday night Cash did let Junius know he had the money. What happened after that is guesswork. But he must 've told someone about it, or he wouldn't have been killed himself. It wasn't necessarily the one he told that killed him. He could 've been overheard."

"Couldn't someone have been watching him?" Ivy said more calmly.

"That's possible. But even someone who knew he'd been tryin' to pry Cash's secret out of him couldn't be certain he'd do it that night, or even that Cash did have any money. I draw the line at the coincidence that someone just happened to pass Cash's room late that night—it was at the back of the house, you know—so he just happened to learn what Junius was learnin' right then. Now, did Junius ever talk to you about the possibility Cash might have some money?"

"Yes, but I think he talked to others about that. He couldn't keep a secret. He hinted that he was going to be too clever for Cash. I didn't take any scheme he might have had too seriously, because I thought Cash the shrewder of the two. And I couldn't believe he had any great amount of money . . ."

"Go on."

"I don't know how. I don't—don't want to admit too much, do I? Suppose I say that one—one person here was restless that night. She couldn't sleep well, and sometime after eleven I—she was going into the bathroom but was still in the hall when Junius came upstairs, and they bumped into each other. He was excited and angry. He told her about Cash, that he'd been, Junius said, 'living off of them all this time and making fools of them when he was rich.' He didn't say how he'd found out, and he didn't threaten Cassius. His only idea seemed to be that they'd 'pay him back' for his trick somehow or other. I—what's the use of pretending?—I wasn't interested enough to go on standing there in the dark."

"It was dark?"

"Oh yes. He spoke when we collided, and then I recognized his voice. I said good night and went on into the bathroom."

"Before Junius came in here?"

"I can't swear that he came in here at once. We were standing in the middle of the hall—the bathroom's there. There was no one in the hall when I came out, but it took me awhile to find the extra aspirin Kitty keeps in the drug cabinet. I didn't hear Junius moving about in here, but I very seldom did, even if this room is next to mine."

"But you didn't hear anyone talkin' in any other room?"

"No. We didn't speak very loudly, but there were times when Junius' whisper was very suitable to the stage. Well, that's all," Ivy said, pushing her hair back from her forehead. "I've told you. I didn't want to, and I was afraid to. But then you made me afraid not to. If you thought I was the person Junius was most apt to confide in, that— well, it—"

"Put you in a spot?" Rocky said. "I hoped you'd see that. Well, I wouldn't worry. You've not really hurt anyone by tellin' what you have. Did anyone from here get to see Mrs. Slack on Friday?"

"That was the day after the fire; the day before she— No, none of us talked to her. You should know."

"I should know no one got in to see her? I'm not apt to forget it. Didn't you an' Mrs. Feather-stone-Quinn talk to her Thursday?"

"Oh yes. Kitty asked me to go with her to pay a formal afternoon call. She said Amelia liked that, and I hadn't ever done it—just talked to her outside. We went, and she served tea."

"Was she wearin' that china brooch that day? Show it to her, will you, Eleanor?"

"She was wearing one like this. I couldn't swear that this was hers unless you told me it was."

"Why? Have you seen any others like it?"

"They're being shown in the jewelers' shops again."

"Have you seen any on that order aroun' here?"

"Y-yes. Mary Anne showed Kitty and me one very much like this. But I did Mary Anne's room for her this morning because she's so busy, and hers is still stuck in a pincushion on her bureau."

"Olivia told Mr. Allan she gave that brooch to Mary Anne, Miss Horne. You don't need to worry about that part of it," the doctor said.

"Oh! I'm glad of that. Yes, I knew Miss James gave it to her. She never wore it."

"What did you talk about that afternoon you called on Mrs. Slack?" Rocky asked.

"Why—we were all very polite and discussed the weather. We admired Mrs. Slack's work. Kitty said she had some material she'd give Mrs. Slack to make tidies for the living room here. She didn't

really want the place decked with pink-and-yellow
roses, but she thought she could pay Mrs. Slack
for the work. We didn't discuss Junius and Cassius
at all."

"That's what I wanted to know." Doctor James
cleared his throat warningly, and Rocky nodded.
"All right. I guess that's all, Miss Horne."

The doctor escorted Ivy to the door, came back
and touched Rocky gently on his good shoulder.
"I know this is all very distressing, but forget it
for a while. You must let me fix this shoulder, and
then lie down."

"I will," Rocky said with unexpected docility.
There was a pinched look about his nostrils and a
fine film of sweat on his forehead. "I'm ready to,
though I haven't talked to quite ever'body. But I
don't suppose it's worth-while."

"I suppose," Eleanor murmured, as James
walked to the table for his bag, "that you wouldn't
tell me why you sent Jazz to Merton?"

"No, honey, I wouldn't. But I'm glad I did. I
don't see how else— All right, Doc, I'll be still."

Someone rapped lightly on the door, and Eleanor opened it cautiously to see Robert Allan standing in the hall.

"Oh, it's just you. Come in. I was afraid— They
aren't coming upstairs yet, are they?"

"Just talkin' about goin' to bed. They'll be up any minute now. Where," Allan said, looking around the room, "is that darn fool son of mine?"

"Setting the stage for this performance of his by prowling around people's bedrooms. But he certainly doesn't want to be caught at it."

"Serve him right if he was," Allan grumbled. "I gave up a long time ago. I'm just waitin' aroun' for my orders. Had he ought to be in bed? I can try assertin' myself a little."

"Do you think it would do any good? Oh, he's all right. He doesn't seem to be running a temperature, and he's behaved himself for at least five hours. What time is it?"

"Nine thirty-five. You said this 'little performance' of his. You wouldn't happen to know what it is, Daughter?"

"I probably know less than you do. You've been here all the time, while I feel there's a good deal I haven't been told. He sent Jazz to Merton to get something, and Jazz came back—"

"Lookin' like he'd had a hard day of it. He put his car in the garage an' shut the doors very careful. Then him and Rocky had some more conversation, an' Mitchell cussed plenty an' went out to look for somethin' else. He's been settin' an' strummin' away on that piano in the livin' room for the last half-hour."

"He can play at almost any musical instrument. He's always organizing home-talent dance orchestras. I wonder if I should warn Rocky? He wouldn't want to be caught out of his room when he isn't supposed to be feeling very well."

"Let him— Oh, here you are," Allan said, looking sourly at his son. "You goin' to light for a while or keep on buzzin' aroun' all night?"

"I'm through. It may work, and it may not." Rocky sat down and threw half a dozen matches on the table.

"What's those for? Well, that was only what you'd call a rhetorical question—if that's the kind you don't expect to have answered," Allan said. "But wouldn't it maybe be possible just to go on an' arrest somebody without goin' through all this?"

"All what? You're goin' to bed an' to sleep—if you want to. Jazz 'll keep guard downstairs."

"Keep guard an' what else?"

"Anyway, who do you want me to arrest?" Rocky said. "What proof have I to arrest anyone on?"

"I don't see, from what I know, that you have a strong enough case against anyone," Eleanor said reasonably. "But you must have some idea what you're doing. There must have been straws, to show you which way the wind blows."

"Sometimes a wind whips aroun' and chang-
es direction. There's one or two things makes me
think I'm doin' the right thing," Rocky admitted.
"But slips that people make when you're talking to
'em are the straws in the wind that you call them.
They aren't enough to convict people in a trial.
You can prove motive against ever'body here, but
not exclusive means or opportunity against any
one person."

"In that case, I'd get me some sleep an' forget
it," Allan drawled. "What is' it you're goin' to do?"

"Find out if you can make thieves fall out."

"You're still certain there are two people involved?" Eleanor said.

"One man could 've managed the business; one
woman alone couldn't— I hear folks comin' upstairs. You go to bed, Dad, an' tell them, if they
ask you, that's where I am."

"An' that's all?"

"Stay awake if you want to, but don't leave your
light on."

"I reckon you know what you're doin'," Allan said disparagingly. "But I ain't goin' to sleep.
Good night, Eleanor."

"What about Jazz?" Eleanor whispered.

"You don't need to do that. People know we're
in here, an' that I'm probably awake."

"I didn't realize I was doing it. There's something in the atmosphere, as created by Mr. Allan, that makes you feel like whispering. What about Jazz?"

"He'll be up pretty soon. Officially, he's on guard tonight, so he'll come up an' make his rounds. There's nothing out of the way about that."

"N-no. You want everything to seem quite natural—"

"Anything doin' this afternoon and evenin'?"

"Nothing worth telling. A feeling isn't a fact."

"What feeling?"

"Oh, I don't know," Eleanor said, beginning restlessly to put the room in order. "Just the feeling that everyone is suffering from nerves. Ivy Horne wouldn't talk at all, Mr. Glidden was outside, painting, and even the fountain of Mrs. Featherstone-Quinn's conversation seemed to be slightly dried up. But I do like her—far better than I do Ivy Horne. Mr. Barnhart and I talked about this and that and nothing "

"There's a pair of handcuffs in that suitcase," Rocky said. "Get 'em out, will you?"

"Do you think," Eleanor said, laughing, "that you know how to snap them on in a 'single, quick movement'?"

"I should, after all the practicin' I did on the bedposts."

"And me. And then couldn't find the key to the things for fifteen minutes, while I sat there, manacled."

"Your tongue wasn't handcuffed, honey. That's why I took to the bedposts. That 'll be Jazz, now. . . ."

CHAPTER XVII
A BELL TINKLES

"Well, everybody's in bed," Jazz said. "I met the Featherstone in the hall, pounded my chest and assured her she had nothing to fear while I was on guard. Told her I was going to sit in the front hall as per your orders. Now what?"

"Do what you told 'em you're going to do, until about eleven. By then ever'body should be asleep, but if any of them should be readin' or still up you'll know that by a light in the rooms. Did you find one?"

"A ladder, you mean? Yes, though Murdoch found me prowling around looking for one and showed me where it was."

"That's all right. Do you think you can manage?"

"I doubt it," Jazz said pessimistically. "I'll probably lose my balance and fall off."

"Oh, you're sure-footed. I don't dare try it myself."

"No one's asking you to. But don't blame me if I make a mess of it. I put on that gadget you gave me."

"Any objections?"

"Objections? Oh—I see what you mean. None at all. I think I managed to fill your specifications pretty well," Jazz said, grinning at Eleanor. She said pleasantly:

"You can both go straight to hell. I suppose you think it would be funny if I burst from suppressed curiosity?"

"I had a hard enough time not answering Nancy's questions as to why I wanted—it. I managed to dodge the reporters. I went into the telegraph office," Jazz said, "and since I manage the place, I glanced through the sent business. The stuff they sent out was O.K. A lot of it-is-rumoreds and it-is-saids."

"Where are they now?" Rocky asked.

"The last I saw they were in the H.M. and J. club, getting drunk. They were drinking gin fizzes, and I slipped Shorty Roberts five dollars to make them double strength."

Rocky laughed. "You'll do. I'm glad they didn't send any of their crack reporters. All right, you go on. I'll be countin' on you." He turned to Eleanor. "You'd better turn the lamp way down low, honey. Then you might as well lie down. No tellin' how long we've got to wait—if anything at all happens."

"You lie down."

"No, I'm all right. We'd better not talk any more."

Eleanor piled the pillows against the wall and sat down across the bed. "I am not going to sleep," she said firmly, "but you happen to have the only really comfortable chair in the room. . . . All right, I'm not going to talk any more."

She had slept badly on the train last night; it would be nice to curl up now and take a nap. She closed her eyes. After all, she could not help waking when anything happened. But in spite of open windows, the room smelled of disinfectant, cigarette smoke and the fumes from the kerosene lamp. This room, the entire house was in thrall to quiet that beat against your ears more loudly than any noise ever could. And Rocky sat so still. . . .

She traced his profile in the air, grew tired of that, changed position with an impatient movement and whispered: "If something doesn't happen pretty soon, I think I'll scream."

"Please don't."

Eleanor sighed. He had spoken so politely and impersonally. She closed her eyes again and began to count seconds: one, two, three—up to sixty and then back to one and two again. She had checked off fifteen minutes on her fingers when she thought she heard a slight, bumping noise at the back of the house. She sat up straight, the bed springs creaking. Rocky looked at her and shook his head warningly. Eleanor sank back against the pillows again, muttering:

"You wait, I'll get even with you yet, mister."

When she thought another fifteen minutes had passed she dared to get quietly off the bed and go to the table to look at her watch by the lamp's dim light. It was eleven-twenty. Rocky's lips formed the words: "What time?" and she went over to him and whispered her answer against his ear. After an instant he shook his head again.

"I'm afraid it isn't goin' to work, and if it doesn't I've tipped off my hand for nothin' at all."

"How long are you going to wait?"

"I don't know—another hour, I guess. Of course, I'd wake up if— No, I don't want to risk that."

"You're not going to sit up all night if I have to get Jazz and your father to keep you from it. Your forehead feels hot again."

"All right. Just a little while longer."

"It's so close and still. Not a breath of air. It must be cloudy. Perhaps it's going to—"

Rocky's fingers tightened on her arm. The house was no longer quiet. Someone was screaming— not shrilly, not loudly. Screaming like a person in a nightmare, with low, hoarse sounds. Trying to evade some nameless terror, thinking: "This isn't real. I know it isn't real. In a minute I'll wake up. But why can't I get away? Why can't I scream . . ."

The choked cry rose to a higher pitch; you felt that it came from between clenched teeth. The sound broke off, began again. There was the dull thud of something falling. . . .

Rocky was in the hall now, muttering: "If I wasn't right about this I deserve to be shot." Eleanor turned the lamp high, caught it up and followed him, her hair suddenly matting damply on her forehead.

Other doors were opening, flashlights and lamps lighting up the hall. There was a dreadful, fumbling sound behind one door, as if someone were clawing at it with shaking hands, trying to turn a key in a lock, trying not to cry out, but still whimpering.

The door swung open, and Ivy Horne stood looking at them blindly. Her mouth sagged. After an instant a long nail file fell from one trembling hand to the floor. Eleanor made an instinctive movement toward her, but Rocky held her back. He whispered: "Wait!" and she realized that no one else had moved out of that first tableau. They were all listening, listening to a tiny sound in the room beyond.

In the darkness there, a bell was tinkling faintly. The noise grew more distinct, coming slowly
closer to them until a big black cat stalked out
into the hall, brushing against Ivy Horne's long,
silk gown.

She screamed again. "Leon! Leon! Oh God! take
it away!" Her white arms were around Glidden's
neck, her face hidden against his dressing gown.
"If it's really there—take it away! I can't stand
it—the bell tinkled, and it was furry and black—I
knew it was black without seeing it! It purred and
tried to rub its head against me. The other one
did that—and then its head was bloody, and it
twisted on the floor—I had to kill it. I told you I
had to! I told you I'd never forget it . . ."

Glidden patted her writhing shoulders perfunctorily. "You told me? You're a little upset, Ivy,
and no wonder. Get a grip on yourself, and stop
talking nonsense. It's just Mr. Allan's idea of a
good joke."

"You see, Miss Horne," Rocky said softly, "you
aren't goin' to get any help from him. He believes in
lookin' out for himself. You've got a lot of explainin'
to do, but you can't be hung for killin' a cat."

Ivy's arms dropped. She backed away, staring
at Glidden. "You—you're not going to say that
I— I don't believe you ever loved me! I think you
were lying all the time! The way you acted about

that money . . . All right, if I've a lot of explanations to make, you'll have more! I'm not going
to save your precious skin for you—and another
woman—by taking the blame! I didn't kill anyone.
You did that! It was all your plan—"

Glidden struck her across the mouth. "You
damned little tramp," he said coolly. "Stop yelling
like that. I should have known better than to trust
any woman. Don't forget there's such a thing as
accessory before and after the fact. I'll take you
with me, my lady, wherever I go. If I go—"

His hand was already inside his dressing gown.
He made a sudden, jerking motion, and Robert
Allan drawled:

"I wouldn't try that if I was you. It wouldn't
hurt my feelin's none to plug you once or twice.
Throw that gun down on the floor."

Glidden stared for an instant at the long, sil-
ver-plated pistol, steady in Allan's brown hand
and dropped his own gun to the floor. It slithered
along the carpet as he kicked at it.

"You should be in the movies, Mr. Allan. Don't
cry, Kitty. After all, you asked me up here and put
temptation in my way. I'd have gotten away with
it if I hadn't been fool enough to trust a damned,
hysterical— Word diluted, as Mary Anne would
say. El Dorado: the search for spirit gold. That's a
joke—please laugh . . ."

Eleanor picked up the breakfast tray and put it on the table. "We think," she said, as Rocky managed to get his fingers on the sixth of half-a-dozen buttered muffins, "that you have eaten enough. We have been very patient with you, considering your enfeebled state."

"Three eggs and six muffins?" Robert Allan said. "Enfeebled—hunh!"

Rocky grinned. "All right. It's not my fault you 'n the doctor stuck me back in bed last night. Well—"

"This is your old maestro, Rocky Allan," Jazz said. "Yowsuh!"

Robert Allan looked at him disgustedly. "Let him get on with it. I heard what the woman said, that Barnhart took down in shorthand an' typed out so nice—"

"I was glad when Dud Williams came and took them away," Eleanor said. "Go on, Rocky."

"I'd be glad to when you all get through talkin'. Of course, Ivy Horne tried to say in her statement that everything was Glidden's idea, and he was responsible for ever'thing. He ain't talkin', but he'll deny all of it, an' on some points he might be tellin' the truth.

"Junius fell for Ivy as soon as he met her, an' she didn't discourage him—privately. He told her right away when he began to suspect Cash had money. She says the scheme to get some of it from Cash was his, but she probably helped him figure it out.

"With Glidden's help, because she told him ever'thing Junius told her. The main thing they wanted to know was if Cash had enough money to make murder worth the risk. If Junius could get some or all of it peaceably, they could relieve him of it.

"Ivy says she didn't think any farther than that, but that Glidden turned out to have his plans all ready when the time came. As soon as Cash bragged to Junius he had money Junius came hot-footin' it back here, talked to Ivy at the door of her room an' told her all about it. It was dark, so he couldn't see Glidden had been in there with her. She calmed Junius down an' let him come in here.

"Then Glidden got Junius to let him in here an' killed him. He stunned him with that nice brass vase over there on the mantel an' then finished him off. He wanted some gloves, so he helped himself to a pair Junius had. Then he produced this plan he had all figured out.

"They took Junius down an' put him in the car. Then Glidden went over to Cash's place an' made some excuse to talk to him. He killed Cash with that poker we found under the stove and disfigured his jaw with it, after he'd done a rough job shavin' him. She was outside, keepin' watch. But he called her in to look things over, an' she wasn't wearin' gloves. She was the one to turn out the lamp when they was ready to go.

"Then, all she could do was come back here. Glidden took Cash's body over to the old Quinn house, then drove out to Deep Lake, walked back an' touched off the fire. It was a nice setup that was supposed to stop us right there, but they'd forgot Cash wouldn't be apt to use a car, and they didn't fill it up with gas or take any of his provisions, like he'd have done.

"Glidden had a flashlight he turned on to see if ever'thing was all right before he lighted the fire. He wanted to turn Cash over on his stomach an' put all the identifyin' objects they had under him, so's they wouldn't be destroyed. Well, of course, he saw footprints in the dust there an' a trail of burned; matches through the house. When they found that brooch while they was fightin' fire, and when he knew, later on, that Amelia Slack had been lookin' for it, he was sure it 'd been her in the Quinn house that night.

"Meanwhile, Ivy 'd got to thinkin' things over, an' she was afraid she'd left her fingerprints on that lamp or in Cash's room somewhere. So she had to sneak in there Friday afternoon while Mrs. Featherstone-Quinn was sleepin'—all doped up with sleepin' powders, though she didn't think she was. She made one of the keys from here fit Cash's door. Glidden wouldn't help her. Well, we've discussed what happened while she was there: how Sultan made her drop the lamp, an' she killed him. She was lucky and didn't get splashed any with coal oil. She kept her head enough to polish off ever'thing either of 'em might 've touched, and that's why some perfectly harmless prints seemed to 've disappeared between Friday mornin' and afternoon.

"Meanwhile, Glidden was scared Amelia Slack might 've seen him that night. He was sure she'd been there sometime or other. She didn't talk all day Friday, but he judged her by himself an' thought maybe she was waitin' the right time to trade her silence for the money. He didn't intend to lose it like that. No one but Amelia Slack knew if she ever had any idea like that. If Junius died first, Cash's money was rightfully hers. Of course, she'd have had to bluff to get it the way Glidden thought she meant to, because she really hadn't seen him.

"Ivy says she begged Glidden not to kill Amelia, but that she couldn't make him take the chance that Amelia didn't know anything. He made her get Mary Anne's painted pin an' go over to Mrs. Slack with it. He'd given the right pin to me so I wouldn't think the person who had it had tried to return it to Mrs. Slack.

"Well, Amelia let Ivy in, all right, said the pin wasn't hers but thanked her just the same. She'd locked her front door—the back one was locked, too—but she left it open when she let Ivy in. So Glidden sneaked into the hall an' listened to Ivy condolin' Amelia on her 'loss.' An' Amelia passed her own death sentence by sayin' she'd like to know if Cash or Junius was killed first, because if Junius was, Cash's money was 'rightfully' hers.

"Whether she meant anything special by that, it was enough for Glidden. Amelia did scream once, when he came in an' started toward her, but no one heard her. He moved so fast she didn't even have time to get out of her chair.

"What saved Olivia was that Tom Slack came blunderin' along toward the house when they'd just left it. He was too drunk to see them, even if it hadn't been so dark. But that meant it was safer to get back here in a hurry. Besides, Ivy insisted that if Olivia had known anything she couldn't have kept still about it for an entire day. An' the next day Glidden managed to hear Olivia talkin' to me, an' from what she said he was sure he was safe, so far's she was concerned. I thought I heard someone outside that office window. . . .

"Glidden had had the money belt hidden in a vacant room here, but he came out Friday night before Ivy did an' hid it in the schoolhouse. By that time he knew we knew about the money, an' he was afraid to have it near him. He wouldn't tell Ivy where he put it, an' that didn't make for a gen'ral feeling of trust an' friendship between them.

"Well, when the inquest 'd been held in the schoolhouse he wasn't satisfied with his hiding place, an' he'd thought of the possibility he might like to make a quick getaway, an' he wanted the money again. He wanted to find some place closer home for it—or I suppose he did. Ivy said he told her he was all prepared if he had to take a powder, an' that she'd be safe—he'd be the one to be suspected. Which wasn't so, and the fact that he had the money in his hands didn't set well with her.

"He sneaked over to the schoolhouse while I was at the Jameses', looking aroun'. Got the money all right, but ran into me. His main idea was to get away without bein' seen, which was lucky for me. An' I reckon that's all."

"Will you," Eleanor said, "take that insufferably smug look off your face? We knew almost all you've told us so far. Get on with it."

"You heard the lady," Jazz said, grinning. "When interviewed, Mr. Allan said modestly—"

Rocky turned red. "Oh, lay off. Between the three of you . . . All right; let's start with motive. Everybody here needed money. But character counts for somethin'. In the case of the doctor, for instance. Slack was too dumb to be behind all this. An' the fact that the money was hidden in the schoolhouse seemed to point to someone who didn't know the town too well. Anyone who did would know they'd hold inquests there and would choose some other buildin' for a hiding place.

"Of course, that idea occurred to me pretty late in the proceedings and didn't matter much, anyway. The fire was more important. The people who'd lived here a long time was too afraid of fire to take a chance, I thought. I couldn't see James or Murdoch bein' willing to risk burnin' up the town.

"Well, about the money—Barnhart gave up a sure salary once, to take a chance writin'. That looked like he didn't think money was so important. Mrs. Featherstone-Quinn seemed too gen'rous to be crazy for money. But you know what Ivy Horne's hist'ry has been so far's money's concerned. And Glidden wanted to get to New York or Paris and, I imagine, to marry this girl, Marjorie. Ever'one said they wanted money, but those two seemed to me most likely to kill to get it.

"Once you knew what Junius had been up to, he was the startin' point. He had to 've told somebody what he'd learned about Cash, unless you were goin' to believe in a lot of coincidences. Junius had been workin' on his scheme quite awhile, but he couldn't keep a secret. He'd given part of it away to his wife an' Amelia. It wasn't unreasonable to think he thought he was in love with Ivy, and if he was it was a pretty sure thing he'd told her everything.

"That birthday ode he started to write helped to clinch that point. Mrs. F.-Q. knew right away it was meant for Ivy, but she lied like a lady an' said it was for her.

"In a case like this you've almost got to make up your mind that the odds are in favor of things having happened a certain way, even if you can't prove it. So you say: Junius confided in someone and most likely it was a woman. But it was phys'cally impossible for one woman to do all that was done the first night, alone. So the woman Junius confided in must 've had help. And not his, because the car, with him in it, drove away before the fire was started—a long time before.

"Any combination of any one of three women, leavin' out Mary Anne, with any one of four men, was possible. But if you cut out the old inhabitants, you have just two men an' two women. A

partnership between one in the hotel and one in
the town wouldn't work out so well. It 'd be hard
for Olivia an' Glidden to work together so well,
for instance. An' Olivia didn't kill that cat because he wouldn't have got near her. Murdoch had
an alibi for that: he was out watchin' Mrs. Featherstone-Quinn's car all afternoon.

"Well, was it Featherstone plus Barnhart, Horne
plus Glidden, Horne plus Barnhart, Glidden plus
Featherstone? I wouldn't have considered that last
one if Glidden hadn't run aroun' with elderly la-
dies in Reno. Ivy Horne did ever'thing she could to
make us think Mrs. Featherstone-Quinn an' Barnhart might be in cahoots. Glidden wasn't above
hintin' at Ivy and Barnhart. They tried mighty
hard to give the idea there was nothin' between
them, actin' like they didn't care much about each
other an' referrin' to this Marjorie White.

"But the first night we were here they spoke
about wanderin' aroun' the city together at night,
lookin' in bookstores. Then Glidden spoke about
Ivy's pet view of the moon over Chinatown—"

"And Mr. McCarthy said she had an apartment
there?" Eleanor said.

"That's it. I've got an evil mind. I thought he
might have seen the moon come up or go down
from her apartment. But to get back to the idea

of two people bein' involved. We knew one person wore gloves—men's gloves, because Junius's was missin' and there weren't any others except Mrs. Featherstone-Quinn who had any, from all reports. There weren't any in any rooms but hers, an' one pair hadn't been worn, an' the others had so many holes they'd have left distinctive marks. But whoever drove the car seemed to 've worn gloves. Also, that was a man's job—carrying Junius' body to the lake.

"But somebody appeared to 've got anxious about fingerprints and gone to the trouble to remove some from Cash's room when Sultan was killed. So that pointed to one person who wore gloves—a man—and one who didn't—probably a woman.

"Also, it seemed to me Amelia wouldn't have let in any man late that night she was killed, except James, Slack or Murdoch. She was too proper to admit Glidden or Barnhart. But she'd have let in a woman who had a good excuse for asking to see her. So that looked like two people workin' together, again.

"I was sure about Glidden, first. We had a talk in his room, an' he got to discussin' something he called creative distortion. If I got it right, which I doubt, he said artists don't always paint a thing

the way it looks, according to their eyes, but distort it to fit what they think is the way it really
is. I thought: if an artist can do that he'd find it
easy to paint a picture that was distorted, to give
the person who looked at it an entirely wrong idea
of the whole thing. And that's just what that first
setup of the fire an' the deserted car aimed to do.

"That was too elab'rate to 've been thought
out in a hurry. I always thought it was ready and
planned for the occasion. The extra little twist
they gave it, to make us think it was Junius' body
in the fire, and that Cash had got away—to confuse the question of motive—took thinkin' over.
Junius couldn't have been told about that. He
wasn't dumb. If Cash's murder had been suggested
to him he'd have sense enough to think: after that,
why not me?

"Of course, there wasn't anything conclusive
about Glidden's talk on artistic the'ries. He said
right away that Mrs. Featherstone-Quinn an' Ivy
knew more about that than he did. His real slip
was made the evenin' I got shot. He said anyone
like Cash, who carried aroun' wads of fifty- and
hundred-dollar bills, was askin' to be killed. Hardpan Reid said Cash carried twenties, fifties and
hundreds. I said at the supper table Friday night
that he carried twenties and hundreds. But Glidden stuck in the fifties because he'd seen them.

"I wasn't sure about Ivy Horne till she told us that story about talkin' to Junius, because she was scared not to. An' she had a chance to cast suspicion on Mrs. F.-Q. and Barnhart. She suggested Mrs. Featherstone-Quinn might 've been jealous of her an' Junius, an' that Barnhart would do anything for 'Kitty.' She meant us to think someone had overheard Junius talkin' to her and didn't stop to think that if that had happened her own life wouldn't have been worth much, knowing what she did about the money.

"And then she *did* give herself away. She was talkin' about Mrs. Featherstone-Quinn offerin' to give Amelia some material to make tidies for the livin' room here, and she said something like: 'not that Kitty really wanted the place decked out with pink and yellow roses . . .' Well, when Amelia was killed she was just finishin' up the yellow roses on a tidy that had pink and yellow ones on it. There was yellow wool in her needle. The only time Ivy was ever in Amelia's house was Thursday afternoon, and she wasn't workin' yellow roses then.

"Because Olivia said that Friday afternoon she went home to get Amelia some scraps of wool so she could finish up the work she was doing. Which almost cert'nly meant the yellow wool was in the scraps she brought. Besides, she worked very fast, Doctor James said. She was workin' a long time

Thursday night and some Friday, so even if she had started that tidy when Ivy and Mrs. Featherstone-Quinn were in to see her Thursday, she wouldn't have much more than started it—not got to the yellow roses—or she'd have finished it before Friday night. That's pretty involved, but there it is. And Ivy couldn't have got her idea about tidies with pink and yellow roses from the ones in the room. They were all black cross-stitch."

"I suppose," Robert Allan said, "it didn't occur to you you could ask Mrs. Quinn or Olivia about that?"

"I didn't need to. I was afraid to ask Mrs. Featherstone-Quinn. She might 've guessed something was wrong and warned Ivy. I didn't even talk to her because I wanted Ivy to think I suspected her. But I've asked her about it, now, an' she says Amelia was crochetin' Thursday afternoon. I wasn't going to ask Olivia about it, either. She's not dumb, but neither can she hide her feelings, if she'd suspected what I was gettin' at."

"So that brings you up to that business with the cat," Allan said. "Which I don't approve of."

Rocky shrugged one-sidedly. "This murder was a rotten, dirty business. I didn't have proof enough to arrest Glidden or Ivy and make the charge stick. I thought Glidden wasn't in love with her, and that she was with him. When two people are to share money they got by murder it often leads to trouble. I thought she'd be most apt to crack.

"About all that business of Glidden's with Mary Anne's kitten did was to show Mrs. Featherstone-Quinn didn't really care much for cats. I couldn't see that anybody had a really deep aversion to 'em. But when Ivy said what she did, about bein' affected so by that story of Poe's about the black cat, it gave me an idea. There was a chance she couldn't get Sultan out of her mind. That was a messy business. So was all of it, but if she did that herself— Well, I'd sent Jazz to get this cat before Ivy gave herself away, and when she did I decided to throw double or nothing."

"And did I have a nice time, scouring the country for one black cat with affectionate disposition?" Jazz said. "I went all over Merton: no luck. Either the cats were not black or not affectionate, or their owners were suspicious—and who can blame them? I finally went out to one of the farms near Monte Verde, where they're overrun with cats and would sell you the farm for five dollars, cash. This pussy—"

"He's a very nice cat," Rocky said, stroking the black head against his knee. The cat said: "Awr-ah" sleepily, curled up again and went off to sleep with a rumbling purr.

"Well, they said they couldn't keep this beast off the beds or out of the house, and that he had an incurably optimistic disposition. 'Makes up to everybody,' the woman said. I brought him up in a basket, and he never even yowled. Put the collar and bell on him and poked him in through the window. He did protest a little when we were going up the ladder, but very sleepily. I think he was born sleepy," Jazz said.

"Or else he's lost his manhood," Rocky suggested.

"Perhaps it's not that kind of cat," Eleanor said.

"Well, the woman said he'd never had kittens yet."

Robert Allan looked at them reprovingly. "That's no kind of talk to be indulgin' in right now. Your scheme worked—"

"I guess he made straight for the bed with that bell tinklin'. Well," Rocky conceded, "it might be enough to scare a person if they had an unpleasant mem'ry of a cat with a bell—"

"Tinkling in the dark, and something furry and purring on your bed and following you— Ugh! I like cats," Eleanor said, "but I can see how that might be pretty awful. Why didn't she light the lamp?"

"I left her one good match an' a lot of damp ones. I figured she'd use the good one lyin' right by the lamp when she went to bed. She couldn't make the others light. She did grab that nail file, but there wasn't anything else in the room she could hurt the cat with. I admit there was a minute or two when I was scared I'd just managed to frighten her into hysterics."

"I wonder if she'll change her mind about squealing on Glidden?" Jazz said. "She signed the statement when Barnhart typed it, but they do change their minds."

"She's in it, any way she figures it. She can do better for herself by pleadin' guilty and throwing the blame on Glidden as much as possible. I think she'll stick to it, hating him like she does now. It happens like that lots of times."

"What about the money?" Eleanor asked.

"Didn't they tell you? We found it," Allan said complacently. "If he run right back here after he shot Rocky, he didn't have any time to hide it any place but here, I figgered, and no chance after that. He stuck it down cellar. We tore the place up an' got it out of a box of old fruit jars an' things. He wouldn't tell us where it was."

"By the way, Dad, you're still pretty quick on the draw. There might 've been trouble, with Glidden still havin' Murdoch's gun. He just laughed when I asked him where he kept it yesterday an' said in back of the radio, in its works, till night."

"You'd better get over them careless ways of yours if you want to live much longer," Allan said. "When do we get out of here?"

"This afternoon, if the doctor 'll let me take the ride. Well," Rocky said pensively, "there's one person in this county's goin' to be mighty happy. That's little Freddie Haynes, our public pros'cutor. He's always wanted to try his hand at a real murder trial, an' now I've got him one."

CHAPTER XVIII
MURDOCH VS JAMES

Robert Allan lighted another cigar, his high-heeled boot impatiently tapping the floor of the car. "Won't that woman ever get finished sayin' good-by to Eleanor?"

"It's a len'thy process," Rocky murmured. "Eleanor's been backin' away from her for five minutes. I hope she don't fall down the steps backwards."

"And you will come back to see us?" Mrs. Featherstone-Quinn was saying. "I suppose if I wanted to try to be funny in a horrid sort of way I'd say: 'See you at the trial.' Well, I suppose I will."

Eleanor took another backward step. "You're going to stay here for a while?"

"I almost have to, don't I? Mr. Allan said he didn't know if I'd be called as a witness, and I certainly hope not, because when I think of getting on the stand and testifying— Well, let's not talk about that. I'd stay here until winter, anyway, because, after all, I own the place, and I may not be able to sell it, and Arthur says he thinks the seclusion—if we can manage to avoid excitement from now on—is just what he wants."

"Mr. Barnhart's going to stay here for a while, then?"

"Don't you think Mary Anne is chaperon enough?" Mrs. Featherstone-Quinn said anxiously. "Because I have made up my mind—Arthur says it seems to him we're old enough not to be romantic any more—and since I will persist in marrying people to look after them, I might as well look after him. He says my talking doesn't bother him at all, that it did when we were younger, but now he simply doesn't pay any attention to me when he gets tired of listening. But in such a polite way that I think it's really a good thing he has a deaf ear like that, and I wouldn't mind at all if he saw me done up in curlers. But it would be awfully bad taste to make up my mind too soon."

"I'm sure you'd get along very well together," Eleanor said, backing down the porch steps. "I hope you'll be very happy if you—"

"Oh, thank you. I really don't know why we never thought of it before, but after all this— Well, luckily I have a hopeful disposition so I'll get over— Oh, do you have to go? Weren't those reporters funny this morning? So angry because they hadn't come back last night to— Good-by, Mr. Allan. And Mr. Allan—both Mr. Allans."

Both Mr. Allans nodded and smiled, the senior rather woodenly. "I'm sorry," Eleanor said, getting into the car. "I got away just as soon as— What is it, Rocky?"

"I'm fresh out of cigarettes, honey."

"Smoke one of my see-gars," offered his father.

Rocky shuddered. "In my weakened state of health? We can get some cigarettes at the store."

"If you insist on having them. It wouldn't hurt you not to smoke . . . No, I'll get them," Eleanor said, stopping the car in front of Murdoch's store. "What kind do you want?"

"Oh, any— Wait a minute," Rocky said, catching her arm. "I want to hear this, since they don't seem to care who does."

Olivia and Lawrence Murdoch were standing just inside the store, "looking at each other like two banties gettin' ready to scrap," Robert Allan whispered. Olivia pushed her hair back from her forehead, put her hands on her hips in a gesture of exasperation.

"You know damn well we can't get any of that money without fulfilling the terms of the will. Otherwise it goes to the next of kin. And it explicitly states we must marry and live together for a year."

"If you want Amelia's money so badly, can't you stand to wait a year to get it?"

"The will says we have to occupy the same house. And that would mean I had to stay here another year, I suppose."

"You're damn right it does," Murdoch said truculently. "If you think I'm going to marry you so you can get that money and then trail around wherever you want to go so we can meet the terms of the will—"

"I never expected anything so chivalrous of you!" Olivia brought her foot down on the floor as if she were stamping on a particularly loathsome insect. "I get the rough end of the deal any way you look at it."

"If we're going to get married to get that money you'll live here and like it," Murdoch said doggedly.

"I suppose you'd even be low enough to hold me to the exact wording of the will? It says 'live together.' Was that Amelia's old-fashioned way of saying this marriage must not be one of these 'in name only' things? Very likely. She'd count on you, of course: 'men will be men, my dear.'"

Murdoch drew back a step, his florid face paling. His nose began to twitch. "I've stood a lot from you," he said slowly, "but that last crack is just a little too much. You asked for it . . ."

"Clark Gable couldn't have done better," Rocky murmured happily. "Boy, was *that* a sock!"

Olivia drew her hand across her cheek, staring at Murdoch with round eyes. "Why—you—you— Do you think for one minute I'll stand for—"

"Hope I didn't hurt you too much," Murdoch said casually. "No you don't." He caught her by the shoulders, kissed her violently and pushed her toward the door. "Don't start a fight. I'll close my hand next time. If you want that money you'll marry me, live here for a year and keep house for me. You're as good a cook as Mary Anne and a lot pleasanter to look at, though her disposition's got yours beat to a frazzle. Think it over."

He disappeared into the back part of the store. Olivia stood leaning against the door, looking fixedly at her feet. One hand smoothed her reddened cheek absently, finally moved up to cover her eyes . . .

"Let the cigarettes go," Rocky said softly. "Let's go. Of course, it probably won't do any good. When she thinks it over, she'll be pretty mad again."

"But she was getting ready to cry," Eleanor said. "And he had sense enough to kiss her. Being kissed like that does things to a woman's morale. You may be right, but I'll bet that romance has at last come to Olivia."

"He shouldn't," Robert Allan said perfunctorily, "have hit a lady. . . ."

COACHWHIP PUBLICATIONS

CoachwhipBooks.com

VIRGINIA RATH

DEATH AT
DAYTON'S FOLLY

COACHWHIP PUBLICATIONS
COACHWHIPBOOKS.COM

MURDER ON
THE DAY OF
JUDGMENT

VIRGINIA RATH

COACHWHIP PUBLICATIONS
CoachwhipBooks.com

VIRGINIA RATH

FERRYMAN,
TAKE HIM ACROSS!

VIRGINIA RATH

AN EXCELLENT
NIGHT FOR
MURDER

COACHWHIP PUBLICATIONS
COACHWHIPBOOKS.COM

COACHWHIP PUBLICATIONS
CoachwhipBooks.com

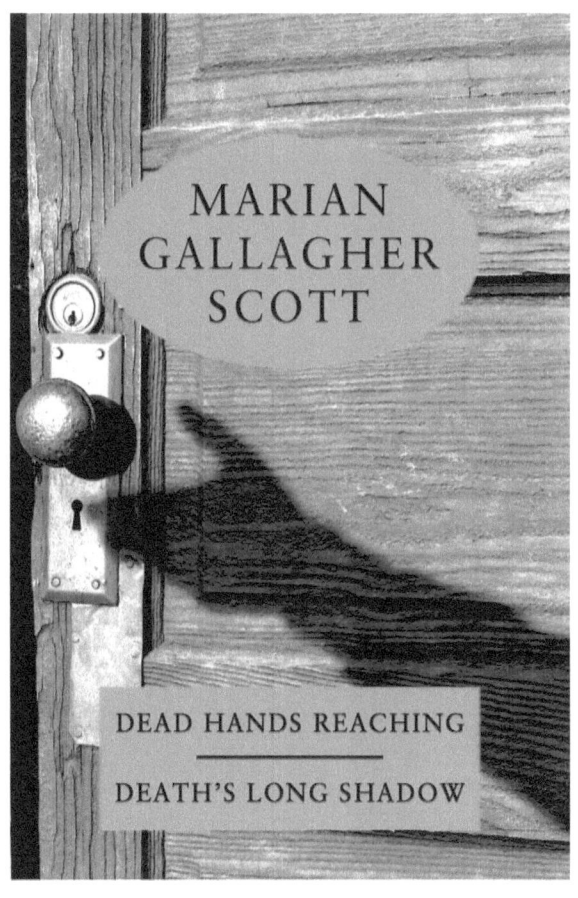

MARIAN
GALLAGHER
SCOTT

DEAD HANDS REACHING

DEATH'S LONG SHADOW